the
assassination
arrow

J. ALLAN SMITH

First published by Dog Ear Publishing
4010 W. 86th Street, Ste H
Indianapolis, IN 46268
www.dogearpublishing.net

dog ear
PUBLISHING

ISBN: 978-159858-753-1

This book is printed on acid-free paper.
This book is a work of Fiction. Places, events, and situations in this book are purely Fictional and any resemblance to actual persons, living or dead, is coincidental.

Printed in the United States of America

To my brother Jerry whose insights and skills have helped me write this story, and to Wayne Qualls for his faith and belief in me. To my parents, my mother who inspired me to write and to my father who showed me the value of hard work and shared his passion for the great outdoors. To my wife whose never-ending love and patience is the one constant I can always rely on.

CHAPTER ONE

We don't always know why things happen the way they do. At times, the purpose or reason for the circumstances we find ourselves a part of is revealed instantly, but at other times, years might pass before we understand why. Still, there are questions we will ponder; the answers we may never know.

This evening, I am wrestling with these thoughts, as I stand knee-deep in the Stillwater River in my youngest brother's favorite stretch of water. I smile as I watch the trout sip the caddis flies off of the river's surface. As I pick a size 16 elk-hair caddis from my fly box to match the hatch of the evening and begin tying it on to the 5x tippet, my arthritic hands move slowly but deliberately. I secure the fly with a clinch knot after sliding the leader through my lips to moisten it and prevent friction as I tighten the tippet's end to the eye of the hook. I raise the fly to my teeth to bite off the excess leader, consciously aware of the bad habit developed from my youth, so I have to resort to using my clippers, as my worn teeth won't make the cut. The bamboo rod I hold in my hand, my most cherished gift from a friend who has long since passed on, is older than I, and yet, as though having a heart of its own, it seems to impatiently anticipate the action for which it was designed.

My eyes, though not as clear as they used to be, scan the surface of the rippling water before me, marking the location of a feeding trout where I can cast my fly. I tilt my head and listen to the river's music. The gurgling, chuckling, sloshing, sucking, and splashing echo of the river's moving force, with the occasional crash of a heavy fish smashing against the current, creates a mood that delivers me from the cares and troubles of life and moves me, as it always has, into a state of peace, tranquility and solitude. I am captivated by the moment.

Although my senses are in tune and harmony with the river's life, my mind keeps drifting back to the night, three months earlier, when my grandson, Simon, who was spending the weekend with me while my daughter Heidi was out of town for the weekend, had mischievously wandered up into the attic and started snooping around. Hearing the ruckus from below in the living room, I hobbled up the stairway, only to find him trying to pry open an old chest that I had put up there more than 30 years ago. After scolding him a little for getting into things that he had no business getting into, I sent him to bed. My own curiosity got the best of me as I stood there staring at the chest, even though I knew the contents that it held. I rummaged around for the key but could not remember where I had hidden it. After a few hits on the old lock with the heel of my shoe, I finally managed to open up the chest myself.

Folders and files of gathered facts from research, interviews, phone calls, letters and emails filled the chest, containing in them a story that I had promised to write so long ago but never did complete. Wrapped in newspaper and stuffed in a cardboard tube on top of the folders, lay the original arrow. It was the arrow that shook the very soul of this nation.

I spent the entire night reading and organizing the information I had gathered so long ago and by the first light of dawn, I had convinced myself that I needed to finish the story that I had started, if for no one else, then at least for myself. It was a story that had never been completely told, and although pieces and bits of it could be found in the pages of history, many of the significant details were left unrevealed.

As I began the long strenuous task of compiling the information, I found myself reliving each moment as if it had just happened. Each and every detail I recalled with vivid clarity.

For the last three months I have eaten very little and practically spent every waking minute of my day, writing and working to complete the story. I have ignored my daily walks and routine visits to the river. My daughter has fretted over my loss of weight and lack of physical activity. She stops by to check on me everyday, afraid that I am about to "cash it in".

Today, I sent the story to the publisher, and this evening, I am here, standing in my Brother Joe's favorite stretch of water, to cast my fly upon the surface and reap the joy I have known all these years that only comes by time spent on the river. Although my body reveals the effects of time, my heart, my soul and my mind feel young and wild and free. The uneasiness and restlessness and to a certain degree, even bitterness, that I have harbored and allowed to be my master, have been flushed from my veins. The irony to my discovery is that it took so long for me to realize what I should have known all along—only the truth can make you free. Perhaps it is more than just the knowledge of the truth, but the revelation. This is my story.

CHAPTER TWO

It had been an incredibly busy and frustrating week. A power outage, early that morning, crashed my computer and destroyed an article I had spent 3 days trying to complete. It was due by that afternoon. To top things off, the fuel pump went out on the truck. Fortunately, I was able to bum a ride from my best friend Tom, but arriving in the office thirty minutes late did not sit well with my chronically constipated, bi-polar boss. So when Hannah, my secretary, or "administrative assistant" as they are now called, buzzed me on the phone, I was not really in the mood to take the call. However, when she paused and stated in a whispered voice, "Mr. Tyler, I think you better take this call. It's him." I immediately stopped my pecking on the keyboard and told Hannah to transfer him to my private line.

The red light on the phone flashed; I let it flash a couple more times, trying to gain composure of my thoughts and what I was going to say.

"Hello, this is Ross Tyler," I said, trying to produce as much confidence and surety in my voice as possible.

"We need to meet—soon," he replied, followed by the immediate click of the phone and the irritating sound of the dial tone.

For a few minutes I just stood there. I knew that voice. It was one of those deep, slow but very deliberate voices that once you hear, you never forget. I was stunned. The man was *alive* after all. I had always concealed my deep suspicions, but without anything solid to stand on, I kept them to myself. He had called me only once and we spoke for about an hour, but then the "accident" came, and that was the last I had heard from him.

My thoughts were interrupted by Hannah's voice over the intercom, "Mr. Tyler...Mr. Tyler..."

"Yes, Hannah, please come into my office," I answered, "and can you please bring me a cup of coffee, and do so quickly. I need to speak with you."

Hannah entered the door to my office in less than a minute, wearing a yellow and white-checkered spring dress, cut just enough to be considered a little suggestive, but at the same time, quite appropriate. Her silky brown hair with gentle highlights flowed across the smooth, bronze skin of her neck and shoulders, enhanced by her dark eyes, which seemed to reveal a subtle hint of mischief, or at least that's the way I interpreted it. She was young and extremely bright. I knew very little of her personal life. I had never heard her mention a boyfriend or even a date for that matter, but a woman as beautiful as she would have at least one romantic interest. She came to my office two and a half years ago, and I knew in my heart that without her, I probably would have been fired from this job a long time ago. The aptitude and proficiency of her organizational skills had kept me out of hot water with my boss on more occasions than I could possibly enumerate.

She handed me the cup of coffee and smiled, anticipating with wonder what I was about to say.

"It *was* him, wasn't it?" she asked.

"Yes, I'm sure of it. I don't think I could ever misplace that voice," I answered.

"What did he say?"

"He said he wants to meet, and soon," I answered again.

"Where?" she asked.

"*That,* he didn't say."

"What are you going to do?" she asked.

"What can I do, except wait?" I replied. I paused for a minute and took her hand in mine without really even giving much thought about the gesture, and then I looked her in the eyes and said, "Listen, Hannah..."

"I know, I know," she interrupted, "I won't say a word."

"Good," I replied, "this story could make us big, but I also believe there is more to it than we know. The last thing we want to do is jeopardize the trust that he has in us."

"Mr. Tyler," she stated, gently squeezing my hand, "you won't have to worry about me."

"All right," I replied, "Why don't you call it a day? I'll see you on Monday." Hannah closed the door behind her as I turned and stared out the window of my high rise office into the hot and humid July afternoon and the smoggy haze of downtown Chicago.

"Where are you hiding?" I whispered to myself. "Why are you calling me?" I thought aloud.

The hours passed and from what I could see, by 7:00 p.m. the entire floor was all but empty except for the cleaning crew who performed their nightly duties. While digging through my old files, memories of the events that shook the nation began to unfold across the computer before my eyes. I found it simply amazing that almost three years had transpired since that time. Strange, I thought, how quickly we forget.

Shortly after 8:00 p.m. I decided to spend the night in the office. All of the other employees had left the office for the weekend. Working my way down to the lounge, I purchased a diet coke and a bag of Cheetos. "Another fine supper," I thought sarcastically to myself, wishing that I hadn't sent my ex-girlfriend packing her bags so soon. She loved to cook

Carefully, maybe even a little paranoid I suppose, I walked down the hall, and stepped into the men's room. Mr. Kendall, a large black man and his grandson Rueben, a young energetic boy who came to help his grandfather clean everyday after school, met me at the door as they had just finished mopping the floor. The aroma of Clorox and Lysol still lingered in the air.

"Good evening, Mr. Tyler. Looks like, sir, you be staying late tonight," Kendall commented.

"Yes, sir, Mr. Kendall. I've got a few loose ends I need to try to get wrapped up."

"Well, sir, Rueben and I have just finished and we're goin' to head home to mama. She's got suppa waitin'. We'll lock up every ting and see ya on Monday. You's have a good weekend now, ya hear?"

"Yes, sir, Mr. Kendall, you do the same."

I pushed the door to the stall, but it was locked. I pushed the door to the second stall, and it was locked as well. "What the heck?" I stooped and peaked beneath the door but did not find any of the stalls to be occupied. I kept trying each door, finding four out of the five locked. The fifth was unlocked. Somebody, perhaps Rueben, was probably just playing a prank.

After taking care of business, I reached for the toilet paper. As I began to unroll it, I noticed something written on the roll in very fine dark ink. "Mr. Tyler, look inside the roll." I disassembled the dispenser and looked inside the roll. A note was carefully folded and stuffed inside: "Mr. Tyler. Phones tapped, computer wired. All correspondence screened, house, office, auto—under surveillance. This bathroom stall is one of the few places that is not exposed to hidden cameras on this floor. Trust NO ONE. Enclosed is a map. July 31ˢᵗ. Be there." It was not signed. I compared the handwriting on the toilet paper with the writing on the note. They were not the same.

I folded the map without looking at it and put it in my shirt pocket, and disposed of the message in the commode.

My chest tightened as I washed my hands. "Who placed the note in the paper roll? How did they know I would be staying late? How did they know that I would come into the restroom? Why would they choose this particular way to get a map to me? Was the person who put it there still in the building? Did Mr. Kendall have something to do with it? How would he know? Who *else* would know? I had known Kendall since I came to work at the Tribune. His family had a contract for cleaning our level of the building, and to my knowledge, they never missed a single night.

Kendall was a soft-spoken, polite and courteous fellow, and I had chitchatted with him on several occasions. Most of the employees, I noticed, didn't give him the time of day, but my daddy always taught me that you treat people the way you want to be treated. It didn't matter what race or nationality they were, nor their religion, occupation, size or sex. Mr. Kendall was a man that put his pants on one leg at a time just as I did. He had just as much right as anyone else to be treated fairly, but what did I really know about the man? Nothing really. If I really was being watched, then *why* was I being watched?" It hit me. Perhaps, someone else had their suspicions about the accident. Maybe someone else believed the man was actually still somehow alive, just as I did. But why, after all this time, was he trying to make contact again? Who did he trust enough to send a message? Or could it be that he himself was here in the building? I doubted that.

Upon returning to my office, I sat down in my leather seat, and folded my hands behind my head, placing my feet upon the desk. Looking around, I wondered if a camera was watching me at that very moment. For some reason, I felt certain that it was true. My inner voice kept telling me, that not only was I being watched, but also something very dangerous was in the making. I must not, as the writer had so specifically stated, trust anyone, and too, I dare not let anyone know that I was sure that something was amiss.

The longer that I sat there, the more I felt certain that I was being watched. The more I thought about it, the more I began to panic. I had already made a mistake, I felt certain. Bringing up the files on my computer after receiving the phone call would certainly be suspect. It wasn't the information in the files that anyone was really interested in, but rather the fact that I had not looked at them in months that might cause someone to be suspicious. They, who-ever "they" were, would know that I must have had a reason to bring up the old files. Maybe I was just being paranoid, but regard-less, I was feeling very claustrophobic. I had to get out of there, only where do I go? Then I remembered the map.

CHAPTER THREE

It would not be safe to return home, I thought to myself, but then again, maybe home was exactly where I needed to go. If I didn't show up, whoever was watching, might believe that I was on to them. However, I did need to go some place where I could take a look at the map, without the fear of revealing what information was hidden in it. I stepped into my Jaguar and started the engine. The car was a beauty and purred like a kitten. The car had been a part of the package that came with the job. Again, I recalled the writing on the tissue paper— "Everything was either tapped or wired or on video surveillance, including my car." Where to go? Friday night in downtown Chicago, I thought to myself, on a hot and humid evening, without a date. "What a life!" I spoke sarcastically aloud to myself. Half a mile down from the Tribune, I decided to pull into a bar, just to kill a little time. It was a joint that I visited frequently.

Locking the Jag behind me, I stepped onto the sidewalk, only to be bumped into by a rather large, muscular black man, wearing a silk stocking on his head. He apologized like he had insulted my mother or something and was trying his best to dust me off and make sure I was all right.

"I'm O.K.", I said, slightly annoyed about his hands being all over me. I figured he was probably going to mug me right there.

His eyes caught mine and held for just a second, and I recognized his face. It was Kendall. He whispered, "Mr. Tyler, you're being followed. Have a nice night."

"Wait! Wait! How do you know?" I asked, but he just kept on walking.

The whole street was lined with cars and people walking along the shops. I tried to see if anything or anyone looked out of place without looking too obvious. "Heck," I laughed aloud. "The only fool out of place in this city is me!"

The nightclub was crowded as usual on Friday nights. People of just about every flavor were there. I had shared drinks with several of them over the last couple of years. Seldom did I ever see anyone else from the paper come to this place. Maybe they had a *real* life to live, I often surmised.

The dim room was filled with cigar and cigarette smoke giving an eerie hazy feel to the night. A small band was playing some sort of rock music in the back. The banging drums and whining of the electric guitar pierced my ears and intensified the pain of the headache I had been developing all afternoon. Several couples were dancing to the music, but the majority of the crowd was drinking beer and engaged in conversation.

Glancing around the room, I did not seem to notice anybody's eyes continually looking in my direction. If people were following me, I concluded, maybe they were waiting outside.

The bartender knew me by name. I had chatted with him many times before, although I never did tell him a whole lot about myself. Filling a mug with draft beer, he broke the ice. "Hey Tyler, I haven't seen you in awhile. You working on some big story or something?" I smiled back as he handed me my beer.

"Tank, (if you saw the man, you'd instantly know where he got the nickname), I haven't had a good story to write about in over a month. My boss has me buried butt-deep in this teacher's union strike. Shoot, why doesn't the city just give the whiny little babies the raise they always get, and be done with it?"

"Tyler, you never do have anything good to say. Drink that beer and loosen up," Tank responded.

"I'll try to remember that, Tank," I replied as he grabbed his towel and went to assist another customer. Maybe I did need an attitude adjustment.

The place was a dive, yet people flocked here every night, to drown their sorrows, send their cares away in smoke, or just to be near other people to keep from facing the loneliness of living in an empty house or apartment. Why I came here, I wasn't sure myself.

Perhaps I, too, was lonely, and I didn't want to face the night alone, at least not yet. Tank brought me another beer. "Come over here," he said. "There's someone I'd like for you to meet."

"No," I told him, "I'm not in the mood to meet one of your sleazy girlfriends."

"Ah, come on, Tyler. You'll like her." Giving me a gentle tug at the elbow, which with Tank, gentle means practically lifting me off my bar stool. He dragged me toward a little table in the back corner at the end of the bar where the noise of the crowd and the music didn't feel like an ice pick in my ears. I finally gave up resisting his steel-like grip on my arm and let him lead me to the table. Upon reaching the table I took a look at her. I immediately realized that I had assumed incorrectly about the kind of girl Tank would introduce me to. I was the one who was the slob in this picture, and I wished I had taken a minute to clean up a little before seating myself at the bar.

"Tyler," Tank stated, putting his arm around my shoulder, "I'd like for you to meet Wren."

"Wren, this here's Tyler."

I extended my hand to shake hers and she firmly shook mine back. "May I have a seat?" I asked.

"Please do!" she offered.

"Wren," I muttered softly, as I looked her up and down, "that's a pretty name. I don't believe I've ever heard it before, at least, I mean, well, you know, as a person's name."

She smiled and chuckled lightly as I wallowed in my ever-deepening hole of despair and embarrassment for stumbling all over my words.

I felt a little awkward at first, sitting there with Wren. Meeting new people, in my line of work, was something I did on a regular basis, so I could not explain the uneasiness I felt, but I was soon to find out that Wren had a gentle and easy way of making me feel relaxed, and the discomfort quickly subsided.

She was absolutely the most attractive woman I do believe I had ever seen. Like a moth drawn to a flame, it seemed impossible to resist staring at her, and I knew that she was very much aware that I was staring. I did not care. Unquestionably, her stunning and striking beauty created a sensual desire that could not be ignored. My lust *of* the flesh and *for* the flesh burned almost uncontrollably.

I guessed she was somewhere near 30 years of age, give or take a year or two, but she had the complexion of a twenty-year old. Her skin was rich and stunning, not the kind smeared with an overdose of makeup, but the kind of skin that comes from expensive lotions and time in the sun. It glistened in the soft lights of the bar. Her brunette hair, long, thick and silky-clean, she wore loose and straight across her shoulders. Her eyes were deep and dark and mysterious and by far the most captivating eyes I had ever seen. Her ivory smile and lightly painted lips mesmerized my stare. I kept thinking, "Man, this girl is gorgeous."

We visited for a little while, just covering the normal formalities when meeting a new acquaintance—small talk, I guess. She told me she was taking the summer off from Harvard to work on her dissertation and was visiting a friend of hers in Chicago, who had flown out of town for the weekend to spend it with her fiancé in Cancun. Her friend had shown her this place before she left, and since she didn't feel like sitting at home, bored out of her brains, she decided to come down and hangout for a while.

"How long have you lived in Chicago?" she asked.

"About 3 years. In fact, it will be 3 years next month."

"What do you do?" she inquired.

I pointed to a newspaper lying down on the bar just an arms length away. "I write for that paper," I answered.

She grabbed it, and I told her where to find my article. She thumbed through it and began to read a little of it. "Somehow…" she stated as she glanced over the paper, folding it back up at the same time, "I doubt you picked the teacher's strike as a topic to write about."

I laughed and said, "No."

A moment paused without conversation, and then she asked, "You're not originally from here, are you?"

"No, I'm not…Truth is I hate this city. Come to think of it. I've never found a city that I really liked."

She smiled at me, "You sound more like a country boy than an editor for a major paper."

"Does it show that much?" I asked. "Well, you hit the nail on the head."

"So," she paused with her inquisitive, searching eyes, "Where *are* you from?" She sat back in her chair and said, "Wait a minute, let me see if I can guess."

She took my hand and turned it palm side up, slowly tracing the lines with her finger. My thoughts raced. When she looked at them, I realized that the calluses on my hands that had taken a lifetime to develop were all but gone. I was a little embarrassed about that. As she ran her fingers softly over both hands, I grew oblivious to everything around me in the club. She brought my hand to her mouth and gently kissed my knuckles and leaned forward toward my face and whispered, "Ross Curtis Tyler, you were born August 19th, 1962, in Billings, Montana. You have three brothers and one sister. Two of your brothers live in Tennessee, your sister and youngest brother live in west Texas. Your parents live on a ranch just outside of Columbus, Montana. You attended high school in Columbus, and graduated in 1981. You attended Montana State University in Bozeman, majored in journalism. Shortly after graduation, you got a job working for the Billings Gazette Newspaper. You worked there for 16 years, until the assassination of the Vice President three years ago, which, oddly enough, connected you with contacts that led you to national recognition, and that's when you were offered this job here. You have never been married. You enjoy hunting and fishing and backpacking and of course writing. You work out on weights during the winter months…

"Hold it right there," I stated in shock, stopping her abruptly and pulling back, withdrawing my hands from hers. The fact that she knew things about me that no one else in this city knew about me was unsettling, maybe even frightening, and one thing was certain- I didn't like it. "How do you know all these things?" I asked.

"Ross", she whispered slowly, "I can tell you how tall you are, what you weigh, the birthmark on your left foot, the last time you've been to the doctor…In fact, I probably know more about you than you yourself do."

No, I didn't like it. "What do you want?" I asked feeling very exposed.

"You have something in your pocket that some very mean and important people must get their hands on. And, oh, yes, you're supposed to be dead by morning."

"How do you know I have something in my pocket?" I asked.

"Ross, you are amazingly predictable. You run the same routine nearly every day.   You leave your office, usually grab a drink and snack, go to the bathroom, loosen your tie, and sit on the toilet all before you leave... and you do the same thing no matter what time of day you actually leave the office," Wren smiled and replied. "Think about it Ross. We know the blind spots that our cameras don't monitor. Our camera in the restroom covers everything except the last stall. We also know how to read people. Your whole demeanor was different when you came out than it was when you went in and whether you realize it or not; you raised your hand to your shirt pocket four times on your walk back to the office. Coupled with the fact that you received a phone call today from a man that has been presumed dead for nearly three years, we are confident that you were given instructions in that stall."

I just stared at her, wanting to believe that she was lying, but I could tell she was not. She knew too much about me already, and I figured there had to be a reason she was revealing this information to me.

"How's it supposed to happen?" I asked.

"I'm supposed to lead you home, and uh, you know..." she let me guess the rest.

"Like a Black Widow?" I sarcastically asked.

"I'm sorry, Ross."

"So I assume since you're telling me all this that you have changed your mind?" I asked.

"Ross, I've been watching you and studying you for over two years, most of it on cameras hidden in your office." I saw a tear swell up in her eye, but I was much too angry to care a whole lot about her feelings at the time.

"Who in the world do you work for?" I asked. I could feel the heat surging to my face as I churned in a torrent of anger, and I started to rise from my seat.

Wren reached for her purse. I thought she was going to pull out some kind of identification; instead, she showed me the front-end of a .38 revolver and flatly, but quietly stated, "Mr. Tyler. Sit down. If you listen to me, I might be able to save your life, but don't you dare think I'll hesitate to kill you, if it appears for one second that you have put my life at risk."

I doubt that anybody else in the dark, smoky haze of the nightclub would have seen the gesture, but I knew she was serious. I just stared at her and slowly sat back into my seat.

"Mr. Tyler. We know you have a map. Our cameras were unable to distinguish exactly where or what kind of map it is. My employers intend on having that map in their hands this evening, and your soul in hell before sunrise. Now smile at me and act like you're having a good time. If you don't, it will certainly be the last good time you'll ever have." Confused and not sure just what to say, I tried to formulate some kind of sense out all of this, but I couldn't. I just sat there in my seat, staring at Wren in disbelief and bewilderment.

"Are any of your people with you in here?" I asked, almost sarcastically.

"Yes, as a matter of fact, there are five of us," she replied. "Don't turn to look, but I'll tell you who they are while you're still flirting with me." She held my stare and smiled slightly, and for some reason I felt a little more relaxed. "The black guy at the pin-ball machine is Tom. He's bad news Ross. He's one sadistic, cold-blooded man. Then there's Kirby, the older fellow who sits at the end of the bar that you often buy cigarettes and a drink for, when you occasionally come in here. He likes to get to know the people he's going to erase. He's worse than all the others put together."

"Is that what you call it?" I asked. "You *erase* someone?"

"Yes, that's what we call it, and I've seen Kirby erase people in the most horrific means possible. He's a butcher Ross and what's more, he enjoys it. Last year, I heard that he slaughtered a wealthy family over in Boston. He shot the man, and then attacked the woman, who was pregnant. He sliced her open, extracted the infant and killed it in front of the woman before she died. I hate him and I despise him. He's told everyone that you're his. His plans are to see you suffer, very slowly."

"What have I ever done to him?" I asked. "Shoot, I've always been kind to him. What could I have possibly done to make him want to find joy in killing me?"

"Nothing, Ross, you don't have to. Like I said, he enjoys bringing as much pain as possible to people before he erases them."

I sat there shaking my head in disbelief still trying cognitively to absorb the information.

"Who else in here is a part of all of this?" I asked.

"The bouncer over by the door, wearing the red bandana and Harley Davidson outfit, the one you call Hog, he's a part of this too. I never did know why the agency hired him."

"Agency," I blurted. "Who are you guys?"

Wren again ignored the question, and stated, "Then there are Tank and I." Our eyes met briefly.

"Not Tank," I said, astonished.

"Yes, Ross. And you might as well know this: Hannah, your secretary, yea, good ol' faithful Hannah, has been watching you since the day the paper hired her. Why do you think she got hired? Do you think the secretary she replaced really died in an auto accident? The Jaguar you're driving, the big salary you're making, all of it, Ross, was to get you here in Chicago where we could keep a close eye on you."

I started to grow uncomfortable, and Wren sensed it. "Just stay put, Ross, I've got a plan."

"And just who are you to be planning my life?" I asked, tight-jawed, muttering under my breath, trying not to raise a scene that would be noticed by the others.

"Because," she whispered, "if you don't trust me, Ross, you won't have a life at all by tomorrow morning." Once again she made that point very clear.

"How do I know that I can trust you, Wren, or whatever you call yourself?" I asked, my lips tightening as again panic swelled up in my throat

"You can't know," she replied. She paused and leaned forward toward me, grabbing my hand and stated, "Ross, listen to me. As far as everything goes for tonight, nobody knows about anything that we have talked about. I would be dead for certain right now, and so would you. They are all here, doing their thing, playing games, drinking beer and acting like they are having a great time, while I'm here trying my best to seduce you and take you home, which is where they plan on making the hit. Ross, you don't even have a clue of the magnitude of the mess you're in. You're in way over your head, Ross, and you don't even know it. To top it off, we are not the only folks who are watching you."

"When you say 'we'—who is this 'we'? Who are you?"

"I can't say, Ross," Wren answered. "However, if somehow, someway, the two of us survive, I'm going to find you, no matter how long it takes, and maybe we can, you know, just go from there and see how it goes."

"You don't seem awfully confident that you can get me out of this mess," I commented matter-of-factly.

"Here's the deal, Ross. I have a plan. I have never given these people the first opportunity to doubt me, and I'm putting my life in serious jeopardy by doing this. It would be a whole lot easier to let them kill you and just forget about it."

I did not like the way the word "kill" came out of her mouth so easily.

"So, why don't you?" I inquired.

"Ross," she impatiently scolded, "it's getting late, and we don't have the time for long explanations. I hope, very strongly, that one day I will have the opportunity to fill in all the blanks. Now, here's the plan. I'm supposed to get you to take me home. Of course, we'll be followed, but you won't be able to know by whom or how many. Remember not to mention anything of our conversation or what we have talked about while we are in your car. Your car is bugged and also has a tracking device on the frame. When we get to my friend's little cottage, you can park your Jag out in front. They have no surveillance of any kind on my friend's place at all, as far as cameras or bugs and so on. Like I said, they trust me. Now listen, someone will be watching through night-vision binoculars somewhere in the distance, so don't be looking around acting suspicious. Walk me to the door, stop, let me get the keys out of my purse; kiss me so whoever is watching really believes everything is going as planned.

"Now listen, when I open the door and turn on the light, I will yell at the burglar that's waiting in my house. You chase after him through the house and out the back door, but do not catch him. He's a young man that I paid well to be there. I will make immediate contact with my people who are watching. I can sound pretty convincing. They will be there quickly, so as you flee out my back-door, you'll pass across the alley. In the alley is a manhole. Open the lid, drop inside, close the lid, and crawl like the devil."

"Where's it come out?" I asked.

"Down on the river. It will come out on the bank. It's hidden pretty well by some river cane. A Smith & Wesson .45 will be duct-taped to the wall at the end of the pipe. A boat will be wait-ing there for you. Only one person will be on board. Ask him this question: 'How's the water?' If he does not say 'It's freezing', fill him full of lead and take the boat yourself. If he does say 'It's freezing', he is going to take you up the river about 25 miles and drop you off in a little cove back in the swamp. I have an extended cab Ford-250 4x4 truck waiting there for you. It has dual tanks full of gas, a cooler of food and water. You should be able to make about 800 miles without showing your face. Of course, if you need to take a nature break, do it somewhere with absolutely no one around. There are a few other things. Your Wranglers and boots, shirt and shorts and socks are in a sack underneath the seat. Change into them as soon as you are dropped off at the truck. It's about time you quit dressing like something that you're not any-way. That tie looks like it's about to choke the life out of you. In the back seat is also a backpack with everything you need, ammu-nition for the .45 and a thousand dollars in cash. You won't need to check it, because you won't have time. Trust me, I know how to pack a backpack," she said. Reaching into her purse, she pulled at a set of keys and handed them to me. "Put those in your pocket. They're for the truck."

"Where am I going?" I asked

"You're going home!" she stated.

"Home?" I asked

"Montana," she answered softly. "I don't know where in Montana, although we believe it is somewhere in the Bob Marshall Wilderness. We have very strong evidence that Mr. Belden is still alive. In fact, as far as we know, he has not left the Bob Marshall since he assassinated the Vice President. My agency has sent six of the best mercenaries that we could hire in there to find him and kill him and they have never come out. What's more, no one has ever found a single clue of any remains. To the best of my knowledge, the FBI has lost eight men who were trying to do the same thing. The Bob Marshall is a big wilderness and we feel very sure the map you have in your pocket will tell more specifically where Belden wants to meet you. We have always believed that sooner or later, he would try to contact you. He did it once before. That is why we have kept a careful eye on you for all this time. Every other attempt to capture or destroy Belden has failed, mostly because we can't find him, and if he is able to go public with what he knows, and prove it, some mighty powerful people in this country are going to be facing the electric chair. My people do not care anything about you; they just want to get their hands on that map, and make sure that you are dead before this night is over.

"I expect that they will be trying to figure out where you disappeared to tonight. That will give you a head start, but once they realize you're nowhere to be found, they'll be looking for you heading west. Destroy your credit cards, don't shave, just go back to looking like the cowboy you've really always been. Oh, and one other thing. Lose the cell phone in the river. Take this one. It's brand new and has 500 minutes on it. Do not call your parents, and do not stop by their ranch. Believe me: my people will be stopping by to ask questions. Do not give them anything to talk about. Ross, you cannot let anyone know who you are or where you are going. It's your only chance."

My thoughts, again, were trying to formulate some kind of sense out of all of the information Wren was revealing to me. It was too much. There were too many loose ends and unfilled blanks for me to put it all together. A part of me wanted to run and try to escape and another part of me believed what Wren was saying.

"How far have I got to crawl down the pipe?" I asked.

"It's about 125 yards. It doesn't get used anymore. I went through it last week myself." Wren stated.

"You," I said astonished, "Why did you do that?"

"I told you Ross, I don't want you dead. Part of it, a lot of it, has to do with you, the other part I'll tell you only if we both survive this ordeal. If we don't, it won't matter anyway."

She paused for most of a minute, searching my eyes, wanting to say something, but biting her lip, held by some kind of restraint from which she couldn't break loose.

"Ross, listen to me. I may never see you again. If they find out that I helped you, I'm dead for sure."

"What are you saying?" I asked.

"Ross, I don't have time. Please, for God's sake, do not trust anyone. I mean *anyone!*" Wren pleaded, trying to conceal her emotion. "Wren, I'm trying hard to trust you, but I don't even know you," I agonized again.

"Ross, you don't have a choice. I've told you that already. If you don't, you'll not see the sun come up in the morning. I'm the only hope you have, and it isn't much."

"Why are you doing this, Wren? I've got to know."

"For two years I've watched you work, eat, sleep..." She looked into my eyes, which suggested that she had developed some strong feelings toward me over the course of time, even though we had never met until that evening. "We have used more kinds of surveillance on you than you can shake a stick at. I always knew the day would come when you would get the information we wanted and we would take you out. We've suspected he's been alive for quite some time now, and we have some pretty strong evidence to support that."

She paused, searching my face for clues that I might willingly share some information, but she didn't press it.

She started again, "I told them about a year ago that I wanted to be a part of the set up. Hannah argued a little, but I let her know quickly that she had better not get in my way."

"Wren, you make it sound like you were fixing to start a cat-fight with Hannah. You really don't look like the fighting type," I stated.

Wren just laughed. "Ross, if you only knew. They don't call me Wren for nothing."

"What do you mean?" I asked.

Wren just chuckled again. "I suppose you thought 'Wren' was for a cute, little bird. Hah!! Wren is for wrench, Ross." She laughed almost hysterically. It must have been an inside joke among her constituents. Personally, I didn't find it to be all that funny.

"Listen, Ross, seriously now, I'm going to try to survive this. I want you to do the same. Even if I don't, remember, remember,

remember—Trust NO ONE. My people are the bad guys. The guys who are supposed to be the good guys are the really, really bad guys. Most of them are FBI. As soon as you can, look at that map, read it, memorize it, and destroy it. Also, if, I mean, when, you get to the mountains, stay low and under tree canopy as much as possible. The FBI has satellite surveillance. My people do not, but we have a mole with the FBI, so it really doesn't matter."

Tank came over and asked us if we needed another drink. "Sorry," he said. "I got so caught up with other customers that I just kind of let you two get to know each other. Looks like you're doing all right."

"Yeah, give me a ticket Tank, and we're going to get out of here," I replied.

"On the house," Tank replied as he turned toward the other customers down at the other end of the bar.

I smiled at Kirby, and shook his hand as we picked our way through the crowd. He raised his eyebrows and tilted his head toward Wren who was holding on to my elbow. He winked at me as if to suggest that he knew what I had in mind. I just smiled and said, "See ya later." I looked across the crowd of people at Tom who was still jostling the pinball machine. He didn't seem to indicate that he was aware of our leaving, but I noticed that he raised his hand and whispered into his cuff. Obviously, he was wired, probably sending a message to the "tail" outside that Wren had told me about. Hog just nodded at me as I made eye contact with him while Wren and I stepped out of the crowded bar into the foreboding night.

The street was not as crowded as it had been earlier, but after all, it was a little after midnight now. I started to the Jag with Wren in tow, holding on to my elbow. Away from the smoke filled club, the aroma of Wren's sweet perfume grew far more noticeable and left me intoxicated. The night was hot, and I was in no hurry to get to the car. If Wren was being honest with me and what she told me was true, it was certainly possible that I would be dead in less than an hour.

Part of me wanted to run, but another part told me that if Wren's plan worked, I might find myself in the middle of a story that had started three years ago and had never finished. It was the story that made me *big*, at least for a little while, and it was the story that brought me to Chicago, but it was also a story that went stone cold and remained untold. I needed that story. Clovis needed that story. Our world needed that story.

Wren was talking as she walked by my side to the car. I really don't know what she said as I was thinking about all that she had told me in the club. I opened the passenger side to the Jag and helped her in. Her long tan legs gleamed in the streetlights of the night and the contour of her body could not go unnoticed. Shortness of breath, fluttered pulses in my chest, and beads of sweat emerging from my forehead, assured me, that I had fallen prey to the talons of her clenching beauty. She caught me looking and smiled but didn't seem to mind. I know I sure didn't.

Stepping into the driver's seat, she leaned over and pecked me on the lips then pulled back and brought her finger up to her lips, reminding me to say nothing of the conversation we had in the nightclub.

She gave me directions, as we headed southwest out of town to a residential suburb where I had never been before. She looked into my CD case and to my surprise, pulled out a CD with a variety of different country singers on it: Don Williams, Kathy Mattea, John Denver, Anne Murray and several others. She put it in. I just smiled to myself as I realized "Of course, she knows what I listen to most of the time. They know everything about me."

In the night air, we cruised under the stars and the lights of the freeway, and sang with the sun roof open and the speakers blaring songs like, *"What Do You Do With Good Ole Boys Like Me?"*, *"Country Road"*, *"A Little Good News"*, and a few others. I marveled that she would like country music, but for some unexplainable reason, I was so delighted and glad she did. Country music was really *all* I listened to when I was alone. As our voices lifted into the night, my thoughts drifted back to a girl that I had known in college. Lisa and I shared almost everything in common including our love for music. She was by far the most compatible girl I had ever dated or even met for that matter. It seemed like the two of us were made for each other and I loved her dearly, but I wasn't ready to settle down at the time and she was. What a fool I had been. Lord, what a fool I had been. Although I had dated several girls since then, I never found anyone who even came remotely close to sharing the same interests as mine, that is, until now. Something about Wren, more than just her intoxicating physical beauty, made me entertain thoughts of a future with her in it...

"Take this next exit..." she pointed, snapping me back into reality. Taking the exit and following her directions, she finally said, "This is it." She pointed at a small, cream- colored, little cottage with a white picket fence around it, and shrubbery on all sides. I parked at the front. She looked at me with eyes that began to well up with tears. I started to say something and she quickly put her fingers over my mouth and shook her head, reminding me again that this was real. Biting on her lip and holding back the crackling in her voice, she asked, "Would you like to come in for awhile?"

I could tell she was just making small talk for those listening to the bug in my car.

"Sure," I replied, "but I best not stay for long."

She smiled, "What's the hurry?"

"Nothing, I guess," I replied.

I walked to her side and opened the door and helped her out of her seat. We walked through the front picket gate and she began digging in her purse for her keys. Without looking up, she whispered, "Are you ready?"

"Ready or not..." I answered.

"OK. Kiss me," she replied.

She lifted her eyes to mine as I began to reach over and gently kiss her on the lips. She teased at my shirt and then tilted her head to allow her lips to touch mine. She kissed me with passion. I knew she felt something for me that I could not possibly feel for her at this time. My desire was the spawn of lust for such a tremendously attractive young lady. Her desire for me had grown over the course of almost 3 years, and yet as I slid my hand around her waist and the small of her back and pulled her to me, I felt as if she was the one person, the only person, whose arms I would ever want to be in again. The firmness of her delicate body next to mine created a sense of desire that my heart and mind kept telling me could not be quenched by anyone else. I did not want to let go. We kissed passionately for a long moment and then she gently pulled back, smiled and said, "You remember that, Cowboy, and don't ever forget it."

She put the key in the door, looked at me and stepped in and turned the light on. The place was a wreck. Immediately, someone took off running for the back door. She yelled loudly and reached for the phone. I saw headlights down the street flash on, followed by the sound of squealing of rubber on the pavement. I quickly turned and pursued the burglar. Crashing through the back door, I cleared the back fence, not having a clue where the burglar had fled.

It took me a second for my eyes to adjust to the darkness of the alley, but the manhole cover was right where Wren had said it would be. I looked around to make sure no one was watching, lifted the cover and dropped inside. The hole was not big enough to stand in, but crawling was not a problem. The problem was the absence of light.

I was uncertain which direction to turn. I remained quiet after moving several yards from the opening of the manhole. I could hear Wren's voice talking and yelling excitedly to some men, but I could not distinguish what was being said. Listening more closely, I could hear a droning echo, and I realized that it was the sound of the river, so I began crawling blindly toward the sound. After 50 yards or so, I could see a faint hint of light at the end, coming from the moon and stars, I figured. The sound of the river grew louder. I crawled as quickly and quietly as I possibly could, in complete disregard for the filth and the mud. My clothes were saturated with sweat as I approached the end of the pipe.

River cane almost completely sealed the entrance, just as Wren had said. I started through the end and almost forgot about the pistol. I reached up and tore the duct tape off of the pipe. I pulled the gun out of the nylon holster and freed the magazine; it was full, so I rammed it home and shoved a round into the chamber, leaving it locked and loaded with the safety on. Peeking through the cane, my eyes found the boat just a short distance up the river. Moving quietly through the cane, I advanced to within a few yards of the boat, and saw the driver looking out across the river. Holding the Smith level at his head, I spoke softly, "How's the water?"

The man was a little startled and jumped, turning toward me, "It's freezing, man. Come on." Breathing hard with a sigh of relief, he whispered, "Cripes, man, you scared the crap out of me!"

After hitting the ignition, we idled up the river a couple of hundred yards, and then he eased the throttle to the max. We didn't converse at all. He was completely focused on getting me to the truck. I sat back, watching him the whole time, keeping the .45 in my right hand and ready to use. Wren had told me to trust no one, and so far, her plan for my escape had gone without mishap. I was not about to blow it now by letting my guard down. I slipped my cell phone from my pocket and quietly dropped it in the water. I actually felt a little naked by doing so. I was amazed that I had grown so attached to it

The only traffic on the river was an old fishing boat that was moving down the river in the opposite direction. I heard my boat captain ease off of the throttle after what seemed like a relatively short ride, and I looked at my watch. It was nearly three a.m. Although I wasn't sure, it seemed like we had been on the river for 20 minutes at the most. The driver pulled into a hidden cove and brought the boat up to the shore. "This is it," he said. "You'll find the truck about 50 yards in that direction," pointing toward the west.

"I hate to do this, but put your hands above your head," I ordered plainly.

"Hey, man, that's cool. No problem out of me." He raised his hands high where I could watch him. I felt as if he had already expected that I was going do something like that.

Easing off the side of the boat, I stepped into the warm water of the river, keeping my eyes and pistol steady on the driver. I moved onto the bank and backed away. "Thanks," I said.

"No problem. Good luck," he answered, still holding his hands above his head.

Backing up a few more steps, I watched him until I couldn't see him any longer, and then turned to find the truck. I could hear him slowly accelerating the throttle as he made his way back out of the cove.

I found the truck right where he said it would be. It was sharp—hunter-green with polished chrome, equipped with a heavy-duty bumper and a large winch attached. I started to step to the door when I noticed the license plates. They were from Montana. I opened it up, and looked in the glove box and found the registration papers. Everything was in my name. Reaching behind the seat I grabbed the bag of clothes and changed. It had been several years since I had put them on. The dry socks were difficult to pull over my wet feet, but once I got them on, I was much more comfortable. I hate wet feet. The familiar fit of the boots reminded me that I hadn't worn them in quite a long time. The Wrangler jeans were a little tight, and I decided it was because I had gained several pounds sitting behind a desk and not eating like I should. I decided right then that I was going to do something about that. The shirt hung loose and my beaver felt cowboy hat was still the exact shape of my head. I smiled to myself as I found it so interesting how the familiar things can so often bring back pleasant memories of the life I had surrendered.

Stuffing my white shirt, slacks, socks, tie and dress shoes into the bag that had held my other clothes; I decided that it would be better for me to dispose of them at another location. Noticing the backpack, I dug into the front pocket and found the cash, which I decided to leave inside, minus a hundred bucks that I placed in my wallet. I also grabbed a handful of cartridges and put them in my pocket just in case I needed them.

Putting the key into the ignition and starting the truck, I put it into gear. The dash was equipped with a GPS, and it was a good thing, because I wasn't exactly sure how to get out of the river bottom and back out to the highway. But after gaining my bearings, I let off of the clutch and whispered to myself, "OK, Ross, let's go home."

CHAPTER FOUR

With the windows down, I pulled out onto a country road, noticing the sound of the tree frogs and katydids for the first time. The night was still humid, but I was comfortable with the wind blowing through the cab. Traveling west along Highway 7 for several miles, it eventually merged with Highway 53. Moving almost directly south, I found my way to interstate 80 at Joliet and pointed the truck west. I set the cruise control on 70 and leaned back into the seat for the long haul. Eventually, the adrenaline wore off, and I found myself growing weary with each passing mile. I was polishing off the Mountain Dews and bottled water Wren had left in the cooler, one right after the other. The long night was taking its toll on my body, and I knew I was in dire need of rest, but I couldn't risk stopping now, just barely out of Chicago.

Scanning through the radio stations, I couldn't seem to find one that I wanted. I reached into the console, and found that Wren had not only left me about a dozen country music CD's, but a couple fresh cans of Copenhagen. I chuckled out loud at the gesture of thoughtfulness, then cut the seal of the can, thumped the lid and put a large pinch between my cheek and gums. "Um, Um, Um…" I found myself mumbling as I foundered at the familiar taste and the satisfaction of a small shot of nicotine in my veins. It was not a good habit, and I knew it, but man, how I enjoyed it.

Michael Martin Murphey kept me company through the last hours of the morning, and the breaking dawn found me nearly two-thirds across the state of Illinois. My thoughts kept returning to Wren. Was she all right? Was she able to convince the men who had been watching us that she had revealed nothing to me? What kind of explanation would she give for my failure to return? Was it possible that they thought that perhaps I had caught up with the burglar and came out on the raw end of the deal? Did they believe that perhaps I had grown suspicious? Maybe they thought I had returned and noticed that they were there at the house and got scared and ran. They would obviously find out that I didn't show up at the Tribune Monday morning, and that would only make them more suspicious. A thousand thoughts raced through my mind, but all of them led me nowhere.

The miles droned on throughout the morning when finally I stopped just east of Des Moines at a rest area. Only a few cars were present. Stepping out of the truck, I stretched and yawned. The long drive, sitting behind the wheel, had caused my butt and legs to stiffen and practically go numb. My whole body needed a little exercise to get the blood circulating a little better, so I walked my way up to the restrooms. The rest area was quiet and looked like an inconspicuous place to rejuvenate for a while. A coffee machine was inside, but I realized that all I had was a 100-dollar bill, and no change, so I had to go without. My mind seemed to be in a glazed-over mode of operation. I could not ascertain if the way I was feeling was due to the lack of sleep, the long miles on the road, or that downward, declining feeling that comes after experiencing a high rush of adrenaline, as I'd had the night before. Too, maybe it was because the recent culmination of events had transpired so quickly that it made it difficult to piece them together in any reasonable, logical sense. Perhaps, this feeling was a combination of all these things, I wasn't sure, but one thing I knew for certain: in my current state of mind it would be difficult to make heads or tails out of anything, and that could be dangerous.

I used the facilities and washed up a little. The water was only mildly cold, but after cleaning my dry, dirty face, I felt refreshed and vibrant and ready to get back on the road again.

Getting back into the truck, I leaned the seat back for a little shut-eye, when all at once I remembered the map. Up to this point, I had not taken the time to look at it. Digging through the bag of my office clothes, I pulled the map from my shirt. Glancing over the rest area, making sure that I was not being watched, I opened it carefully. The map was badly worn, but upon opening it, I immediately recognized the area. It was a map of the Bob Marshall Wilderness in Montana, just south of Glacier National Park. A friend of mine in college and I had spent a couple of weeks there back in the summer of '86, backpacking and fishing. The route had been marked with a black marker, starting at the trailhead, Benchmark, going north up the South Fork of the Sun river and extending west along Moose Creek, then running north again along the Chinese Wall. The meeting point was marked with a small 'x' at Larch Hill Pass.

As I studied the map carefully, the scenes of nearly 20 years ago began to unfold. For a moment, I relived the trip that my college buddy Vance and I had taken. Larch Hill pass was a milestone for us during that trip. We had been hiking for seven days and we knew when we reached the summit of the pass that the remainder of the journey to Benchmark would be all down hill. It was also the place where we encountered our first grizzly, who was intent on showing more interest in us than we desired. I smiled to myself as I recalled the memory of that night. Vance and I had spent the entire day ascending the pass and dropped off to the southeast toward the headwaters of Moose Creek. Grizzly scat and tracks were everywhere, giving us a feeling of uneasiness, always ready, always alert, and always cautious. As the day gave way to twilight, we made our camp in a small stand of spruce, a campsite that lacked a lot to be desired, but with darkness and a heavy, summer snow coming down quickly upon us, we didn't have much of a choice.

We built a fire and got supper started, and then quickly pitched our tent. Wet and cold from a snow we didn't expect, our teeth chattered as we shook and trembled while we ate our hot soup beside the warm, life-giving fire. Wrapping a hot rock that we had taken from the campfire ring in a piece of canvas, we placed it at the foot of our sleeping bags to warm our feet. Eventually, the cold, wet chills that we had developed relinquished and we both drifted off into a deep sleep. Somewhere, deep into the middle of the night, I was awakened by a sound, or at least I thought it was a sound. I don't really know, even to this day, if my subconscious actually heard something in the darkness, or if that unexplainable sixth sense that many humans seem to develop after spending time in wild country alerted me to encroaching danger, but I awoke with a start. Lying there without moving a muscle, I strained to listen, trying to tune my attention to whatever had awakened me. For a long moment, the heavy breathing of Vance, deep in his sleep, was all I could hear. Tense and taut for a minute or two, I began to relax and I convinced myself that it was just my imagination causing a state of paranoia. Closing my eyes with a long sigh of relief, I slowly started to slumber back off to sleep. No sooner had I closed my eyes, than I heard the unmistakable "woof" of a bear just outside our tent. This time the sound woke Vance. He quickly sat up and started to speak, but I quickly covered his mouth with my left hand and brought the forefinger of my right hand to my lips. In an instant we had our hands on our pistols. He was packing a .357 magnum, and I, a .44 magnum.

We sat there in the tent, upright, still in our sleeping bags, listening intently, scared, worried and uncertain. The side of the tent moved as the bear brushed by, or so we assumed. Vance screamed at the movement, causing the bear to spook and run deeper into the timber away from our camp, knocking the tent-poles away from our tent, making it collapse over the top of the two of us.

Scrambling and squirming to locate the tent flap in the darkness and fumbling for our flashlights at the same time, we finally managed to free ourselves from the opening. I'm sure that we probably looked like a couple of idiots, but at the moment, it wasn't funny, and it became even less so, when our flashlights revealed that the tracks left behind in the new snow were made by a grizzly.

Quickly, we started adding kindling to what remained of the hot coals of our campfire, and in short order, we had a hot blaze burning. Even under the light snow, there was plenty of dead, dry wood to burn. We both discussed our opinions about whether we thought the grizz would return or not, for which neither of us could be certain, but we both agreed that going back to sleep would be impossible.

Nearly two hours passed as we sat there in the light and the heat of the fire, adding to the flames to keep it bright and hot. We really needed rest and even tried to take turns, one of us sleeping while the other stood watch, and then swapping off, but for fear of the worst, both for ourselves and for each other, we couldn't do it.

At just a few minutes before five a.m., we were sitting on a log near the fire, sipping hot coffee, longing impatiently for the first light of dawn to appear, when I spotted a movement in the timber just a few yards opposite our fire. At first, I thought it might have been just the shadows of the fire dancing in the darkness, but then, the beady, red eyes of the grizzly appeared, not more than perhaps 12 steps from our position, and slowly moving closer.

"There he is," I whispered.

"I see him," Vance replied.

We both stood, with only the fire between us when the bear began to circle to our left. Standing near the flame, side by side, we stood together, talking to the bear, with pistols poised and ready. I fired a shot over its head in an effort to spook the grizzly, but he barely flinched.

At about 8 steps, just across the fire from our position, he stopped. His long silver tipped hair between his shoulders was bristled and standing on end, his ears laid back, and he began popping his teeth.

"I'm going to take him," I flatly stated to Vance without taking my eyes off the bear. "When I shoot, you shoot, make it count and don't stop until he's dead."

There are moments, for which I still cannot explain, when immense danger is present and threatening, that, instead of becoming overwhelmed with fear, as one might expect, a deep, soothing, calmness seeps throughout every fiber of my body, causing a feeling of invincibility. This was one of those moments. I beaded down on the grizzly with the .44 magnum and squeezed the trigger, dropping him like a ton of bricks. A follow-up shot was not required. After looking closer at the grizzly, it turned out that he was an old boar. His snout was covered with scars and one ear was mostly gone. His teeth, mostly worn down to the gum line, revealed to us a bear that had lived a long life, and probably would not have survived another winter.

Although we tried to roll the grizzly over and down the hill below our camp to better conceal his body, we couldn't do it. Afraid of getting in trouble with the law for killing the bear, even though we did it out of self-defense, we never did tell the authorities.

That was a long time ago, but it seemed like only yesterday when we were there. Walking back up to the restrooms, I took one last look at the map, shredded it and flushed it down the commode. "Larch Hill Pass, July 31st, I can make it," I thought to myself.

As tired as I was, sleep should have come easily, but I just couldn't do it. After about half an hour of trying, I finally gave up and moved the truck on down the road.

By the time I hit North Platte, Nebraska, I was spent and needed fuel. Filling up both tanks took the better part of two hundred dollars and I opted to purchase some coffee and Little Debbie donuts. The sun was just beginning to set as I pulled into a rest area just 20 miles west of town. I parked, pulled my cowboy hat over my eyes and drifted off to sleep.

Sleep had barely overcome me, when I was awakened with a start to the wrapping on my window. "Hey mister, do you think you could give me a boost. My battery is dead."

My hand had subconsciously tightened its grip on the .45, as I looked through the window at the wiry man, dressed in a suit and tie, standing outside my door. I slipped the weapon underneath my shirt into the waist of my Wranglers. Only then did I realize that the dawn was again breaking, and I had slept the entire night.

The wiry little man already had his jumper cables out and ready to attach to his battery as I crowded my truck up close to his car and popped the hood. His Lexus appeared to be relatively new. Something didn't seem right, although I couldn't place my finger on it.

Hooking the other end of the terminals to my battery he got into his car to give it a try, but nothing happened. Simultaneously, I got out of the truck as he got out of his car. Looking down at the battery, I realized that he didn't even have the jumper cables hooked up to his battery, and the positive terminal was completely disconnected. I just started to comment, "Hey, you don't..." when out of the corner of my eye I saw him swinging his revolver at my head. The split-second glance caused me to duck, receiving only a scrape along the side of my ear and knocking my hat to the ground. Grabbing his revolver, I twisted it quickly. I heard the bones break in his hand, before I crushed his nose with the butt of my gun. Grabbing him by his shirt and tie and slamming him against the side of the truck, I held the .45 to his nose.

"Who are you?" I demanded.

"You're a dead man, Tyler," he responded defiantly, not willing to give up his identity.

Quickly glancing around, it was apparent that the rest area was vacant. "Get up against the front of that truck, now!" I ordered.

"Spread 'em out," I ordered again. Reluctantly he did as I commanded him while I frisked him, something I had never done before. I found no other weapon on his body, but located his wallet in his jacket. Flipping it open, the badge and identification looked legitimate, at least as far as I could tell.

"Agent Jonathan J. Jones, FBI," I read aloud. "What are you doing? How did you know I was here?" I asked.

"I guess it was just my lucky day, Tyler. I saw you back there getting gas last night and I wasn't sure if it was you or not, so I followed you until I was certain."

"Who else have you told? I asked, getting more nervous and anxious with each passing second.

"I called the agency an hour ago, Tyler." They'll be all over this place any minute," he answered.

"You're a liar." I rebutted, hoping he really was. Kicking his legs out wider, I asked him again, "Who knows you're here?"

He just laughed sarcastically, ticking me off even more. Nothing burns me more than someone laughing in my face when I'm serious, and I certainly wasn't in the mood for playing around.

Holding the muzzle of the pistol pointed at the back of his head, I stepped back and kicked him in the groin. He screamed and groaned as he bent over and fell to his knees. Coughing and gagging on the blood that was spilling from his broken nose, I asked him again, this time flipping the safety off of the .45. "Who else knows you're here?" Glaring at me with hatred in his eyes, he just stared. "One more time," I said.

He lunged at me with both hands, but I hit him hard across the bridge of his nose with the butt of the gun again, jerked him up, twisting one arm behind his back, ripping muscle and cartilage and dislocating his shoulder. "Who knows you're here?" I growled in his face.

"You ain't nothing, Tyler."

Pulling his broken arm around the front of the truck, I dangled his fingers into the motor fan. He screamed, cursing and struggling trying to free himself, so I hit him hard across the back of the head, again with the butt of the pistol, causing him to fall backwards unconscious into my arms. Dragging him to his car, I stuffed him back inside his Lexus. Taking some bottled water from the truck, I used his shirt and tried to wipe off his face, then wrapped it around the bloody nubs of his mangled fingers. As he slowly began to come around, I asked him one more time, "Agent Jones, who knows that you're here?"

He coughed hard a couple times and whispered hoarsely, "No one, nobody knows. I was going to take you in myself. You know...be the hero."

"I'm sorry, Jones. You didn't give me much of a choice. Now what am I supposed to do. If I don't kill you, you'll have the whole FBI on my tail before the day is over."

"God, don't kill me, Tyler. Please. I'm begging ya," he pleaded. "I won't tell a soul. I'll make up a story."

Deep in my heart, I wanted to believe him, but the possible consequences of doing so were something I wasn't sure I could risk. "I don't know, Jones. It's mighty risky. If I leave you here, what are you going to tell the Agency?"

Staring across the steering wheel, I noticed that the bridge of his nose was swelling and he appeared to be in considerable pain. He coughed a couple more times and tried to lean out the door to spit the blood out onto the ground beneath my feet. "I'll tell the agency I got jumped by a couple of thugs," he suggested. "I'll request a week of R and R. No one will know."

Scraping my boot back and forth on the pavement, I contemplated and wrestled with the idea. "How do I know I can trust you?" I asked.

"Listen, Tyler, one thing I am not is a liar. I won't reveal to anyone that I found you, but I won't lie to you either. When I get healed after this mess, I'll be looking for you again. You can bet on it."

"Jones, you've got me in a hard place." I replied, "I don't want to kill you, but I have no other option except to leave you here, and like I said earlier, that's a risk I'm not sure I can take."

Thinking about it, I knew in my heart that I couldn't kill him in cold blood. I grabbed the handcuffs from his belt and locked his wrists to the steering wheel. "If I see you again, I'll kill you right where you stand. No questions asked." I shoved the muzzle of my .45 in his nose. "I do have one question right now though. Why does the agency want me dead? Why not just take the map and leave me alone?"

Jones chuckled and coughed, groaning at the pain that the movement brought to his body, "Tyler, if you live long enough, you'll find out real soon. There are some things that the FBI cannot afford to let the public know about." I could tell that he was not about to reveal any more information to me.

"Alright," I replied.

Spinning the cylinder on his revolver, I emptied the cartridges into my hand and tossed his gun into the back seat of the Lexus. I slammed the hood on the truck, and stepped back to the Lexus. Using my pocketknife, I severed the fan belt. I looked at Jones, and he just stared, groaning in pain. I gave him a bottled-water and some cookies Wren had left in the cooler. "I gotta go, Jones," I said. He just grunted. I stepped into the Ford, and pointed it west again on Interstate 80. My adrenaline was still running high, like a river overflowing its banks during the late spring runoff. I did not like fighting and I always try to avoid a fight whenever possible, but Dad had made darn sure that if we boys ever had to, we would know how to take care of ourselves. Right now, I was feeling very appreciative for all the training he had given my brothers and me.

CHAPTER FIVE

It was July 22nd. I had nine days to make it to Larch Hill Pass. I figured that once I reached the trailhead at Benchmark, I could make the hike in two days, three at the most if I ran into bad weather. The miles of the interstate began to unfold before me, and by late afternoon, I was turning off Interstate 80, just outside of Cheyenne, Wyoming, at a truck stop to refuel. Digging more cash out of the backpack, I paid for the fuel and a quick burger. I had grown tired of the snacks Wren had left in the cooler. There did not appear to be anyone watching me. Caution was in order and my survival depended upon staying alert. I could not afford to let my guard down or become slack in my vigilance.

I started the Ford and punched it onto I-25 north. This route was very familiar to me, like a favorite pair of work boots or an old hat that has molded and shaped itself to the contour of your head after years of wear. Many times my brothers and I had traveled it along with my father, either moving livestock or farm equipment or attending the rodeos during The Frontier Days that were held annually in Cheyenne. Those days were long gone, and it seemed as if that time was a million years ago in another world.

The summer sun was hot during the day and the air was dry. The taste of dust upon my tongue reassured me that I was indeed back in the West. After two days in the same clothes, I was beginning to smell a little ripe. I really needed a shower, but I figured that would just have to wait.

Mile upon mile of sagebrush, antelope, jackrabbits and mule deer passed behind me as I kept the Ford pointed northwest toward

Montana. Somewhere between Casper and Buffalo, I lost all track of time. "How did this all get started?" I asked myself as I thought back over the last three years. How did I get so wrapped up in such a complicated mess? How had I let my life get so entangled in the pursuit of money and fame? Why had I resisted Dad's invitation to stay and work the ranch and take it over after he got too old? Tears rolled down my cheeks as my thoughts turned to Mom and Dad. Alone on the ranch, all of their children had ventured off to live somewhere where the winters were milder and the money was better. It was ironic to me that the good money that my brothers and I were making could never seem to quench the thirst and desire each of us felt to return to a life that was simpler than what we were now living. Whenever we spoke to each other on the phone, the conversation always turned to our dreams of trying to get together and meet again in Montana to fly fish the Madison or Yellowstone, or backpack into the many lakes of the Beartooth Mountains or hunt bugling bull elk or monster mule deer with our bows in the Missouri Breaks. Responsibilities and obligations, mostly due to the chains with which money had so tightly ensnared us, kept us from making those dreams come true. Only on occasion were we able to return home, and seldom could we arrange our schedules so that we could do it at the same time and be together. Still we remained a close family and kept in touch often, but all of us knew that time and distance had pulled us apart, and either we had to get comfortable with that reality, or decide somewhere, somehow to try to change it. I resolved right then that if God let me live through whatever it was that awaited me in the next few weeks, I was going to do something about it.

I was the oldest and the last to leave Montana. Working for the *Billings Gazette* had kept me close to home. In 45 minutes I could be back on the ranch to visit or to help Dad work the cows, build fence, or at times, we would grab the fly rods and head down to the Stillwater River and fish until dark, but since I left to take the job in Chicago, I had only been home twice. "Oh, the things we take for granted... and what for?" I asked myself. "All for the buck," I said aloud answering my own question. I just shook my head in disgust at my own selfishness. At a time when my parents probably needed me the most, I chose the city lights of Chicago.

"My Lord, what a fool I have been," I muttered to myself again and again, as I continued north on I-25.

Mile after mile and hour after hour raced on by the road as my mind drifted back to the life that I had lived and what it had now become. "Time," I was thinking aloud again, "is something you can never buy back. Once it's passed, it is forever lost." For certain, I realized that the last several years had been completely focused on the two newspapers that I had worked for and making a name for myself in the process of doing so. The money was good and I had made some wise investments, but deep in my heart, I felt certain that I would give it all up to simply return to the life I had left behind. "How had my life turned out to be wanted by the FBI?" It was difficult for me to fathom.

I looked to my left, west, toward the skyline. The horizon, outlined with a hot-pink brush-stroke of fading sunlight, assured that the close of another day had finished its course. Nowhere have I ever seen sunsets that could match those found in the West. It was refreshing and breath taking at the same time to witness once again. The evening air was fresh and my lungs gulped it inside as if they could never get enough.

Adjusting my hat on my head and my butt in the seat, I got comfortable again for the long drive into the night. I popped another top on a Mountain Dew, got a fresh pinch of snuff, and began to think of the story that had shaken the nation only three years ago, and how it had completely changed my life. In less time than it takes to tell, my simple life as an outdoor editor for the *Billings Gazette* changed to a complex one as a major field editor for the *Chicago Tribune*, not to mention the fact, that my face had been televised around the world. Little did I know back then, the kind of trouble I would be facing now.

CHAPTER SIX

Clovis Belden had grown up all of his life in Montana. He was born in 1946 on the ranch his father had inherited from his father, who had homesteaded the land in 1878. Clovis had worked the ranch, running Hereford cattle and Quarter Horses and refused to allow sheep ever to be raised on the property. His hatred for sheep, a very prevalent feeling found with the cattleman of Montana, was passed down from his grandfather, through his father.

Clovis attended school in Augusta and excelled in athletics. He stood only 5'7" tall and weighed about 150#, but he was always in perfect physical condition. Football and wrestling were his favorite sports, but cross-country track was the sport that earned him a scholarship to the College of Great Falls where he graduated with an associate degree in Agri-Business Management. It was there that he met Judy. They courted for only six months and were married. The two were made for each other. Where you saw one you would see the other, and it seemed they had managed to slip into each other's lives without ever skipping a beat. The life of each was complemented by the other, and after receiving his degree the following month, the couple moved back to the ranch where Clovis had been born and raised. After fixing up an old trapper's cabin that had been on the 5200-acre ranch for years, the two settled down with the plans of working the ranch and building a larger home in the future.

Judy had also grown up on a ranch, east of Havre, and was very much accustomed to the ranching lifestyle. Within four months of their marriage, Judy was pregnant, but only two months later, Uncle Sam decided Clovis needed to spend a little time in Vietnam. Their daughter Kelli was born while he was halfway around the world.

The three and a half year hitch in the jungle is a period of time that Clovis never spoke about. Judy had asked him once about his part in the war, and Clovis politely told her to never bring it up again. It was only some time later that I, while doing some research on the man, discovered in greater detail, this dark and mysterious period in Clovis's life.

It turns out that Clovis's woodsmanship and marksmanship that he had so well developed as a boy growing up in Montana were quickly noticed and utilized by the U.S. Army. After Six months of intense training, Clovis was receiving military mission assignments as a sniper and assassin. Considering that the average life-span of a sniper during 'Nam, after being spotted by the enemy was only seven minutes, Clovis was meticulously careful to never be spotted by the enemy. He was a master of concealment. Later, in an interview with Colonel Jackson, the only officer Clovis reported to, Jackson told me that Clovis was like a ghost: "He could sneak up on you in a vacant parking lot, in the middle of the afternoon and cut your throat without you knowing it." Jackson would not further comment on the individual targets given to Clovis, except to say that he "always got his man".

The assignments given to Clovis were pretty much routine in design. Clovis would be dropped from a helicopter in North Vietnam with a map and the identities of individual targets and a rendezvous point to return to for evacuation. In most instances, he was given his sniper's rifle, a knife and a .45, while food, water, shelter, and the basic elements of survival, were completely left up to him. Under the cover of the jungle and often the darkness of night, Clovis would advance toward his target, living off of the land's animals and vegetation. He would destroy the target, either by a well-placed bullet or at times with his knife, depending on what the situation called for, and then quietly make his escape. Clovis had earned a reputation among the Viet Cong for striking his enemy so swiftly and lethally. They titled him "The Mongoose" and had placed a very high bounty on his head.

With only a month left of service, Clovis was sent on his final mission. It really was not much different than the others, but given his orders, he had ten days to accomplish the task and meet back at a given locale. He didn't show. It was later learned that on the second day after the night drop into North Vietnam again, Clovis had stepped into a bamboo snare. The snare was anchored by a strong young sapling, which, after being triggered, hoisted Clovis's body into the air, similar to a catapult, impaling him backwards and upside down on sharpened bamboo stakes. Four of the stakes had completely passed through his body. One had entered from the backside of his left thigh and protruded out the front side, less than a quarter of an inch from his femoral artery. The second was through his buttocks on the same side, protruding upward, narrowly missing his kidney and exiting out the front side of his hip. The third had entered under his armpit on his right side and protruded through the upper high portion of his chest, and the fourth had entered the side of his right calf muscle and rammed into the leg bone, protruding out the front on both sides of the shinbone.

Clovis knew the Viet Cong could and probably would at any time show up, and if he were captured, death would be very slow, torturous and agonizing. He had heard that the Viet Cong would often torture a man by every imaginable means possible just to observe how much pain and agony he could endure.

Clovis fought the horrifying pain as he tried to remove himself from the wall of stakes by breaking the individual stakes that held him imprisoned to the wall, but the bamboo was too tough to break. One at a time, he pulled his body loose from each stake, trying not to fall to the ground in the process. Hanging upside down, he wasn't sure if his body was trying to pass out due to the adrenaline shock often associated with a major injury, the loss of blood, or the blood rushing to his head. To this day, no one else is certain how he managed to pull himself off, or how he treated his wounds or kept himself hidden from the Viet Cong, but seventeen days later, he hobbled into camp to report to Colonel Jackson, who immediately had him flown to Saigon, where he was treated for two weeks and sent back home to Montana, wearing a purple heart and a Medal of Honor. It was his last mission and the only assignment that he did not complete.

Upon his return, Judy noticed a dramatic and remarkable change in Clovis. More often than not, the changes that might occur in a man, during and after wartime are for the worse, but not so with Clovis. Clovis seemed to have developed a deeper and greater appreciation for life. His love for Judy and his new daughter, Kelli, was magnified by his commitment and devotion to make every day special in some small way. Judy told me that often during the late spring and summer months, Clovis would pick a bouquet of wild flowers growing from a meadow in the high country and bring them to her. She never grew tired of the flowers. At other times, Clovis might be working on the far end of the ranch and just decide to drop what he was doing and come home and spend the rest of the day with her. At times she would ask him "Why?" and his eyes would just tear up, but he could never really verbalize his feelings or give an explanation for his actions except to shrug his shoulders and say, "Because I love you and I want to." For Judy, that was enough.

The greatest change Judy noticed in Clovis was his incredible patience. Ranch work can certainly try anyone's patience, but Clovis just seemed to accept the problems that surfaced as a part of daily living, dealing with them as they came. Unlike his father and grandfather, he believed strongly in taking the time to enjoy the "finer things of life" as he was so often quoted. The finer things in life for Clovis, I learned many years later, mostly included his wife and family, second to God, and then hunting, fishing, and a fondness for new and wild country.

For Clovis, hunting and fishing were never simply a matter of killing or catching, but he prided himself more in the method used. He was a master with a fly rod and enjoyed tying his own flies and proudly claimed that he had never caught a fish on another man's fly. He had an uncanny ability to read water, and could often catch fish when others around him were getting skunked. It was said that he would often give other people a pointer, using the rod and the fly that they had been fishing with to demonstrate a particular cast or presentation, and Clovis would catch fish while trying to help them improve. He was never a show-off. He just loved to see people enjoy the feeling of a rainbow, brown, cutthroat or brook trout on the end of their fly line. "Life's too short to be snobbish about it," he would say. Anyone who had spent a little time in the fly-fishing world knew exactly what he was referring to. Clovis loved his vintage bamboo fly rod and braided line, and found that using it always brought him the greatest satisfaction. It was not that he sneered at anyone for using a more modern type of rod; it was simply a matter of preference. Again, it was never about catching fish, but rather about how he caught them.

As much as he loved fishing, he loved hunting even more, and while he enjoyed casting his fly on the river in the presence of friends and family, when it came to hunting, he always preferred to go at it alone. The solitude and seclusion of hunting alone was more important to Clovis than the taking of an animal, which, like his assignments in Vietnam, he never seemed to fail. Judy never fussed or worried about him, knowing that Clovis, more than any man she ever met, could very well take care of himself in the mountains. She asked him once, "Clovis, don't you ever worry about grizzlies?" Clovis casually replied, "Honey, I'm careful, but if I end up bear crap on a mountain somewhere, some day, then just take comfort in the knowing that I died doing something that I love. There aren't many men who can say that."

In the guest room of the log house that he and Judy had built, the walls were lined with a complete arsenal of guns and mounted animal trophies. He loved to shoot, as did Judy and Kelli, and Clovis was known to be an incredible shot. Friends were always trying to get him to enter competitive matches and shoots in Great Falls or Billings every year, but Clovis always declined. The truth was he seldom ever hunted with a gun any longer. Oh, he kept his .220 Swift in the truck for the occasional coyote found snooping around his cows during calving season, and he kept a .22 rifle on the gun rack for plinking gophers all summer long, but when elk and deer season rolled around, he always reached for his longbow.

Clovis had built several bows throughout the years. He built his first bow from a chokecherry bush that had been in a brush fire. The fibers in the wood were well seasoned and he found it to be quite a challenge. For his first bow, he was quite proud, but he realized that he had taken a little too much wood from the belly of the bow and it only pulled about 35 pounds when he was finished. The second bow was made from an Osage orange stave that had been given to him by a friend of his from Oklahoma. Both bows had been backed with rattlesnake skins, and the second bow he had built as a takedown model to carry as a backup in the event that his first was broken or destroyed in some way. His favorite bow, made from hickory and backed with bamboo, was extremely smooth and quiet. Clovis loved working with wood and during the long winter months in Montana, after the cattle and horses were fed and Kelli was off to school, he and Judy would spend many of their days in the workshop building all kinds of crafts. Judy always built shelves, stools, quilt racks, bookends and other things as Christmas gifts for the following year.

In the past several years, Clovis had started crafting his own arrows. He would take willow from the river and bring it to the workshop where he would skin the bark and let the raw shafts slowly dry and season near the wood stove, but he found that very few shafts had enough spine to fly correctly from his bows. He then started experimenting with Douglas fir, liking the heavy weight and density of the shafts. Although difficult to produce straight shafts, he found them to be very tough and durable. Wing feathers taken from turkeys were split and used for fletching. More recently, Clovis had learned the art of flint knapping and started crafting his own arrowheads. Of course, he said that he preferred the "Clovis point", a name given to the arrowhead of ancient southwest Native Americans. His reason was obvious.

Years passed by and Kelli had excelled academically in high school, earning herself a hefty scholarship. She applied to Harvard and was accepted. She was the only child Clovis and Judy had reared. Finding themselves alone together, after Kelli moved out, they found that, unlike so many other parents they knew, they did not suffer from the "empty-nest syndrome." Instead, their love and passion for each other only multiplied, and Clovis found that Judy would spend longer hours helping him run and maintain the ranch. Clovis, in his own way of thinking, considered himself to be blessed by God with a life that most men would die for, if they could only live it for but one year. With no boss to answer to, a ranch to maintain in some of the most beautiful country in the world, a beautiful wife and daughter that he adored more than anything, and ample time to hunt and fish, it was as close to heaven on earth as a man could get. He was often quoted saying, "I am, of all men, most richly blessed." The ever-present smile on his face would certainly make a person have a difficult time doubting his sincerity.

It was early fall, the second weekend of September. Clovis had been anxiously waiting for this day as he did every year. Opening day of archery season had finally arrived, and every year he spent 10 days backpacking into the Bob Marshall Wilderness, hunting bull elk. The elk rut was his favorite time of year and nothing stirred his adrenaline more than the sound of bulls bugling from deep, dark-timbered canyons or high alpine meadows. The screams, growls and chuckles of a mature bull, was to Clovis the sweetest sound in all of nature, and when you mixed in the fresh, clean, crisp, mountain air of autumn, along with the dancing, quaking, yellow aspen leaves, against a brilliantly blue sky, surrounded by the piercing peaks of the Rockies, life gained a new perspective. Clovis's passion for elk hunting burned in his heart, and the promise of another trip made him ecstatically restless. Two days before opening day, Clovis was already packed and his restlessness was about to drive Judy crazy.

"Why don't you just go ahead and go now, Clovis?" Judy asked with annoyance. "At least you can be where the elk are by opening day. Besides, you ain't getting anything done around here anyway," she added.

"Are you sure?" Clovis asked. "I don't want to make you think I'm anxious to get away from you."

"Get outta here, Clovis Belden. You're driving me nuts," Judy loudly insisted.

"Well, if you insist," Clovis chuckled.

Grabbing her, he pulled her to him and kissed her passionately and was greeted to the same kind of passion in return. He always knew that hunting in wild country presented all kinds of unforeseen dangers, and while he was quite adept in the wilderness, the thought of not returning always lingered in his mind. After all, he wasn't as young as he once was, and anything can go wrong when spending time in rugged, uninhabited country. It was this thought that kept him cautious and careful. Returning to Judy was always the drive that kept him from taking unnecessary risks.

For a minute, they just held each other. "Be careful, Clovis, and good luck," Judy stated. In a conversation I shared with Judy, many years later, she revealed to me that she always worried about Clovis a little more than she would allow herself to show. She knew that Clovis would not enjoy himself nearly as much if he knew that she was at home worried about his well-being, so she had learned to keep her fears and emotions hidden.

"I will, Baby...thanks," Clovis replied and turned toward the door.

He hooked the stock trailer to his old truck and proceeded to load the llamas. For hunting, he preferred his llamas to horses. They could eat almost anything, so, unlike a horse, he didn't have to consider packing in feed. They were able go long stretches without water, which made choosing a campsite a little easier. The llamas could also traverse terrain in which a horse would certainly break a leg, and with four llamas he could easily pack in all of his gear and bring out his elk as well. He had decided that he was getting too old to pack an elk out of the high country on his own back. However, the one thing that had sold him on the llamas several years earlier was the fact that when they are alarmed, they make a loud barking sound. Clovis, therefore would stake out his llamas around his tent, knowing that if a grizzly were to snoop around in the night, he would be alerted by the llama's alarm calls. He found great comfort in the vigilance of the llamas. Hunting elk all day was tiring business and the older Clovis found himself becoming, the deeper he found himself sleeping—not a good characteristic in grizzly country.

The ranch was situated where the property boundary connected to the border of The Bob, as it was often referred to in the local area. However, Clovis wanted to hunt the burn area of the North Fork drainage this year, which was on the western side of the Divide. So, with his gear ready and his llamas in the trailer, Clovis pointed his truck west to the North Fork of the Blackfoot. He had no way of knowing, five days later, his name and photographs of his face would be televised around the world.

CHAPTER SEVEN

President Anthony Watson and Vice President Charles Peterson swept the nation during the election. Watson had been the governor of Georgia and Peterson had served with him as Lieutenant Governor. They had met at Stanford and became the best of friends, choosing to be roommates for the remainder of their time in school.

After graduating from Stanford, they both returned to their home state of Georgia, where each of them worked in private firms out of Atlanta. In spite of the long hours and the heavy work load of their jobs, they continued to remain close and keep in touch, which was not a difficult task, seeing how they lived on the same block and attended the same church each Sunday. Their religious beliefs and faithfulness to God were never something to be considered as an option or a matter of compromise.

Both of them found love within the first two years living in Atlanta, and decided to have their wedding day at the same place and time, which did not seem to bother their fiancés in the least, since both of them were sisters.

The years passed and both were blessed with successful careers. Eventually they moved away from working for someone else's firm and opened up practices of their own. Each of them had two children. Watson had two boys, and Peterson had one boy and a girl. All of them spent so much time together with one another, that they were almost inseparable. It would have been unheard of to even think of celebrating any special occasion or event without the other. Christmas, birthdays, Easter, Thanksgiving, all of them, they were always together

Watson was the first to turn to politics. He made his debut by becoming a member of the local district's school board, something he said he wished he had done a whole lot earlier. From there, his life of politics just went ballistic. When he made his way to the Capitol, he invited Peterson to join him, and through a long series of events that takes too long to tell, Watson was eventually elected as the Governor of Georgia, Peterson in tow.

The people of Georgia loved Watson with his no-nonsense approach. The liberals who stood for things that violated his conscience were hard pressed to make any progress when they tried to pass a bill through the legislature. Watson stamped his veto on many of them and found support in his administration, most of whom shared his uncompromising moral beliefs.

Watson and Peterson both discovered a deep affection and fondness for politics. Anyone could see by simple observation that these two men loved their work and they loved the people of Georgia, and most Georgians loved them. You never heard a word about the two of them taking vacations on the peoples' hard-earned tax dollar. Scandals and rumors of self-interest were just not in their political agendas. They related well with every class of people it seemed, and regardless of race, color or creed, the two worked to make Georgia proud of their leaders.

Both men were very benevolent men and although they never tried to seek public recognition for contributions that they had privately made to care groups or charity organizations, somehow the public would find out and their esteem of the two men would only heighten. What Watson and Peterson gave of themselves manifested and magnified the public opinion a hundred times over.

Although they were careful to admit it, their interest in politics was second only to their shared love for the outdoors, and both of them would work overtime just to be able to take a fishing trip on the river, or hunt whitetails in the thick pines of northwest Georgia. The people of Georgia loved to hear about their highly esteemed leaders engaging in the same kind of outdoor recreation that so many of them enjoyed. It built an incredibly and extraordinarily strong rapport with the people, a by-product Watson and Peterson never expected.

Perhaps the one simple thing that the people noticed shortly after Watson and Peterson took office that brought credibility to the promises they made while campaigning for office is the fact that the two men did not use the State's vehicles to take private trips. In fact, Watson had an old, white, rusty '79 Ford pickup that the two of them would take on their hunting and fishing trips. The press had picked up on this and it only added to the growing admiration and respect the public had for these two men.

Watson was a masterful speaker. His command for the English language was superb. He always seemed to know what to say and when to say it. Coupled with a good sense of humor, he could get a crowd on their feet, yelling and cheering. He ran on a platform that touched the issues of real life in Georgia: education, government spending, tax relief, drug prevention, health care, tougher crime laws, and environmental depredation. When he was voted into office, he did everything in his power to bring improvement to the State of Georgia. So much so, he was beginning to receive national recognition.

On Thanksgiving Day, as Watson reminisced with me years later, the two families were together to celebrate the holiday. Watson asked Peterson to go for a walk with him for a few minutes. Watson revealed to Peterson that he was considering running for President on the Democratic ticket and would be honored if Peterson would consider running with him as the new Vice President elect. Peterson was dumbfounded. The idea that Watson might actually run for President had crossed his mind before, but he had never, for one minute, entertained the idea of sharing the Oval Office with his best friend. Peterson was speechless and could only stare at Watson.

"Tony," Peterson finally replied, calling him by his first name as Watson had always insisted. "I don't know what to say."

"Say 'yes'," Watson replied. "I won't do it if you're not my right hand man."

Exasperated, Peterson stated, "Tony, you know I'd do anything for you, but…"

"Then do this," Watson interrupted.

"Give me a few days to think about it Tony and talk it over with Holly. It's a big step, and I want to make sure she's comfortable with making it."

"Fair enough," Tony replied, "but please let me know by Wednesday of next week. I told the Democratic Party leaders I would let them know by Friday. Listen, Charles, I'm not trying to put pressure on you, but I meant what I said: If you don't agree to run with me, I won't run at all. I need you that much."

On Monday evening Peterson walked over to Watson's house after supper and told Watson that he would be proud to run with his best friend and would consider it an honor. Watson was elated because he had told Charles that he needed him and that running without him was not even a consideration, and even if Watson would have wanted to go on ahead without Peterson, he wouldn't haven't done so for the sheer sake of principle. He had given his word, and in his own way of thinking, a man is only as good as his word.

Watson and Peterson campaigned "low-budget" style, as they were often quoted. While they would accept donations from supporters, they traveled by bus from state to state and city to city. They often requested the crowds not to spend their money on large campaign parties and expensive meals, telling them it would be better put to use by giving it to a charity or putting it to a savings account for their children's college education.

Watson's masterful speaking ability that he explicitly demonstrated so well as the governor of Georgia, winning the hearts of the Georgia people, had the same affect on most Americans. "What you see is what you get," Watson would often say. "It isn't much but it's the best we have to offer, and we offer to you the best we have."

Both men were still handsome men by most standards. Watson was 5'11 inches and Peterson was 6'1 inches tall. Both in their mid-fifties, they were showing a little gray and Watson was developing a small bald spot on the crown of his head. Since their days at Stanford, they had made it a point to work out at the local fitness center at least three days a week early in the morning, often training together.

The left-winged liberals hated them. PETA despised their deep love for hunting and considered them to be barbaric. The gay and lesbian groups along with the abortionists protested often at their campaign speeches, but Watson always made it perfectly clear that he would not compromise on his religious convictions for anything and for no one.

His campaign speeches mostly consisted of the issues he stood for including better education, beefing up the military, toughening up on immigration laws, lowering health care costs, tighter regulation on government spending, more pride in American industry, lowering taxes- the usual conservative spiel. He sounded more like a Republican than a Democrat. However, Watson had a way of convincing the American public that he could do it, and when November rolled around, the silent majority, the often unheard backbone of this country went to the polls and put Watson and Peterson in the White House. A Democrat with some sense of morality had made it into the Oval Office. It had been a long time.

Once in office, the two went immediately to work. Watson did not just put Peterson on the back burner where it appears most Vice Presidents find themselves, but Watson had such a deep love, respect and admiration for Peterson, that he included him in every major decision. Seeking advice from his cabinet members and advisors, Watson would nearly always seek Peterson's input on the matter and more often than not would follow any recommendation that Peterson would contribute. They would bounce alternative scenarios off of one another and address subject matters from a variety of perspectives and almost always come to an agreement on the most efficient and beneficial means of serving the American people.

After being in office for a little more than a year, Watson and Peterson did find one subject that they could not agree upon. The high cost of fuel prices had prompted the need to seek out alternative fuel resources. The push for ethanol, made from corn, seemed to be the hottest idea to surface and find acceptance in the fuel industry. Ethanol burned cleaner, meaning it would lower automobile emission problems, providing cleaner and purer air, especially in the large metropolitan areas, which could mean fewer health problems and perhaps decrease the possibility of global warming. The need for more corn production would better subsidize the American farmer, especially in the Midwest, providing an increase to a much-needed income.

America needed to look to alternative fuels to secure the future. On that, both Watson and Peterson agreed. The problem was not with the idea or the concept, but rather in the ethanol production process. Research was indicating that in order to produce a single gallon of ethanol, it required more than 1700 gallons of water. This water was being drawn from America's rivers, irrigation ditches, and in some cases, pumped from the underground water tables. "Water," Watson would argue, "is the one thing we cannot live without. When you consider the droughts we have had over the last decade, and if there *is* any truth to the theory of global warming, we cannot afford to deplete our supply, even if it appears to be unlimited at the present."

Peterson would argue, "We owe it to the American people to find and produce an alternative fuel. We don't have any idea just how much water we have in our underground water table, but if we don't find a means of supplying this country with fuel, this country will find itself in an economic depression bigger than it has ever known throughout its history."

Watson agreed, but rebutted, "Until we find a means of producing the ethanol without taxing our water supply at such a great expense, I cannot support it. Too, the reports that I have most recently read indicate that the cost of fuel used to make and transport ethanol supersedes the benefits of producing an alternative fuel. Until we find a way to solve or eliminate those two problems, I cannot, in my own good conscience stand behind it. "

Rather than succumbing to a stalemate, Peterson replied, "Then let's find a way."

"Exactly," Watson answered, "and I know no better man in this country than you to see it gets done."

"All right then, I'll get it done, Mr. President," Peterson responded.

"Charles, it's still Tony; it will always be Tony to you."

CHAPTER EIGHT

Late in July, Watson and Peterson were visiting with one another in the Oval Office. Peterson was staring at the picture of both of them on a fly-fishing trip on the Green River in southwestern Wyoming more than ten years earlier.

Peterson, without looking up from the photograph, asked, "Tony, do you realize that we have not wet a line since we moved into the White House?"

Watson noticed Peterson's stare at the photograph and moved closer to it to examine it himself. "You're right," Watson answered, pausing for a minute, and then asked, "What do you have in mind?"

"Well, about a month ago, I was reading about the great cutthroat fishing on the North Fork of the Blackfoot River in the Bob Marshall Wilderness, and it's been itching under my skin ever since to go and give it a try," Peterson commented.

"What's my schedule look like?" Watson asked.

"Busy," Peterson answered. "Nothing open until the second weekend of September."

"Let's do it," Watson answered. "The fresh air might do us some good."

"It could get a little chilly up there that time of year," Peterson commented.

"I don't care if we freeze our butts off." Watson answered. "I'm ready for a break. I need one something fierce. It doesn't even matter to me if we catch a fish. Set it up and let's go. Keep it quiet though. I really don't want the press following us all over the wilderness. Tell the Secret Service to provide half a dozen men, get Security to make sure the area is clear, and let's go fishing."

Peterson looked up at his friend and could see the excitement in his eyes, something he hadn't noticed in quite some time, and wryly commented, "I've already started looking into it." Watson looked at him in bewilderment, so Peterson continued, "Well, I've wanted to surprise you with a trip, but I had to wait for the right time you know. Let me tell you a little more about it.

"There's an outfitter out there who has agreed to take us on horseback about 15 miles up the river. He says the best fishing is on the upper stretch of water. He'll provide everything we need: tents, food, fly rods, flies, the whole nine yards. All I have to do his give him a call and tell him we're coming. He also assured me that if we choose to come, we can fly in on his private airstrip and the public will not have to know. Just give me the 'thumbs up', and it's done."

Before the day was over, Peterson had made all of the arrangements, and both of them looked forward to the five-day trip anticipating the much needed rest and relaxation. Peterson suggested that he might start on a second book during this trip. He had published one two years earlier, *THE BIOGRAPHY OF PRESIDENT ANTHONY WATSON*. Peterson enjoyed great success among the American people as an author and who better than his best friend to write the biography of the President? Of course, Peterson was able to share insights about Watson that certainly no one else could have. Watson and Peterson were like brothers and not even their own wives knew them as well as they knew each other.

The Watson and Peterson family shared Labor Day Weekend together. They had left D.C. and the White House to spend a weekend in a cabin on a secluded lake in north central Maine. As always, the Secret Service had several agents posted for security reasons, but both families had grown so used to their company that they seldom ever noticed the presence of the service men and were certainly by no means annoyed by it.

Watson and Peterson on several occasions discussed the fly fishing trip on the North Fork, which was scheduled for that following weekend. They were to fly to a ranch just outside of Condon, Montana, and be transported to the trailhead from there. The owner of the ranch was Cody Newsome who owned and operated Newsome Outfitters, which specialized in fall hunting trips for elk, deer, bear, mountain lion and fly fishing pack trips into the Bob Marshall and Scapegoat wilderness areas. Normally, the fly fishing trips were completed each summer by the end of August so that Newsome could accommodate archery hunters on the second weekend of September, which is when the season starts, but for the President of the United States, he gladly made the exception.

On horseback they would travel up the North Fork for one long day and set up camp along the river and fish different sections of the river for the remainder of the time. Peterson assured Watson that the horses were trail horses accustomed to taking fishing clients into the mountains all summer long and should not present any type of problems, other than the fact that each of them knew that, since they had not been on a horse in many years, they would certainly re-discover muscles that they had forgotten they even had. Fired up and ready to go, the two of them were filled with anticipation. Everything was ready. The weather forecast was looking good, reservations and contacts were made, and transportation and security was assigned. It was just a matter of waiting for the day.

The three and a half hour flight was uneventful. Arriving on time Watson and Peterson found Newsome waiting at his private airstrip on his ranch and introductions were made. Newsome was 38 years old, clad in Wrangler blue jeans and a long-sleeve shirt, wearing a vest, boots, and Stetson. He stood 6'3" tall, with brown wavy hair and a walrus-style mustache. He had inherited the cattle ranch from his father and had started his own guide service to supplement the working ranch with additional income. Hospitable and courteous with a deep western drawl, Newsome was likeable and cordial.

Since it was still early morning, Newsome suggested that they go ahead and get started. With any luck at all, they could have camp set up by evening and maybe even a little time to rig up a fly and make a few casts on the river.

"That's what we came for," Watson and Peterson said in unison, and so the trip began.

After an hour of saddling all the horses, Newsome had everything ready to go. By 10:00a.m. Newsome, Watson, Peterson, and
five Secret Service Agents, along with four pack mules, were on
the trail heading up the North Fork drainage. The weather was
clear and mild. A person could not have asked for more. Around
2:00 p.m. they stopped to give the horses and themselves a break
and to eat a small snack. Everyone agreed that they could wait
until supper for a real meal.

It had been such a long time since Watson and Peterson had
been in the wild outdoors of the West, that they found themselves
absorbing every little detail that triggered memories of days gone
by. The aroma of pine trees, the Indian paintbrush and Columbines
and other flora that filled the mountain meadows, the clean air, the
rushing sound of the river, the scream of an eagle, the squeak of
saddle leather, even the taste of dust on the trail or the smell of
horse sweat created an intoxicating mood that seemed to evaporate
all the other cares and concerns that filled their lives.

Just shy of 7:30 p.m., they arrived at the place where Newsome wanted to set up camp. Everyone except Newsome was sore
and stiff. Three of the five agents had never been on a horse, and
they were all feeling a little saddle sore.

Newsome commented that his hired hand had gone back to
college, so he was short on help, but everyone jumped in and
helped Newsome get the tents set up and the horses put in the pole
corral that he had built there years before.

"Is this grizzly country?" one of the agents asked.

"Yes, sir," Newsome answered, "And wolf country now," he
added. Seeing the look of worry on the agent's face, he added, "I
doubt we'll have anything to worry about though."

By 9:00 p.m., camp was set up and Newsome had rib eyes
cooking along with baked potatoes and cornbread. Alcohol was
never allowed in Newsome's camp. It wasn't that he opposed
drinking so much; he liked to take a nip now and then himself, but
not when guns were present in camp.

When everyone had eaten their fill, on what they called "the
best meal they had ever eaten," collectively they washed up the
dishes and crawled into their sleeping bags.

For two days the men fished the river, casting flies to hungry
cutthroat. It didn't seem to matter much what fly they used, the

fish were hungry, but the pheasant tail nymph was the most consistent producer.

Peterson had struck up a friendly relationship with Newsome and while Newsome tried to divide his time equally with Peterson and Watson, it seemed that Newsome found conversation to come easier with the Vice President.

The Secret Service Agents had never tried fly-fishing before, so Watson suggested that they give it a try. At first, it looked like it was a lesson in futility. Tangled line wrapped around each other, flies snagged in the overhanging branches of the trees growing along the river, and one half-way embedded hook in the earlobe of Agent Carol that required punching the fly on through his lobe so the barb could be cut off and the rest of the hook extracted. Nevertheless, after a lot of laughs and a great deal of assistance from Watson, Peterson and Newsome, all of the agents eventually enjoyed the thrill of setting the hook and landing a trout of their own.

On the morning of the final day of fishing, the weather was still clear and gorgeous, although the mornings had been a little chilly. It had been a great trip and at the request of Watson, politics was not allowed in conversation. No one argued to that. Everyone enjoyed the rare pleasure of going unshaven and getting up in the morning to a hot cup of cowboy coffee and dressing in clothes that did not require starch or neck ties.

At breakfast Newsome suggested, "If you men are up to a challenge, there is a section of river about a mile hike from here. It funnels through a canyon with steep cliffs along each side. It *never* gets fished, but I found a trail on the other side last year that leads down to the river. It's not really that tough, and I found that the fish in that section of the river are considerably larger because no one ever fishes down there. In fact, I landed a cutthroat last year that weighed nearly four pounds. It would be a wonderful way to top off a great trip before we have to head out in the morning. It's up to you."

Watson looked at Peterson and asked, "What do you think?"

"I'm in," Peterson answered.

Cleaning up the dishes and hanging the food back in the trees to prevent unwanted visitors messing around camp while they were gone for the day, they packed their vests with lunches, fly-boxes, and leaders and grabbed their fly rods and began the hike up the river. Shortly before reaching the mouth of the canyon, Newsome paused to let everyone catch up. "We'll cross here," he instructed. "The trail is on the other side about a hundred yards up the river."

The water ran a little swifter than the stretches they had been fishing and the round river rocks were slick, but by holding on to each other, they crossed without mishap. Finding the trail, Newsome stopped to explain. "The trail works its way up toward the top of those cliffs, near the crest of that hill." Pointing as he described the trail, "Then," he continued, "it drops off gradually toward the river. It's really not that tough. It's a trail used by the mountain goats and bighorn sheep and to my knowledge, no one else knows anything about it. I really don't believe it will be a problem."

Everyone listened and simply nodded in agreement, understanding what Newsome was saying and trusting his judgment. The hike uphill was rather slow. The elevation was a little troublesome on everyone except Newsome, but he was patient and stopped whenever they needed rest. As they neared the top, the trail made a bend and began slowly and gradually winding down toward the bottom.

Newsome commented, "Okay men, just stay close to the cliff wall on the right and don't look down," pointing at the valley approximately 300 feet below. "The only tricky part of the whole trail is just ahead."

Fifty yards down the trail, a large rock protruded into the trail making the trail rather narrow. The trail also made a 90-degree bend back to the right directly on the opposite side of the rock. However, Newsome had discovered that by leaning forward and hugging the rock, stepping with a left foot first and then bringing the right leg around, it was really very simple. However, the thought of falling 300 feet below was fearfully intimidating. Given the same situation without the danger of falling, a person could probably do it with his eyes closed.

Newsome stood with his back toward the valley to assist the men and said, "Alright, one at a time."

Watson was first in line behind Newsome, so he went first and stepped around the rock with the assistance of Newsome.

Peterson was next. Peterson stepped around the rock, first with his left foot, as Newsome had instructed. Just as he swung his right foot around the rock and placed it on the trail directly behind Watson and out of sight from everyone else, he suddenly fell backwards with arms flailing and appearing to be in a panic of helplessness. Newsome, reaching out to catch him, was slightly off balance. He grabbed Peterson by his fly-vest who instinctively turned to grab Newsome by his shirt and arm.

The momentum of Peterson's fall coupled with the fact that Newsome was off-balance and not adequately braced, forced both of them to spill over the edge onto the canyon floor below. Standing and staring in disbelief, everyone watched as the two men fell helplessly to the canyon floor, seemingly in slow motion, striking pieces of protruding rock from the jagged cliffs, and finally landing into the boulder strewn bottom with a hollow, nauseating thud that could be heard, even at the height of the place where they stood.

Watson screamed in disbelief, "Charles, Charles…My God, Charles!!! Somebody do something." Everyone scrambled to the edge to witness the disaster lying below. Stunned and shaken, Watson kept screaming at the top of his lungs, "Somebody, do something!" The agents, in a state of shock and confusion themselves, kept looking for a way that they could get to the bottom but were having a difficult time of it. Even from 300 feet above, their eyes told them as they looked at the mangled bodies lying in the rocks below next to the river, that both men were dead. No one could have survived that fall.

Agent Carol, running his fingers through his hair, trying to decide what course of action to take, pulled his satellite phone from his pocket and hit speed dial to Headquarters at the Pentagon. "Sir," he stated, trying to suppress the quivering in his voice, "we have a situation here. Vice President Peterson has had an accident and is dead…He fell off a cliff, sir, along with Newsome, the fishing guide," he commented, obviously answering questions from Headquarters.

"No, sir," Carol continued, "We have not found a way down to his body yet, but we can see him, sir, and it's obvious that both of them are dead… No, sir, I did not see it happen. I mean, I saw both of them fall, but I'm not sure how it happened... Yes, sir, President Watson is all right, but he is very shaken up. I think we need immediate evacuation. Can you record the coordinates from my phone...? Yes, sir, we'll be here waiting on you. You'll need to send a chopper and some men who can rappel down to the bodies..."

"Yes, sir, the other men and I will move the President up to the top and keep him safe there. We'll build a fire and wait."

Agent Carol put his arm around President Watson, who kept staring down at the body of the friend who had been closer to him than a brother. With tears rolling down his cheeks he sobbed to the point his entire body was shaking. Carol was worried that Watson's knees might buckle at anytime and fall as well. "Max, John, Jason," Carol commanded, "help me with the President. Pete, go up to the top and get a fire started. I think the President may be in a state of shock."

Within minutes, the men had moved Watson to the top of the mountain and had a fire blazing. Appearing terrified and worried, Agent Max approached Carol, "Do you think we ought to try to find a way down to the bodies? I mean, I just hate to leave Peterson down there."

"No," Carol answered. "He's dead. Right now, our top priority is the President." About that time Carol's phone rang. "Agent Carol speaking... yes, sir... yes, sir, we're standing right here beside him now. We'll make sure nothing happens. Yes, sir, of course we're armed... Yes, sir. I understand. Thank you."

Carol hung up the phone. "That was headquarters," he commented to the others and to Watson, who seemed to be oblivious to anything around him, "They said they have a bird flying out of Malmstrom Air Force Base as we speak. It should be here within the hour. He also asked if we were armed. I find that a little strange. Of course we are armed. Why would he ask that?"

Carol looked at his watch; it was 11:40 a.m., not even noon yet. At 12:26 p.m. they heard the choppers, two of them, coming in from the east. They chose a nearby meadow to land, because the place where the President and his agents were standing was not favorable for landing a helicopter. Upon landing, the military paramedics were quick to assist President Watson and encouraged him to fly back to the base with them immediately. Watson, who was starting to regain his senses, could not be persuaded. "I'm staying right here until we get Charles out of that hole. Now get down there and get him," he ordered.

Two men from the Air Force base, Captain Smith and Lieutenant Reams, began rigging up their rappelling gear and strapping on their harnesses. Giving Agent Carol a headset and microphone, one of them stated, "Here, put this on. We'll use this to communicate when we get down to the bodies."

Quickly, the two men rappelled to the bottom and rushed quickly to the bodies of Peterson and Newsome. Newsome lay face down, twisted and tangled and obviously dead. Peterson also lay face down, most of his upper torso pointed downward in between two large boulders, his broken legs extending upward toward the sky. From the bloody mess on the larger rock, they could tell that he had landed there and then rolled off into the crevice. They could not see his face, but the amount of blood on the surface of the rocks and the twisted distortion of his body suggested he was dead as well. Working quickly, the two men hoisted his body up on to the surface of the large rock.

Rolling him over, they noticed something protruding from both sides of his throat.

"What in the world is this?" Reams asked Smith.

"My God..." Smith proclaimed. "Better call Carol."

"Agent Carol," Reams spoke into his headset. "This is Lieutenant Reams. We have a problem here."

"What kind of a problem?" Carol asked impatiently.

"Uh, sir, it appears that Vice President Peterson has been shot," Reams suggested, having a hard time believing it himself.

"What do you mean shot?" Carol asked.

"Yes, sir, affirmative, I mean shot, through the throat, uh, sir, with an arrow," Reams answered.

"That's impossible," Carol replied. "I was right here when it happened."

"Yes, sir, but how do you explain an arrow protruding from both sides of his neck?" Reams rebutted.

Carol paused. He didn't know what to say.

"Reams," Carol inquired through the headset, "they are both dead, right?"

"Yes, sir," Reams affirmed.

"Is the arrow still intact?" Carol asked.

"Yes, sir, Mr. Carol, the arrow is still intact, although I don't know how after such a long fall," Reams returned.

"Listen carefully, Reams," Carol ordered, "Do not... I repeat, do not remove the arrow! Be as careful as possible not to touch or harm that arrow in anyway. I am going to call and have some investigators flown in to examine this scene right away. We're going to send this chopper out over the canyon to get you guys out of there. Attach Peterson to the lift first and be careful not to break or destroy that arrow."

"Yes, sir," Reams answered.

Carol just shook his head and turned to the other agents, motioning for them to step aside from the President while the paramedics thoroughly looked him over. Carol didn't want President Watson to hear what was being said. Carol quickly explained what Reams had reported to him. None of them could believe it.

President Watson noticed the five men talking to one another and could tell something was up.

"What is it?" he asked.

Looking at the ground, Carol was not exactly sure what to say. "I asked you a question, Agent Carol. Now give me an answer!" President Watson demanded.

"Sir, well, uh, Sir, well you see, Sir," Carol stammered, "It appears that Vice President Peterson was shot."

Almost verbatim to the same question Carol had asked, Watson, standing up from the rock that he had been sitting on, asked, "Shot, what do you mean when you say shot?"

"Lieutenant Reams, one of the men down in the canyon right now with Mr. Peterson and Mr. Newsome, said that Mr. Peterson had an arrow protruding through his neck. I'm calling Headquarters to send in our investigators right now."

Watson stared at Carol, speechless; stumbling, he fell back to his seat on the rocky ground. "An arrow!" he declared in stuttered confusion. "How could that have happened...? An arrow through his throat? This can't be an accident! Nobody is accidentally shot with an arrow!" A torrent of emotions commingled with fond memories raged through his bewildered mind. Nothing made sense. "Why would somebody shoot Charles?" He asked under a blank stare fixed on the canyon floor. "My Lord, what will I tell Holly?" he wailed. He pressed his hands against his face, weeping again almost uncontrollably. His concern remained focused on his best friend and his family. Suddenly the thought surfaced, but he kept it to himself: "Was that arrow meant for me?"

Carol ordered the remaining rescue crew to get the chopper out over the canyon and get a cable down there to the men. The crew did as ordered. Peterson was hoisted up first and lowered on the mountaintop where Watson and the men waited. Upon seeing Peterson, Watson began to weep bitterly again. Deformed, disfigured, and saturated in blood, Peterson was unrecognizable. Agent Carol, worried about the President's condition, put his arm around Watson and stated,

"Mr. President, you are going to have to try to get a hold of yourself..."

Watson cut him short, "You mind your own damn business, Carol. Peterson was the best friend I ever had." Startled, Carol stepped back. It was the first time that he had ever heard the President use anything even close to profanity.

"Yes, Sir, Mr. President. I'm sorry. I was just thinking that Mrs. Peterson might need to know about her husband, and I thought it would only be appropriate if you were the one to make the call." Watson started to snap back at Carol again but realized that he was acting a fool. Wiping the tears from his face and running his fingers through his hair, he turned to Carol.

"Agent Carol, I apologize for my behavior. You have been beside me for almost two years now and have been nothing but loyal and dedicated to my well-being and best interest. You are right; I need to call Holly." Extending his hand, Watson looked Carol straight in the eye and humbly continued, "Agent Carol, I say it again, man to man, I hope that you will accept my most sincere apology."

Carol, readily taking the President's hand, shook it with pride and honor, and replied, "Yes, Sir, absolutely, Sir."

Carol handed Watson the satellite phone and Watson turned from Peterson's body and moved down the mountain a few yards to where he could be alone. This really was not a phone call he wanted to make and he really did not feel that it was a situation that needed to be handled over the phone, but knowing that the death of Peterson might be leaked to the media before he could speak to Holly first was not a chance he was willing to take. He called his wife Sarah first, only to find that Holly happened to be visiting with her at the time. No one could hear the conversation, but their hearts ached inside themselves, as all they could do was imagine the horrible degree of weeping and crying that must have been taking place on the other end of the line.

The process of evacuating all four men from the canyon, Newsome, Vice President Peterson as well as Captain Smith and Lieutenant Reams, took a little more than an hour. They were just finishing up as Watson had finished his phone call.

"Agent Carol," Watson affirmed, "I have a family I need to get back home to in the White House. I am going to take the other agents with me on this chopper back to Malmstrom and then we're going to take a private jet from there back to Reagan. I need you and agent Maxwell Caruthers to remain here. I have just spoken with FBI Director Kenton at Headquarters and they have their best investigators in the air right now. When they get here, you will need to explain the events of the day, just as you remember it."

"Yes, Sir," Carol and Caruthers answered.

"Oh, and listen up, men," Watson continued, "Director Kenton told me to tell you not to be snooping around. Under no circumstances are you to disturb this scene. Stay put. When they are finished with you, I'll see you back at the White House."

"Yes, Sir," they answered again.

"Mr. President," Carol inquired, "Has anyone made contact with Newsome's family? I was just wondering what we were going to do about Newsome's horses?"

Watson thought for a minute and assured Carol that he would get someone to take care of it.

CHAPTER NINE

Medical examiners quickly examined both Peterson and Newsome upon their arrival at Malmstrom. Newsome was left behind and arrangements were made for his family to be notified. A separate jet transported Peterson's body back to D.C. while Watson and his remaining three agents returned to the Capitol via Air Force One. Holly, Sarah and all of the children were at the airport waiting. It was 3:00 a.m. upon arrival in a cold, insistent rain that fell heavily upon a devastated Capitol. Gloom and despair enveloped the entire family. It would be a very sad and gloomy occasion for the entire nation when the press released the news in less than three hours.

Peterson's body was immediately taken in for an autopsy. The arrow was removed and the information was immediately relayed to Watson.

The medical examiner reported that there were no identifiable fingerprints on the arrow. The arrow, however, was not an arrow most modern day archers used. Rather than being made from aluminum or carbon or graphite, it was made from Douglas fir, fletched with Merriam turkey feathers, secured with sinew. The nock was filed across the grain of the shaft, and the arrowhead was made from obsidian. It had entered in from the top of Peterson's neck, suggesting that the arrow was shot from above, passed through his windpipe, connecting with a lobe on a vertebrae in his neck, which is probably the reason it had not passed completely through. Of course, most of these details meant nothing to the common public, but considering Watson's hunting experience, he was quite familiar with the details of this assassination arrow, and although Watson really did not desire to hear the details, his own curiosity also wanted to know the truth about his best friend's murder. He ordered the report to be sent to the FBI immediately.

Ten minutes later, Chief Investigator Chuck Mitchell called. A thorough investigation of the area had found nothing for most of the afternoon the preceding day, until, on a hunch, Mitchell, standing at the rock from where Peterson and Newsome had both fallen to their death, began to look upward at the cliffs to see where a man might sit in wait for an ambush. Looking around there was no apparent sign that would indicate that anyone had been there. About to leave, Mitchell noticed something that caught his eye. It was a fiber of material clinging to the rough edge of a rock. It appeared to be camouflage and made of wool. He had bagged it up to be further examined at the lab. From the given position of the fiber, Mitchell concluded that it would have been a rather easy and concealed place for such an ambush, the distance appearing to be no more than 20 yards, at an angle of about 30 degrees.

Watson, after patiently enduring the details, asked, "So, what are you going to do about it?"

Mitchell replied, "We have all trailheads and access roads to the Bob Marshall Wilderness blocked off with officers at each point. We have three whirly birds in the air. We have contacted the local lion hunters to bring in their dogs and have explained to them that the man we are looking for could be very dangerous. Mr. President, not a single one of them backed out. They loved Mr. Peterson."

"Good," Watson answered. "What else are you doing?"

"Well, Sir," Mitchell continued, "we have contacted the National Guard who is transporting men from the Mountain Brigade at this very moment. We intend to comb every inch of this God-forsaken wilderness until we find that man or whoever is responsible for Mr. Peterson's death, and, Sir, we may already have a suspect."

"Who would that be?" Watson demanded.

"A Mr. Clovis Belden from over near Augusta. It's a small town just east of here." Mitchell answered. Continuing, he added, "We found a truck with a stock trailer parked at one of the trailheads that is registered to his name. I took the address and phone number from the papers. I spoke to his wife a few minutes ago on the phone and she was very cooperative. She told us that he was elk hunting in the North Fork drainage of the Blackfoot. I asked her what type of weapon he would be using, and she informed me that he was archery hunting. When I asked her what type of arrows he used, she got a little nervous about all of the questions and wanted to know why I was asking. Obviously, she has not heard the news yet this morning. She finally consented and explained that Mr. Belden built his own arrows using some kind of fir wood, turkey feathers and his own flint arrowheads. Mr. President, he's got to be our man."

"Then catch him!" Watson ordered loudly in the phone. "I don't care what it takes. You and your men are to stop at nothing until you have him by the throat. Do you understand, Mr. Mitchell?"

"Yes, Sir. We will do everything in our power to bring him in," Mitchell answered.

Watson started to hang up and then added, "Oh, and Mitchell. Just between you and me, I don't care if he's brought in alive or in a body bag."

"I understand, Mr. President."

CHAPTER TEN

The six o'clock morning news on the Eastern seaboard was first to break the story to the American public. By 9:00 a.m. the news had reached the headlines for every newspaper, radio station, television news-broadcasting network and talk show throughout the nation.

Businesses and schools from all over the country chose to take the day off to mourn and honor the memory of Vice President Charles G. Peterson. The news was much the same no matter what station or program a person tuned in to. The following is a news release as it was given on national public television:

President Watson and Vice President Peterson were engaged in a fishing trip in the Bob Marshall wilderness area, south of Glacier National Park in Montana. Vice President Peterson and local hunting and fishing guide Cody Newsome had fallen from a cliff while descending a trail down to the river to fish a particular stretch of the North Fork River. It appears that Vice President Peterson was shot with an arrow through the throat from somewhere on the cliff above. The unusual characteristics of the arrow have got the FBI puzzled. There is a rumor that the FBI has a possible suspect, but no names are being released at this time. An area-wide manhunt is underway at this very moment to locate and capture the suspected assassin. Many questions are still left unanswered. A motive has not been determined for why someone would shoot and assassinate the Vice President. It has been suggested that the arrow may have been intended for President Watson and missed, inadvertently striking Vice President Peterson instead. The fact that the culprit used a primitive weapon, which would require him to shoot from such close proximity, has also puzzled investigators. Perhaps this is a possible act of a terrorist group. These questions and others like them remain unanswered, but Americans from all over this great country are saddened today by the loss of such a great man.

Photographs of the arrow had been taken and released to the press who displayed them to the public eye all around the world. The arrow was fashioned much like the arrows used by the Native Americans for hundreds and perhaps thousands of years. People just shook their heads in disbelief. Peace-loving radicals and anti-hunting groups of all sorts were having a heyday exploiting the tragic news, arguing, "This type of behavior is what we should expect when we allow people to 'murder' innocent animals. Hunting only promotes violence." Psychologists were being interviewed on nearly every television talk show providing their expert opinions and giving their analysis of the personality and character of the man responsible for this heinous crime.

By noon, the name of Clovis Belden had been leaked to the public. Photographs and portraits of Clovis Belden were on display across millions of television screens. Upon learning of his living address, reporters flocked to his log home and ranch near Augusta. Live broadcasts were made from his home. One camera crew displayed the workshop where Clovis and Judy spent so many of their winter days building crafts. Judy felt as if her privacy was completely and inappropriately invaded. Many, many hours were spent together alone with Clovis in this workshop; laughter and joy, dreams and plans for the future and just a whole lot of good heart-to-heart conversation had been shared there.

"Could this be the very place where Mr. Belden crafted the arrow that took the life of our beloved Vice President Peterson?" one reporter asked.

Judy had undergone intensive questioning from the FBI. She held up rather well. She admitted that she had a difficult time trying to understand why Clovis would do such a thing and could not force herself to believe that he would have done it without a very legitimate reason, but she was also convinced that the arrow was indeed an arrow that Clovis had built. She reported that all of the arrows Clovis built were crested with the same design and pattern and that the arrow taken from the Vice President matched those that Clovis had built. She even found a few that Clovis had finished building, but had not taken on his hunting trip, and indeed, they were nearly identical to the "Assassination Arrow", as it was now being called. Questions about the personality and character of Clovis revealed nothing out of sort. In fact, anyone who had known Clovis would tell you much the same thing. Clovis was a good man, a patient man, a great outdoorsman, loved his family, etc... The FBI decided that Clovis may try to return back home to the ranch, so a complete audio and visual surveillance system was set up around the ranch's headquarters. Video cameras and trail cameras were posted back inside the woods a short distance from the house; the phone was tapped, and Judy's personal computer was screened. She didn't know it for certain, but she suspected that her truck was also rigged with some sort of tracking device. She protested the treatment, but decided that bucking against it was a waste of time.

It seemed that everything about Clovis's past was brought to the public's eye. Again, nothing about the man seemed to match the hideous crime that he was allegedly accused of committing, that is, until his military files were made public. When the nation heard about his service in Vietnam and the fact that he had served as a trained assassin and sniper and had successfully completed over 80 assignments, the verbal picture created by the ruthless media painted Clovis as a sadistic killer. I later learned on one of my many visits with Judy that it was the first time she had learned anything about Clovis's history in Nam. As she sat there listening to the news story over CNN, she explained, she could not believe her ears. Certainly, the tender, patient, compassionate, loving man, the man who brought her flowers, who adored her more than his own life, the most unselfish human being she had ever known, could not be the hideous and repulsive individual that the media was making Clovis out to be. None of the details about the personality that the media was portraying matched with the true personality she knew of her husband. However, the more she contemplated it, the more she realized that everything about his skills, talents and abilities as a shooter and his uncanny vigilance and prowess in the woods matched perfectly with the portrait of Clovis that the media was painting.

It was nauseating for Judy to think how the media could twist and turn information around and mold the public's opinion of anything and anyone to whatever they desired. It wasn't fair or just, and it was obvious that they had created the image of Clovis to be a ruthless, killing monster. She grew angry and disturbed to see her man so unjustly portrayed in such manner. Her gut feeling told her that Clovis was somehow responsible for the death of Vice President Peterson, but she also believed just as strongly that there had to be a logical explanation. While she struggled with her emotions of anger and uncertainty, she wrestled with worry and concern for Clovis's safety more than anything, although, even then, something deep inside her soul assured her that he would be alright. Clovis was a very capable and confident man, and not until now did she really realize how significant that was to her.

Colonel Jackson, who had long since retired from the Armed Forces, was interviewed live from his home in California. When asked about Clovis, Jackson commented, "Belden was one of the best soldiers I have ever seen, and without a doubt, he was the best at his job. I've had many good soldiers serve under my command, but there are very few who, even after all these years, still stick out in my mind Clovis Belden. His character was above reproach. His deep, strong voice was gentle and polite. He didn't say a whole lot, but when he did, everyone listened, and he never shirked the duties of a soldier. He was well respected by his comrades. While I am not at liberty to discuss the details of his assignments, I will say this, if Belden is indeed the man who assassinated Vice President Peterson, they'll never catch him. The Viet Cong never could, what makes us think we can?" Jackson's interview was televised nationwide.

Upon hearing the news, Kelli called her mom back home on the ranch. The FBI invaded the house and listened to the entire conversation. Kelli burned with fury, but like her mother, was worried about her father more than anything else.

"Mom," she asked, "do you think Dad did it?"

"Yes, Baby, I do. It's definitely one of his arrows, but I have no idea why he would have done such a thing. I cannot believe he would have killed him without a very good reason."

"Mom, I want to come home," Kelli pleaded. Judy paused, wrestling with the idea for a minute, and then replied, "Kelli, I think you need to stay in school. The FBI are here at the ranch. I'll go to town and see if I can hire someone to help take care of the place."

"I can't stay here at school, Mom. Everybody is harassing me, asking me all kinds of questions, and I don't know what to say." Judy listened and was uncertain about how to respond to her daughter. "Mom, did you know those things the media said about Dad?" Kelli asked. "You know, when he was in the war?"

"No, Baby. I had no idea. He never spoke of them, and I've never even heard your dad talk in his sleep. I knew he was very good in the woods and all, but it never crossed my mind that the army used him in that way during the war... Maybe you need to come on home after all. I hate for you to drop out of school right now, but maybe after this is over, you can pick up where you left off."

"Good!" Kelli exclaimed. "I'm already packed."

Judy chuckled. Kelli had always been headstrong and determined, and the more Judy considered the idea of Kelli coming home, the more she found herself liking it. Kelli was a capable, tough, intelligent young lady, and she could help with the chores until the situation was resolved.

Three days after arriving back at the Capitol, Vice President Peterson was laid to rest. Although the services were private, scenes of the funeral were televised and the American people wept along with his family and friends. A dark cloud hung over the nation.

Rather than making a State of the Union Address, President Watson called for a press conference. He expressed his sorrow for his dear friend and associate, Vice President Charles Peterson, explaining that every possible means of action was underway to locate Mr. Belden. He would be given a fair trial, and if proven guilty, he would be punished to the full extent of the law. "To that," Watson boldly stated, "I give you my solemn word."

CHAPTER ELEVEN

Clovis had put the arrow exactly where he intended. Without hesitation, he eased out of the cleft of the cliff that he had used to conceal himself and where he had been waiting. Carefully stepping on the scattered rocks to avoid leaving tracks or any sign of his presence, he meticulously climbed over the top of the ridge, working his way into the timber. Once inside the pines on the other side of the ridge, he stepped up his pace to a steady run. He felt certain that it would be a few hours before any kind of search for him would be underway, so he knew that he needed to put as much distance as possible between himself and the others. He had staked the llamas near a stream in a small mountain meadow. Knowing the search team would eventually discover them, he decided to use them as decoys, and not return to the llamas, but move in the opposite direction. This might possibly buy him a little more time. Utilizing the cover of the timber and maintaining a steady pace, he moved northeast toward the Chinese Wall, a 13-mile stretch of cliffs running the course of the Continental Divide. There are only 4 well-known passes that a person can traverse from one side to the other.

Aware that the dogs would certainly be on his trail, Clovis would ford a stream and wade it for a while, hoping to lose his scent. The tactic slowed his progress, but he knew it was well worth the extra time and effort.

IIe carried a day pack with him that contained a first aid kit, knife, matches, fishing line and hooks, his take-down bow, moccasins, a few granola bars and trail mix. Strapped to the pack was his quiver full of arrows and a light-weight, camouflage wool jacket. In his hand he carried only his other bow. It was not much of a load, and he knew that he really didn't need all of it. He had certainly survived on much less, but for now, it would be useful.

As the sun began to set, Clovis decided he had better find a safe place to camp for the night. He selected on a small, hidden, natural cove found under a cluster of downfall created by an avalanche several years earlier. While cleaning out the debris to form a comfortable bed in the pine needles, he could hear the rap-tap-tap of helicopters flying toward the river.

The sky darkened, and the evening air was chilly. He used his jacket for a blanket, and even contemplated the idea of a fire, but he feared that doing so might give away his location.

Friends of Clovis knew that he was a good man. He was honest and fair, and a pleasant man it seemed, in all kinds of weather, but no one really ever knew that he was a praying man. Clovis, however, prayed all of the time, I later discovered. He shared with me that he had learned well how to pray in the jungles of North Vietnam. Numerous times, he found himself hiding in the foliage in the darkness of night trying to avoid detection from the Viet Cong, while he listened to the sounds of their footsteps as they searched for him, sometimes stepping only inches away from his presence. Clovis told me that he always believed the reason he lived today was because there was a greater power on the other end that listened to his prayers. It was this close relationship that he kept with heaven, he exclaimed, that had taught him to make the most of each day and find joy in the journey of living.

Late into the night, sleep finally came, although he was awakened on several occasions by the cold chill of the air and finally, well before the dawn began to break in the eastern sky, he was moving again. Muscles stiff and sore from the poor night's rest, hiking was difficult at first, but soon he began to feel the circulation of blood move through his extremities and found he had to shed his jacket to keep from becoming saturated with sweat. Stopping at a small tributary he paused for a drink of water, casually noticing the tracks of moose, deer, elk and bear that had recently used the water source. He then realized that, like them, *he* was now the hunted, and, like them, his survival would depend upon utilizing every ounce of wariness and caution in his possession.

Dawn was finally breaking and just as the sun was beginning to give birth to another day, the sound of the choppers in the distance assured him that they would be searching for him soon. Moving quietly through the deadfall and timber was difficult as the blow-downs densely covered the terrain. It was the kind of habitat moose preferred and by the abundance of droppings that littered the ground, it was obvious they used this area often. The sound of several bull elk bugling further up the canyon brought a smile to his face- after all, they were the reason he was here in The Bob in the first place.

Clovis had a particular destination in mind. He was hoping to continue northeast toward Larch Hill Pass and then move south along the easterly side of the Chinese Wall to the source of Moose Creek. Years ago, while hunting mountain goats near the Wall, he had found a small, hidden cave about fifteen feet from the base of the cliffs. It appeared to be inaccessible at first, but he located several small rock outcroppings that served as steps, and the climb proved to be relatively easy. The cave entrance itself was just big enough to crawl through, partially hidden by a small pine that grew on the ledge near the front of the entrance, but upon entering, it immediately opened up into a large room. Toward the back of the cavern, several small cracks in the ceiling revealed the sky above, and he discovered that by building a fire out of dry wood, the openings created an upward draft, much like a flue in a chimney, and what little smoke was created by the fire spread and dissipated quickly before reaching the summit, making it impossible to detect. He had gathered wood there years ago in case he ever found himself in a situation where he needed a place to wait out the weather while hunting in that region, and through the years established several places such as this throughout The Bob. However, this particular site was the most suitable and best concealed. Because of the route he was taking, he figured it would take him a day and a half to get there, two at the most.

Around mid-morning, Clovis stopped for another drink and decided he needed to eat one of his granola bars for some energy. He recognized the fact that he was burning a lot of calories, and staying energized and hydrated were key factors to maintaining a high level of performance. Scooping water from a small stream, he splashed it on his face and hair, feeling cooled and refreshed. He stepped away from the stream to listen and was certain that he could hear the baying of hounds in the distance. From the sound of the excitement in their voices, it was obvious that they had discovered his trail. The sound of the choppers sounded like they were coming from the northwest, which meant that they had probably discovered his llamas. He wondered what they would do with them.

Trying to put himself in the shoes of the pursuers he began to strategize what possible measures would be taken for his capture. Always before, during 'Nam, he had managed to think one step ahead of his enemy. However, *this* search would be massive; of that he was certain. You don't assassinate the Vice President of the United States and expect Barney Fife to oversee the investigation. "No doubt," he said to himself, "they'll block off every road and trail that leads in and out of The Bob. They've already brought in the dogs. The FBI will bring in their best agents. The National Guard will probably send a thousand men or more and probably from every direction, aircrews will cover every square inch of this place, and they'll use satellite surveillance. Technology has come a long way since 'Nam. This is going to be tough."

Clovis had a habit of speaking aloud to himself when it was safe to do so. Hearing his own voice allowed him to get a clearer picture in his mind of the present situation. For now, he felt he needed to put as much distance between himself and his pursuers and then go into hiding, something he had learned well in Vietnam. He recalled a couple of circumstances where he was forced to hide from the Viet Cong. On one particular instance, he spent 28 hours in a treetop while the enemy searched frantically for him below on the jungle floor before they finally gave up on the area. It had rained the entire day and night and was one of the most miserable nights that Clovis could remember. On another occasion, after making a hit on a North Vietnamese General, he was working through a very large patch of bamboo, on his way back to be air lifted out, when he accidentally walked right into a small enemy platoon. Gunfire erupted as soon as they saw him and the chase was on. For two days, it was cat-n-mouse, and his pursuers were closing the gap. Knowing that it was just a matter of time before his enemies caught up with him, Clovis, in broad day light, hid himself, submerged under the water among the reeds, breathing through a small bamboo straw, while the enemy marched within feet of his location. He waited until nightfall and escaped under the cover of darkness. Now, a little more than 30 years later, he was being pursued again. His survival, just as then, would depend on his stealth and most importantly, the ability to make the right decisions at the right time.

As he strapped his pack upon his back, he noticed a patch of chokecherry growing in a small coulee. He began to gorge himself on the purple tart berries that had already started to wrinkle and dry from an early frost. He hastily stuffed as many as he could in his pack and turned toward the creek to continue his chosen route, only to be stopped short. A large sow black bear, cinnamon in color, with two cubs not quite half grown were standing right in the trail, obviously coming to the chokecherry patch for the same reason he had. An arrow instinctively jumped from his quiver to his bow, but he felt kind of silly standing there with a stick and a string. The large sow was standing on all fours less than fifteen feet away. She laid her ears back and began popping her teeth. The hair on the back of her neck and shoulders stood on end. She made a false charge at Clovis, who, while standing his ground, felt his heart jump into his throat. "It's alright, mama," Clovis whispered, noticing her ears twitching, meaning she had heard his voice, "just let me get out of your way, and you and your children can have this place all to yourself." Stepping aside of the trail, Clovis slowly and cautiously moved into the brush, not turning his back to the bear, but careful to avoid direct eye contact with her. He did not want to pose a threat. The sow stood her ground and watched him as he moved off and then proceeded forward into the chokecherry patch. Clovis sighed heavily, "I've got to be more careful."

Evening brought Clovis to a ridge looking down into the South Fork of the Flathead River. He would have to be cautious and careful here. This was a popular drainage among fisherman, hunters and back-packers. It was also easy to access by horse, and it was certainly possible that some of his pursuers were already in the drainage.

Again, he moved into the black timber and found a well-hidden place to sleep for the night. This time it was under a ledge of a large secluded rock. Gathering firewood for the night, Clovis believed a fire in such a place would not be detected. The lack of sleep and the cold nighttime temperature from the night before had taken its toll on him today. He needed a warm, good night's sleep, and a fire against the rock cleft would reflect the heat on him all night. In less than 20 minutes he had built a fire against the rock, cut a few pine boughs to sleep upon, knowing that not only would they be more comfortable than the cold hard ground, but would also provide insulation as well. This time, rather than using his wool jacket as a blanket, he put it on and wore it. Placing his pack beneath his head for a pillow, he quickly fell into a deep sleep.

He was quickly awakened by commotion in the canyon below. The morning sun had already risen well above the eastern horizon and was beginning to warm the day. Clovis kicked himself for sleeping so deeply although it was certainly needed. Listening to the sounds coming from the canyon below, he quickly erased all traces of his presence, and carefully moved into a position for a better vantage point. Along the east side of the South Fork, soldiers were camped and moving about; what they were doing, Clovis could not tell. He regretted leaving his binoculars back with the llamas and the rest of his gear, but he had opted that they were too large and bulky to justify carrying for what little use he would get out of them.

As he evaluated the situation, he wondered why they were there. Obviously, they were looking for him, but what made them come to this place? Clovis could think of only one possible explanation that made any logical sense. They had figured out his direction of travel, anticipated his rate, and were trying to sandwich him from the northeast and the southwest. Traveling directly north was out of the question. It led him farther away from his desired hideout on the Wall, and it also led him into country that was not intimately familiar.

Most likely, he had a lead of a day or so on those from the east, and he seriously doubted that those in the canyon below would suspect his proximity to be so near. It might be wise to rest for the day and wait until nightfall to move. With so many after his skin and some of those so close, moving during the day light hours would be rather risky. In the concealed shadows of a cluster of lodge-pole pine, he sat watching the valley far below. On several occasions choppers flew directly overhead searching painstakingly from above. He knew that his presence would go undetected as long as he stayed put. As he sat and watched he could see the choppers in the valley below dropping off more men and taking others to where ever they were going. Not all of the men were clad in military gear. Some of them, he was certain, were FBI and perhaps even local hunters who knew the area well. It appeared that something *big* was happening.

Sipping on water from a small spring, Clovis ate his last granola bar, leaving him enough trail mix for a couple of meals. He added some chokecherries to the trail mix to make it go further. His rations were low and he needed to replenish them as soon as possible. He desperately craved some kind of meat. The creek below was teeming with trout, but it was also swamped by people who were trying to capture or kill him. Patiently, he considered his options, weighing and measuring each one carefully, trying to determine his next course of action.

The long afternoon hours slowly dwindled away as Clovis tried to establish a plan to evade his pursuers and avoid capture. Finally, he smiled to himself, "Why not wait until dark and just slip right through the middle of them?" At first, he thought it might be too foolish, but the more he pondered the idea, the better he liked it. No one would expect him to make a visit late at night. Chances are they would not even have anyone on night patrol. Besides that, he might be able to confiscate a few needed items. It had become quite obvious to him that his best chance of survival was to remain in the wilderness, and doing so would require taking advantage of every opportunity that became available. Content with his plan, he curled up to get the much-needed rest that the forth-coming night would require. As the sun dipped into the horizon of the western sky, Clovis whispered, "Oh God, make my footsteps light tonight and keep me from harm's way." With that he drifted off to sleep.

CHAPTER TWELVE

The early morning chill woke Clovis at 2:00 a.m. He jumped to his feet and stretched, shaking his arms and running in place to improve his circulation. He slipped out of his sweaty hiking boots and pulled on his moccasins. It was a habit of his to carry them with him while he was hunting. When the moment came to stalk an animal he would put them on to quietly avoid making a sound that might alarm his prey. They would serve well in his plans for the night. Adjusting his quiver to ascertain easy access to his arrows, he grabbed his bow, and set out for the canyon below.

The descent down the mountain to the valley floor was rather easy. The sky was filled with a bright moon and a million stars illuminated the entire canyon, making visibility possible. The distant howling of wolves stopped him for a moment. Like most ranchers, he did not appreciate the reintroduction of the wolf to Montana. He had lost several calves to a pair that had decided to call his ranch their home. Although he never mentioned it to anyone, knowing that the fine for killing a wolf was more than he could afford, the destructive days of the two wolves were put to an end one early winter morning when Clovis was going out to feed his cattle. They had killed a yearling heifer the night before and were too engrossed in filling their stomachs to notice Clovis's approach. His .220 Swift found its mark both times.

When he approached the west bank of the river, he could see that he was only about two hundred yards from the camp. The fires were all out, and it did not appear as if anyone was stirring about. He removed his socks and moccasins, pulled up his pant legs and began fording the creek. He did not like wet feet and besides that, the water in his moccasins had a tendency to make a sloshing noise that, if heard, could reveal his presence. Stepping gently into the river, the frigid water bit his toes and the round rocks were slicker than a fish's belly. Using his bow as a staff he waded carefully across the river. When he reached the other side, he quickly donned his socks and moccasins. He got to his feet and looked up the river toward the camp. "OK, Lord, this is it. Direct my steps as you always have."

Reaching the edge of the camp, his first observation had been true. No one was up and about, at least on this end of the camp. Judging on the number of tents in the camp he surmised that there had to be at least 300 men sleeping there. Staying in the shadows, he quietly moved closer, testing each step with his feet to avoid stepping on a twig or rolling a rock. Several M-16 rifles were leaning against the tent post of the mess hall. He smiled at his good fortune. Pulling the magazines quietly from 3 of them and putting them in his jacket, he grabbed the last remaining loaded gun. Army rations were scattered on the tables and a full bag of coffee was sitting next to the coffee maker. He stuffed his pack with salt, pepper, sugar, as much as his bag could hold. On a table inside, near the far corner of the mess tent he found a map of the area. In grid pattern it had been drawn on, indicating the areas that had been searched. A satellite phone, binoculars, pencils, paper, coffee cups, Coke cans, potato chips were scattered all over the table. It was a mess. Clovis grabbed the phone and binoculars. As he started for the tent flap, he turned back to the table. Scribbling on a leaf of notepad, he wrote, "Leave it alone. It's not what you think." Looking out from the mess hall tent to observe any kind of danger, he found it clear. Withdrawing an arrow from his quiver, he pinned the note to a large aspen tree that grew in the camp. From within the tents, Clovis could hear the snoring from many of the men. They were tired and were completely unaware of the fact that the very man that they were looking for was standing in their camp, and could easily bring harm and destruction upon them if that had been his intentions.

Clovis just smiled as he imagined the note and arrow being found the next morning. Someone would certainly catch the brunt of a lot of yelling and shouting. Oh well... Clovis moved to the east side of the camp and disappeared into the timber just as subtly as he had entered. North of here, just a few miles away is Needle Falls. It was near there that Clovis had another secure hiding place he had located while fishing the river only the previous year. He didn't feel this was a good choice at the time, so he kept moving on toward his hideout on the east side of The Wall.

As graceful as a deer and just as naturally, he moved through the timber. Gliding through the trees like a ghost, the miles melted away behind him. Dawn was only minutes away, and he knew that when the note was found, the dogs would be flown in. The pack he carried was considerably heavier with the added weight from the items taken from the soldiers' camp including the rifle that he strapped to the other side. He really hoped that he didn't have to use it.

As much as possible, he focused his thoughts on devising an escape plan. He was quite confident that if he reached the cave on the east side of the Wall, they would never find him, but still, a man couldn't hide there forever. He needed to do something unexpected.

The morning passed quickly. Stopping to take a break, he sat with his back against a large rock to eat a little and drink some water. The sun's radiance and warmth soothed his face, and he felt himself beginning to doze off. Again, he didn't want to stop, but he knew that a little rest might do him some good. An hour later he woke again to the baying of hounds, but this time they were close. Grabbing his gear, he took off at a hard run. Traveling less than half a mile, he stopped to listen again. This time he could tell the hounds were rapidly gaining on him. Moving to a place that gave him better visibility down the mountainside, he could see the dogs below him about a fourth of a mile and behind the dogs another half a mile or so were a group of men in hot pursuit. Perhaps it was time for a little "showdown".

Finding a large rock, one that was too steep for the dogs to climb, Clovis scaled it to the top and waited. The dogs were quickly approaching from the valley below, the scent of his trail strong in their nostrils. Within minutes they were standing at the base of the rock, yelping and barking excitedly at Clovis. There were four of them—two redbones and two mountain curs. Without a moment's hesitation, although feeling a deep sense of remorse, Clovis moved to the edge of the rock and started drilling arrows into the throats and chests of each dog, three of them dying instantly beneath the rock. The fourth yelped and started back down the trail from which it had come, but expired within 25 yards of the others. Clovis understood the love a man had for his dogs. It is a special bond that is unlike any other relationship a man will ever know. A good dog will love you even when you mess up or get mad or do something stupid. He'll lick the sweat off of your face and lick your wounds. He'll snuggle up beside you in your tent to help keep you warm on a long winter night. He'll stand guard and defend you with his life if he has to. Clovis had loved several dogs throughout the years and it always broke his heart when he lost one.   No doubt, the owner of these dogs was going to be extremely angry.

Scrambling down off of the rock, Clovis withdrew two of the four arrows. One was broken and the other was wedged into bone and could not be withdrawn. Wiping them off quickly in the grass, he replaced them in his quiver. He could have used the M-16, but the report would have further given away his presence. Now, the pursuing men did not even have the voices of their dogs to listen to. This would buy him a little more time. He had to make it to the top of the mountain. Running, climbing, scratching and clawing, he struggled toward the top. The timber was thinner here and he hoped he would not be spotted. Choppers were buzzing all over the canyon below him. One passed directly over his head, forcing Clovis to dive into a patch of brush. Somehow, they did not see him. The pressure was on. He cocked his head to listen, and he could hear someone shouting all kinds of obscenities. They had found the dogs.

Sweat trickled down Clovis's face, burning his eyes. Glancing at his watch, it was only 2:14 p.m., a long way until dark. Looking up, he was only a few hundred yards below the summit of the Divide. It was rugged, steep, and a little more exposed than Clovis had hoped for. He had no choice. To remain was to be captured for sure.

Looking at the area before him that he must cross, it was all uphill and no place to really hide until he reached the summit where the tree line started again. He could hear voices below, and they were getting closer. Surely more dogs would be brought in soon. Even if he reached the summit, it would be difficult to hide; he would be on top of the Chinese Wall, which provided very few passes to descend and little cover to hide in. He knew of one particular pass that he was sure no one ever used. People who visited the Bob used the other four more often. If he could make it there, he would descend down into the upper drainage of Moose Creek and move north to the cave.

Trying to build up his nerve, he was uncertain of the location of the men who were after him, but he knew they were close. Taking a couple deep breaths, he was just starting to make a break for it when a bullet shattered a limb directly over his head. Screaming and hollering, gunfire rang out and bullets started spitting everywhere. Clovis took out up the hill as fast as he could go. Rocks and dirt kicked up all around him as bullets sprayed the hillside he was ascending. A hot surge of pain ripped and burned across the bottom of his right forearm, but he never broke stride. When he was less than 10 yards to the tree line, an Apache AH-64 chopper flew in from the canyon and opened fire but did not make contact. Zigzagging through the trees, Clovis ran as hard as his legs and lungs would carry him, with the chopper hovering in the trees above him, trying to determine his location. The chopper kept making circles, which assured Clovis that they were not exactly sure of his whereabouts. He kept running and running. He stopped suddenly, realizing that the area around him looked familiar. He did not think he had come this far, but, yes, there in front of him was the large tree growing atop the edge of the cliffs that marked the hidden pass to the bottom below.

The "pass", as Clovis called it, was really nothing more than a steep chute that was formed by years of erosion through a crack in the cliffs. Taking one look and listening to the sound of the choppers, he determined they were still working toward his direction. Pulling a magazine full of rifle cartridges from his coat, he dislodged several bullets from the brass. Pouring the powder on the ground, he knew the dogs would sniff it into their nostrils as they followed his trail. This would immobilize their ability to locate his trail for a few hours. He piled off the side of the cliff, dropping nearly 15 vertical feet to the top of the chute, sliding most of the way down on his rear. The loose shale and dirt made descending relatively simple, and running downhill, his tracks were quickly eaten up by the loose shale, covering and hiding any track he might leave behind, much like leaving a track in water.

Arriving at the base of the cliffs, he dusted himself off and began running toward Moose Creek. Here, the heavy timber provided adequate cover for keeping hidden. Darkness was encroaching upon him. Gazing through the binoculars he had lifted out of the mess tent, he could see helicopters still flying over the Wall and men and dogs were moving at the top of the cliffs. It would be difficult to locate the place where he descended and hopefully, between the use of the gunpowder and the vertical jump, they would lose his trail, at least until nightfall.

Moving through the dark timber, it seemed as though darkness had already fallen. He stepped into the creek and waded up stream to further hide the scent of his trail. In a sense, this was leading him back into the direction of the Wall closer to trouble, but only farther north. If the place were not located where himself descended from the wall, anyone pursuing on foot would have to hike all the way to Larch Hill Pass to come down off of the Divide.

He moved away from the creek a few yards and found a large, tight cluster of brush. Quickly cleaning out a small opening at the base of the brush, he crawled up under the canopy. By raking away the dead leaves and branches he soon had a comfortable place to sleep. Once that was completed he placed some brush back in front of the entrance to better conceal his camp for the night. He was unusually warm and the evening temperature did feel as cool as the last few nights. Staring up through the brush, he realized that he was unable to see any stars. It had clouded up and threatened to rain. Changing his wet socks and moccasins, he put on a dry pair of wool socks and his hiking boots. It was then that he remembered the burning pain in his arm. He withdrew his jacket and shirt and found that a bullet had grazed the bottom of his right forearm. The wound was not deep, but it had ripped a nasty gash, one that could use a few stitches. It would have to wait until sunrise when he could see what he was doing. For the night, he wiped it clean with his wet socks and dressed it the best he could.

Lying back under the pile of brush, he contemplated more and more his situation. He had a story to tell and one that needed to be told; although, there was no way that he could prove his story was true. If his story was not told, the truth about killing Vice President Peterson and his motives may never be known. His thoughts turned to Judy and Kelli. All he could feel when he thought of them was hopelessness and despair. Would he ever see them again? Would they want to see him? Clovis started to slip off into a deep depression but immediately gathered his wits. "Stop it." He said aloud. "A pessimistic attitude will get you killed quicker than anything."

Digging through his pack, he tore open a bag of army rations. The dehydrated food, once mixed with a little water, was quite tasty, even if it was cold. The United States Army had come a long way with Army food in the last 30 or so years.

Sitting back in his little cubbyhole of brush, he tried to contemplate a way of escape, not only from his immediate pursuers, but also for a means that would clear his name. Suddenly, a thought came to him. He reached into his pack and pulled out the satellite phone and dialed 411.

When the automated operator answered, Clovis spoke, "Billings, Montana...Ross Tyler."

He was immediately connected to the number. The phone rang a couple of times and then was answered. I remember the conversation as if it were only yesterday.

"Hello?'

"Is this Mr. Tyler, the outdoor writer for the Billings Gazette?"

"Yes. Yes, it is. May I ask who is calling?"

"Oh, I'm just a big fan of your writing, and I was wondering if perhaps you might be interested in a story that's a little different than what you are accustomed to?

"What have you got in mind?" I asked.

"A story about a man who assassinated the Vice President of the United States," Clovis answered.

I sat there in silence for at least a minute. I wasn't sure what to say, but I had a hunch, one that I have never been able to explain: that the man on the other end of the line, was in fact, Clovis Belden.

"This is Clovis Belden isn't it?" I finally asked.

"Yes, it is. In the flesh," Clovis answered.

"Mr. Belden, I'm a little puzzled about why you would call me?" Little did I know at the time what that one phone call would do to the rest of my life. I did not think it would be appropriate to ask Belden about his location, at least not at this time.

"Like I said, Mr. Tyler, I have read your work in the Sunday Gazette for years. I have a copy mailed to me every week. I admire the way you write. Your love for fly-fishing and hunting, especially with a longbow are so much like my own, that although I have never met you, there's something about you that says you're a man I can trust. I cannot explain exactly why I feel that way, but the way I figure it, if you're not, I'll let you be the one to prove it to me."

"And if I'm not someone that can be trusted," I asked, "are you going to kill me too?" Immediately, I was kicking myself for saying such a thing.

"Probably," Clovis casually answered, "but unless I've read you wrong, living with the idea that you violated someone's trust, would probably hurt you worse than dying."

"Okay, Mr. Belden, that's fair enough. It's obvious that you and I must have several things in common, among which is our strong belief in being men of our word, and you have expressed that you feel you can trust me; but Mr. Belden, I am wondering why I should trust you? After all, I have never killed anyone, and I certainly did not kill the Vice President of the United States."

Clovis paused. I could tell he was thinking about it for a minute, and again, I was afraid that perhaps maybe I had come on too strong, and Clovis might decide to hang up on me. We both sat there in silence.

"Mr. Tyler, you don't beat around the bush, do you? However, you are right. I should not have assumed that you or anyone else should trust me. However, let me tell you this. Presently, I am sitting at the upper end of the Moose Creek drainage looking at the Chinese Wall, and watching flashlights stirring all through the night. With one phone call, you could put them on to my location right now. I would not risk this call if I didn't believe you were someone I could trust. I cannot give you a reason to suggest that you should trust me, but the way I figure it, if you do this story right, it could make you big and perhaps at the same time, pardon me from the crime that I have allegedly committed."

"Are you saying that you did not assassinate Vice President Peterson?"

"No. I am not saying that. I *did* kill him; however, I had a reason. It was nothing personal at all. Shoot, I liked Mr. Peterson."

"What possible reason could you have for killing such a fine man?" I asked.

Clovis paused for a minute and thought, but decided that it could wait.

"Mr. Tyler…"

"Call me Ross," I interrupted.

"Okay, Ross, when I am able to find some way to prove what really happened and what this is all about, I will tell you and you alone."

"And what happens if you are killed before you are able to do that?" I asked.

"Then I guess the world will never know and my name will forever be disgraced," Clovis answered.

"So, what is it that you would like for me to do now?" I asked, uncertain to what Clovis really desired.

Clovis considered the question carefully. "I'd like for you to tell the world my story. Start it off with a piece about who I am. Do the research. I think you'll discover that, although my assignments in 'Nam appeared to be brutal, I am not a murderer. Ask some rhetorical questions to get people to thinking. Shoot, I don't know, Tyler. I'm not a writer. I just need some help."

Considering that for a moment, I replied, "I'll see what I can do, Mr. Belden, but it almost seems like you are asking me to try to prove you're innocent and you've given me no reason whatsoever to believe that you are."

"You're right, Tyler," still calling me by my last name, "but go ahead and get started, and perhaps in a day or two I'll call you back with some more details that you can work with."

"A day or two," I shouted loudly through the phone, "you'll be dead in a day or two…Mr. Belden, do you have any idea how many men are looking for you at this current moment. The

National Guard alone has deployed over 5,000 men throughout the Bob Marshall. There's a one million dollar bounty on your head. The FBI, local law enforcement, civilians, and just about everyone and their dog are up there now. The entire search is being filmed live on CNN. We, that is, the entire world, are watching it 24/7. Your entire ranch, because it borders the Bob Marshall Wilderness, is being patrolled in the event that you may try to come back home. Glacier Park is surrounded and shut down. One film clip on television got you running toward the summit of the Divide earlier today with bullets flying all around you. Oh, and the part that really made the American public mad was the footage of the dogs you shot. That did not go over well. I'm telling you, Mr. Belden: your days are numbered. I suggest you get a good lawyer and just turn yourself in." Belden said nothing.

"Mr. Belden, I sense that you did not realize that the search for you was so magnified...I also have the suspicion that deep in your heart, you doubt that you'll ever be caught."

Belden seemed to ignore the perilous situation he was in. I suspect that the idea of really being caught was something he didn't really have time to entertain. It wasn't that he was cocky or overconfident, he was just sure of his ability to disappear better than most.

"Tyler," he finally said, "what if I gave you 50 thousand dollars cash to get started on my story?" Clovis asked.

I gulped, "Uh, well, uh, where are you going to get your hands on cash like that?"

"Will you do the story?" Clovis asked.

"Yes, I'll do it, but I don't want the money. Not if it has something to do with the death of Vice President Peterson," I stated.

"Oh, it has everything to do with his death, Tyler, but it has nothing to do with why I killed him."

"You're not making sense," I replied.

"Do you know where Silvertip Mountain is?" Clovis asked.

"Yes, I do. I have never been on it, but I have hunted in the area surrounding it."

"Good. If you are interested in the money, you will find it stashed under a few rocks at the very peak. There are a lot of rocks on the peak and nothing looks out of place, but there's a pink and gray, granite stone lying next to a couple of larger stones. You'll find it there. Better get it before the heavy snow comes."

"I'll think about it, Mr. Belden." I replied, continuing to ponder everything Clovis was telling me and scribbling it down in my notepad as fast as I could at the same time.

"Mr. Belden, can I tell the press about this call?"

"Yes. Please do. However, do not mention the money."

"Okay, Mr. Belden. I'll write your story. I may even try to get up to Silvertip in a couple of weeks to see if the money is really there. I could stand a break anyway. Is there anything else you would like for me to do?"

Clovis paused for a long moment, then he started, his voice cracking, and I knew he was weeping and fighting for words to say. Finally, he spoke, "Tyler, could you please tell my wife Judy and my daughter Kelli that I am sorry about all of this, and that I love them so very, very much? Tell them that I didn't mean to hurt them in any way. Tell them," he paused again, "tell them that I have always been proud to be their husband and father, and nothing or no one has ever brought me more joy in my life than the two of them. Tell them that for me, Tyler, will you?" he asked.

CHAPTER THIRTEEN

As far as I know, I was the last person to speak to Clovis Belden. Two days later, the military and FBI were still searching the area in the upper drainage of Moose Creek when they came upon a scene that looked similar to where a small bomb had exploded. In reality, it was where a grizzly had killed a young cow moose. Approximately 20 yards off of the creek, searching for Belden, a few soldiers smelled something dead. Looking around to identify the source of the odor, they discovered the partial remains of a young cow moose, one that had mostly been devoured by a large grizzly, based on the size of the tracks left behind. However, that was not all they discovered. A short distance from the carcass, army rations, scattered arrows, a broken bow, an M-16 and several magazines, a satellite phone, binoculars, moccasins, first aid kit, and a shirt that was ripped and shredded, and saturated with blood (presumed to be Clovis Belden's) were found scattered all about. The body of Clovis was not discovered, but he was declared dead based upon the items recovered, the supporting evidence surrounding the scene, and the fact that the large amount of blood taken from the recovered shirt and moccasin proved to be his blood. It appeared as if Clovis had been trying to make his way up the Moose Creek drainage and ran into some serious trouble with a grizzly that was determined to protect his kill.

A light snow started to fall that afternoon, so if there had been any kind of scent left behind, it was soon either washed away or covered up. A solid week had been spent looking for the man, so Mitchell and the rest of the FBI were ready to head back home.

The National Guard lingered around for another two days and decided to give up the search as well. Perhaps Belden really did succumb to death by a grizzly. All evidence seemed to indicate that's what happened, and there was nothing new to suggest otherwise. The search was called off and within a couple days, the story was "old news".

A few specialists were left behind on duty in secret search, but even they were unable to discover anything that would suggest that Belden was still alive. Friends and family held a memorial service in honor of his memory.

Even though he was dead, I began my research on Clovis Belden, including a phone call and an hour conversation with Colonel Jackson, Belden's former commanding officer, who actually was now a retired general in California. So far, everything I found out about the man, Clovis Belden, exhibited a lifestyle of which I found myself envious. I needed to know about the character of the man, and after a week of writing and trying to put together his story, I asked the boss for a week off. I had told him about the phone call, and we leaked it to the press, via a short editorial I had written for the paper. The word got out fast, and calls poured in from all over the country. Everyone was curious about the story I was going to write and why Clovis had chosen me to contact. It was time to go and visit his wife and friends. I had heard that Kelli had gone back east to school to work on her doctorate degree. After spending three years teaching high school English, she wanted to go back to school to receive her Ph.D. I also heard that she did not want to answer any more questions. I felt it best to respect her wishes.

Arriving at the ranch, after a long four hour drive, I was immediately impressed with the cleanliness and tidiness of the place. Everything seemed carefully organized and in its proper place. Ms. Belden, who later insisted that I call her Judy, was just finishing up with the morning feeding of the cattle when I pulled into the driveway. Her hair, mostly gray and pulled back in a ponytail, hung down nearly to her waist. Just guessing, I would say that she stood just a little over 5 feet tall, and I doubt she weighed more than 110 pounds. Although time and many years spent in the hot summer sun and the brisk winter wind had taken its toll on her skin, she still remained extremely attractive. Her smile shone brilliantly white and her eyes twinkled softly as she firmly shook my hand and invited me into the log house.

The living room was a showcase. At the far end, stood a massive stone chimney with the finest stonework I had ever laid my eyes upon. The walls of the high, cathedral-style room were adorned with trophies of elk, deer, moose, bear, mountain lion, goat, sheep, antelope, as well as mounted trout, including golden, brook, cutthroat, rainbow and brown. A stuffed turkey gobbler was mounted as if it were strutting for a hen in early spring; a pair of rooster pheasants, fighting for breeding rights, was encased in a glass showcase; sage grouse, blue grouse, ruffed grouse, sharp-tail, and ptarmigan were posed in a variety of stances, on the mantle of the fireplace. Hungarian partridge, and prairie chicken, hanging on the log wall, were displayed as if a pointer had just flushed them. Meticulously in place, each piece was mounted and placed as if it were in its own natural setting. I felt as if I had stepped inside a Cabela's or Bass Pro Shop. Judy noticed me admiring the room. "These are only a small representation of some of Clovis's hunting and fishing trips. I finally had to tell him that we didn't have any more room and that we had spent a small fortune already in taxidermy expenses."

Handing me a cup of coffee, she asked, "Would you care for anything in it?"

"Just black is fine."

"Well, let's have a seat then."

We sat there for several minutes just sipping our coffee, both of us trying to figure out how to break the ice. Finally, she looked at me over her coffee cup, "You know, Mr. Tyler, Clovis thought the world of your editorials. He loved the way you write. You're the only reason we had a subscription to the *Billings Gazette*."

"Thank you, Judy, for sharing that with me. I appreciate it more than you know."

Again, we sat there in silence. I figured it was my turn to restart the conversation. "Judy, I guess you have heard that Clovis called me shortly before his death?"

"Yes, I know." She paused for a few seconds. "Would it be too presumptuous to ask you about some of the things he said?"

When I told Judy about the conversation with Clovis and reiterated the things he made me promise to say, her soft brown eyes began to well up with tears that were soon rolling down her cheek. I offered her my bandana.

"It's ironic you know," she stated, as she removed her glasses and wiped away the tears.

"What do you mean," I asked.

She laughed a little, turning her head to the side and staring out the window into the mild, sunny afternoon. "I used to ask him if he was afraid of grizzlies, you know, out there hunting all by himself for weeks at a time. You know what he used to say?" I shook my head. "He'd say, 'If I end up bear crap somewhere, someday, at least I'd die doing something that I love. Not many men can say that.' I never thought it would really happen."

"You know, Ms. Belden, there are those who don't believe it really happened," I responded.

She looked at me really closely, as if she knew my thoughts already. She thought hard for a long time and then spoke with a sigh, "If he's still alive, he will not be found until he is ready, and I doubt that he will do anything to inform me if he is. I *know* Clovis. He will not permit his emotions to overrule his good judgment. This whole place, or at least around the perimeter of the house and barn are under surveillance. I don't know what all the government has as far as tracking devices, but I'm sure that Clovis knows, and he'll stay away from here. I know my phones are tapped, and it wouldn't surprise me if our conversation is being listened to right now as we speak." She looked at me and said, "Let's go for a walk. I'd like to show you our workshop."

We stepped out onto the porch and then walked toward the barn and workshop. Judy stopped and turned toward me, "If there's something you want to ask that no one else needs to hear, do it out here, away from the buildings."

"OK," I replied. "Can I ask you now?"

"Shoot!"

"Do you have any idea why Clovis would want to kill the Vice President or the President? I mean, it *has* been suggested that the arrow might have missed President Watson and errantly hit former Vice President Peterson?"

Judy laughed somewhat sarcastically. "I doubt it. I've watched Clovis consistently shoot golf balls at 30 yards with those bows and arrows of his. When he draws an arrow, it goes where he wants it to. In the past 14 years, he has never failed to bring home a bull. As far as the answer to why he did it, I do not have the slightest idea. Both of us voted for Watson and Peterson. Clovis always said, 'It's about time they put some good men in the White House.'"

"If, let's say, you know, hypothetically, Clovis is still alive and somehow, some way he informed you, would you let anyone know?"

"No. Absolutely not. Clovis would not permit it," she answered very sternly.

"Ms. Judy, do you think Clovis is alive?" I asked, knowing it was a very tough, personal question.

She looked at me again with her soft brown eyes, and they started to swell with tears again.

"I'm sorry, I..."

"No, it's alright, Tyler. It's just that it's hard for me to picture Clovis being dead. Without his body or any evidence of it, and knowing his ability to survive, I can't help but to harbor a little bit of hope. Hope is all I have. Maybe it's all for naught, but still, I cling to it anyway."

I decided right then that I was going to tell her about the money. Even as much as I could have used 50 thousand dollars, providing that it really was where Clovis said it would be, I felt it really belonged to her.

"Ms. Judy, there is something else that I need to tell you. Your husband offered to pay me 50 thousand in cash if I wrote this story about him, and he told me where to find the money."

"Fifty thousand dollars," she almost screamed. "Where would he get that kind of money? We don't have that kind of money. Shoot, we've *never* had that kind of money."

"That's what he said," I told her as she stood there shaking her head in disbelief. "He said it had something to do with the assassination, but it had nothing to do with the reason he shot Mr. Peterson."

All of this was confusing Judy. She could not formulate the first lick of sense out of any of it.

"Ms. Judy, I want you to have the money," I finally stated.

She looked at me and shook her head in disagreement. "If I have that kind of money, what am I supposed to do with it? If I deposit it in the bank, somebody will get suspicious. If I buy things with it around here, somebody is going to question that, too."

"What if I brought it to you, and you find a place to hide it for a year or so?" I asked.

Thinking about it she said, "No, you take it. You write a story about Clovis, the man. You write it and cause people to question his motives for killing Mr. Peterson. Even if Clovis is dead, just the idea that some day, the truth might be revealed is enough for me."

We spent the better part of the afternoon visiting together. She showed me the workshop and the barn and some of the livestock. Admiring her horses, she asked, "Would you like to go for a ride?" It had been months since I had been on a horse, especially in wild country, so I took her up on the offer.

While we rode, she told me of her love for Clovis. She told me about the first time they met, about their wedding day, how she had given birth to Kelli while Clovis was off to war, and all about the changes she noticed in Clovis when he returned. "He loved Kelli, more than his own life," she commented, "and he loved me too, just as much."

We rode in silence for a while. Judy was riding a small gray Appaloosa filly while I sat on a bay gelding that I could tell had been well trained and well taken care of. I stopped to make a few notes in my notepad so I wouldn't forget anything that Judy had shared with me already. As the sun started to close out the day to the west, we turned the horses toward the barn, arriving long after dark.

"Mr. Tyler, why don't you stay and let me fix up some supper for you? You can sleep in Kelli's room and get on about your business the first thing in the morning if you would like."

I thought about it for a minute and gladly accepted the invitation.

CHAPTER FOURTEEN

I woke early the next morning to the smell of bacon and eggs frying in the kitchen, and hot coffee brewing in the pot. While Judy and I ate our breakfast, I shared with her my plans for going into the Bob and looking for the money Clovis had told me he had hidden on the Peak of Silvertip Mountain. In a hurry to get started, I didn't linger long at breakfast.

I packed lightly, carrying a small sleeping bag, some trail mix, and my .44 magnum pistol, along with some dry clothes, matches, knife and a few other items that I really hoped I wouldn't need. I had no intentions of staying long, but in Montana, a person never knows when the weather will take a turn for the worse. Parking at the trailhead, I locked the truck, grabbed my gear, and hit the trail at a good pace.

I had been too many weeks in the office, so the clear mountain air cleansed and refreshed my lungs. The day was comfortably warm, making my hike enjoyable, and I could not think of another place on earth that I would rather be. The lustrous blue sky, always so big in Montana, enveloped the landscape while golden-yellow aspen leaves quaked in the gentle breeze. Birds and squirrels scurried about across the trail, going about their daily business. Archery season was still open for another week, but since the assassination, somehow I hadn't given a whole lot of thought to hunting, although I couldn't ignore the occasional bugle of a bull elk or two in the canyon below. The high, piercing shrill and guttural grunts and chuckles of a mature bull are, in my opinion, the sweetest music to be found in all of Mother Nature's orchestra, and

I found myself stopping frequently to listen to their song. I was a little saddened that I wasn't hunting those bulls in the canyon below, but I was frightened at the same time. Frightened, because I found myself giving up what I loved so much in order to "do the job", and in this case, a job that I really didn't have to take. "My Lord," I whispered aloud to myself, "what are you allowing yourself to become?" Here, surrounded by what I loved the most, the answer to my own question was distinctly obvious. I was becoming a man, consumed by the pursuit of money, and in the process of doing so, the time to enjoy the wealth and riches attained by saturating myself in my own passions and desires, was swiftly passing me by. I found this struggle to be very frustrating. In my mind, I could reason that time was far more important than money. After all, a man can lose all of his money and still get it back, but time, once it is gone, is lost forever. There are no "do-overs" or "reruns", and it was this extremely vivid reality that disturbed me the most, because even though I knew it, I felt trapped, obligated and compelled to keep doing what I was doing. So forced, like most other problems in my life, I decided that I would just have to worry about it later. Dismissing the thought for the moment, I proceeded to burn-up the trail, stopping only occasionally for a quick snack and a drink of water. No one seemed to be in the mountains that day, and judging from the tracks of horses and people, it had been at least a week since anyone had passed through.

As evening started to fall, I chose a campsite at the base of Silvertip Mountain. I did not bring a tent, so I cleaned out a dry place on the ground in between two spruce trees. Stretching a rope from one to the other, I draped a small tarp over the line and staked it down to form a cover to keep any moisture off of me during the night. The sweat that had saturated my clothing while hiking was now beginning to cause me to feel chilled and cold and my body began to shake and shiver lightly. This was nothing I had not experienced before, but I realized that it could become more severe if I didn't take a few necessary measures to warm my body. Quickly building a fire, I heated up a cup of Ramen noodles and added some jerky pieces. It wasn't exactly elk tenderloin on a bed of asparagus spears, but eating something hot rejuvenated my body, and my fingers found warmth and comfort as I wrapped them around the cup. Adding more fuel to the fire, I sat close and absorbed the radiant heat from the flames, allowing my tired and exhausted muscles to rest and relax. Night had long since fallen, my eyelids were heavy, and I was finding it more and more difficult to stay awake, but I sat there on a log for a long spell, staring into the glow of the flames, poking with a dead pine stick at the blazing, red embers, while listening to the lonely cry of a wolf somewhere in the far distance. I pondered the mournful sound and for a reason I could not fully explain, somehow, I was acutely aware that the wolf and I had a lot in common—we were alone. Recognizing the futility of trying to deal with my emotions at this moment, I put out the fire, dousing it with water from the nearby stream, and then I threw a rope over a high pine branch several yards away from my bed and secured the rope to my pack, which I proceeded to hang high enough to keep out any bears or other critters. Folding my jacket to use as a pillow, I slid my .44 underneath where it would be handy and ready if the need to use it should arise. I crawled into my sleeping bag, not even bothering to remove my smelly, sweaty clothes, and fell asleep almost immediately.

I woke up to the chirping of songbirds and the squawk of a pinion jay. Peeking from the tarp, the morning dew still clinging to the fabric, I could tell that the morning was well on its way of making a day out of it. Crawling out, I stretched and yawned. I was sore and stiff and my muscles felt somewhat like a pretzel, but I quickly rolled my bag, and carefully packed my backpack again. After a quick bite of trail mix, I was back on the trail.

Ascending the mountain took the better part of the day. As I climbed, I pressed my hands against the top of my thighs, pushing downward to relieve the burning sensation in my muscles, covering at times only ten to twelve steps before needing another break. Physically, I was in pretty good shape, but I hadn't been at that elevation for quite awhile. The temperature was considerably colder halfway up the mountain than it was in the valley. A group of mountain goats, all nannies and kids, stared at me as I walked by, not seeming to consider me a threat. Focused and determined, I did not allow my mind to drift to anything else except the goal at hand, and before I realized it, I was standing on the summit. Looking at the mountain from below, it appeared to be rather sharp and rugged, but the summit was actually sort of rounded and strewn with rocks. Moss and lichen clung to the stones, but the timberline was more than a thousand feet below. I sat there for a while enjoying the view, but I was chilled, as my sweaty, saturated shirt did nothing to keep me warm. I took it off and put on a dry t-shirt and my jacket, leaning my back against a large rock, out of the wind. A strange feeling came over me, and I felt myself wanting to cry. I was having a difficult time understanding the reason for these emotions. As I sat there, it occurred to me that I had not been in the mountains for quite some time, at least not like this—alone and completely on my own. Rather than feeling like I was a part of the wilderness, as I had most of my life, I was feeling more like a stranger or an outsider, perhaps, even an outcast. The attachment that I had always known was missing. For too long I had been separated from the mountains' touch.

From this lofty perch, in every direction I looked, the mountains surrounded me. For as far as my eyes could see I could not observe anything that would reveal a trace of human existence. Loneliness set in on me like nothing I had felt in a long time causing me to ponder long and hard about my own life for a while. It disturbed me to think about how meaningless my life had become. I was neither married, nor was I dating anyone at the time, which, I figured, should have given me ample time to enjoy my favorite passions, hunting and fishing, but I had not. I was always buried up to my neck with my job. Life, I felt, was just passing me by. I had nothing to show for the time that I had lived so far. I thought about my brothers and sister who were all married and raising children, but not me. While they sat in the bleachers watching their children play soccer or baseball or football or whatever they were involved in, I had no one to share my life. The more I reflected on my life, the deeper I sank into melancholy.

After sitting there, engrossed in my own pity party for a while, I finally got a hold of my senses. Speaking aloud, I scolded, "You dumb fool. If you don't like the way things are, then do something about it." I determined in my mind right then and there that I would. But at that moment, I needed to look for the money.

Just as Clovis had said, an unusual pink granite stone lay tilted against a few other rocks. It was a little larger than I had expected, but I pulled it away from the others, and there below was a plastic bag lightly covered with dirt. I pulled it free and opened it up slowly, looking about, feeling as if, all of a sudden, someone was watching me. Thumbing through the bills, it appeared to be all there. For some reason, I had expected crisp, clean, new bills, but these were not. They were used and worn. "Maybe I've been watching too many movies lately," I spoke aloud to myself.

Stuffing the money inside of my pack, I thought back to the conversation with Clovis. I wondered if this money was already here when he spoke to me on the phone, and if it was, I could not piece together a time frame for when he could have brought it here. Or did he bring it to me after he spoke to me on the phone, which of course would mean that he was still alive? I turned to descend the mountain, and there it was, as plain as day—a footprint, left in the dirt mound of a mole that recently had been digging for roots. I examined it carefully. The edges were still crisp and clean, indicating that it had been made recently after the last rainfall—no more than a day or two at the most. I searched to find another track, but to no avail. Then I noticed that there were actually very few mole hills present, and I wondered why the individual who made the print would have stepped on the mound? It must have been done on purpose. Maybe it was a clue. Was it Clovis's? Was he still alive? Perhaps I would never know.

I made record time back to the trailhead and called Judy to report to her that I had found the money and to ask her one more time if she would be willing to take it. She gave me the same answer. I did not mention it to her, but I decided that I would put it into a trust fund and leave her and Kelli as beneficiaries. I told her I was on my way back to Billings to get started on the story of Clovis.

In the course of a month, I wrote only three editorials about Clovis. The first, of course, was about the conversation that Clovis and I had on the phone. I titled it "A CONVERSATION WITH CLOVIS." In it I described everything in detail that I could remember about the conversation Clovis and I had shared on the phone, minus the money. The second was titled, "CLOVIS BELDEN, WHO WAS HE?" In this editorial, I wrote a biography about his life, describing every detail I could possibly research and discover, including interviews from friends, family, local business owners and ranchers from the area, an old college roommate, school friends, army comrades; the message was much the same, seeming to have a common thread that ran the full gamut of Clovis's life. He was a loved man—strong, quiet-spoken, a natural leader, enjoyable and pleasant personality, and a man who loved life. Not a single person I interviewed could believe that Clovis would murder the Vice President of the United States or any other person for that matter.

The amount of publicity the two articles generated was more than I would have ever believed. People were reading the article on the internet, and the phone calls to my office rolled in incessantly. Interviews and two appearances for a couple of televised talk shows set the stage for the third editorial. It was titled, "WHY DID CLOVIS KILL VICE PRESIDENT PETERSON?" In it, I included every possible rhetorical question about motive that I could possibly imagine. It was obvious that the murder did not fit the character of the man. "Unfortunately," I concluded, "the tragic death of Clovis to an angry grizzly bear may leave us forever pondering the questions. Perhaps we will never know." Two weeks later, I was offered a job as a field editor for the Chicago Tribune, making more money than I ever dreamed of. I took the job. Looking back at it now, I am astonished at my own greed and stupidity. In fact, when I reflect on many of the poor choices I have made in my life, it literally exhausts me to contemplate the magnitude of my ignorance. All the things—family, the mountains, hunting, fishing, the big skies of Montana, the things that I love most— could never be purchased with money, and yet, when the temptation to make the big bucks was dangled in front of my nose, I grabbed it like a hungry trout attacks a dry fly. My Lord, what was I thinking?

CHAPTER FIFTEEN

Time, it seems, has a way of erasing many of the memories we do not care to carry around. In some ways, I find myself thankful for that. However at times there are unanswered questions and unsolved mysteries that forever beg us for an answer. They may not be questions or mysteries that we dwell on every day, but often enough, they somehow, reenter our minds and force us to ponder and seek for answers or solutions. Sometimes the answers are eventually revealed to us. On the other hand, some of them never are.

Here I was, three years later, still searching for answers to questions that had plagued my mind. Seeking those answers and perhaps finding them might be detrimental to my life, but this was a risk that I had to take. I had never met Clovis Belden. In fact, most everything I knew about the man was post facto, but his story and his life were so intriguing to me, I could not convince myself to walk away.

The morning was still fresh and young when I pulled into Billings. I stopped to fill the truck with fuel and kicked myself for not doing it in Sheridan. Hopefully no one would recognize me here. Billings had been my home and place of employment for years. Fortunately, the convenience store attendant did not give any indication that he knew me.

In about 45 minutes I could be home with my parents, but Wren had told me not to stop there. I felt confident that someone would be watching anyway. I took Interstate 90 toward Livingston, with plans of turning north toward Big Timber on Highway 191.

Driving along, looking down from the highway into the valley at the Yellowstone River, my thoughts turned back again to the days of my youth, fishing with my family along this river. Lord, how I missed those times. Whatever happened to the days when life seemed so simple? Could they ever be that way again? "Yes," I said aloud, "they can be that way again." Maybe I was wrong, but I refused to believe that I was. Life could be simple again. Oh, it would never be the same as it once was. The past has passed, and there's no going back, but I am confident that so much of the turmoil and disdain to which we find ourselves enslaved is brought on by our own doing, and it becomes our undoing. The rat race we make of life is as much our own fault as it is anybody's, probably more. In fact, more often than not, I am convinced that we are our own worst enemy. Drawn away and enticed by our own lusts, we yield to the temptation of material indulgence. We spend most, or at the least the better part of our lives, chasing after those things, which as I have come to realize, eventually rust or rot. Rather, we should dismiss the notion from our minds that possessing more is better and adopt the idea that life is really made up of making memories, moments in time, precious jewels that never decay. These are what we remember, cherish, and value most. Looking across the valley to the far distant mountains, I realized that right there on that ranch were the two people who, although they may not have been wealthy enough to provide me with all the toys that so many of my friends seemed to always have, they gave me more. They gave me their time.

My thoughts turned to Mama. Every spring, she would put the television up into the closet and would not get it out again until hunting season was over at the end of November. Mom and Dad never had a whole lot of money to purchase fine toys for their children like so many other parents seem to do, but what they did for us was something that money could never buy. They made time to spend with their children, quality time. Two, three, sometimes even as many as four times a week, after the work was done, we would grab the fishing poles and head out for a nearby lake or river and fish until dark. I can visualize the scene in my mind as if it were only yesterday. Trout sipping caddis flies and mayflies off the surface of the water, fly-line swishing back and forth in the mild summer Montana evenings, laughter and shouts of excitement echoed through the night air as one of us hooked up with a good fish. More often than not, as the sun began to set in the west, the fishing would become more exciting as the feeding behavior of the trout would intensify. At times, each of us would be hooked up with a trout, all at the same time. Eventually, darkness would envelope the sky, although the slurping sound of the trout and the swishing sound of fly line torpedoing through the air could still be heard. Dad would finally holler out loud, "All right, it's time to head for the house," to which we would always respond, "Ah, Dad, just one more cast." Dad always relented to our pleading, and "one more cast" would some times turn into a hundred more casts.

Those memories hit me like a sledgehammer, and a feeling of regret, remorse, and guilt pounded my conscience. Dad and Mom always had enough time to take their family fishing and even stay long enough for one more cast, and yet it became vividly clear to me, that in the last three years, I had only taken enough time to come home and visit with them but twice.

As I neared Columbus, tears began to flood my eyes and a lump developed in my throat as I looked across to the Beartooth Mountains and thought of my parents' ranch, nestled up there against the distant timberline. From here, it was barely visible, but of course I knew the exact location and the distant landmarks that identified the ranch's boundaries. I pulled over onto the shoulder of the road, wiping my eyes and runny nose, doing my best to bridle my emotions. Suddenly, I remembered the cell phone that Wren had left with me and dug it out from the pack in the back seat. Plugging the cord into the power adapter, I began dialing my parents' number, but stopped myself short. Calling them would not be a wise decision. If their phone was tapped, making contact with them could be dangerous for them as well as for me. Oh, but how I wanted to speak to them, just to hear their voice. I cancelled the call.

Sitting there in the truck, I decided to call my brother in Texas. I needed to speak with someone who could understand what I was feeling, and I was certain that there was no danger involved by doing so. I dialed the number to his cell phone. He answered.

"Hello."

"Hey, Joe, how are you?" I asked, still fighting the lump in my throat, which only seemed to worsen at the familiar sound of his voice.

"All right, I guess. You sound like crap. What's the matter?"

"Oh, I'm sitting here looking toward the ranch, just outside of Columbus, and it's killing me to think I ever left this place."

"What are you doing in Montana?" Joe asked.

"Well, I just needed a break from the windy city," I lied.

"So, how's the weather up there?"

"It's great. The wind is blowing a little this morning, but Brother, the weather is splendid. Right now, I'm sitting here on the interstate. Below me is the Yellowstone and it looks like it's just begging me to come down there and wet a fly. There appears to be a massive caddis hatch taking place on the water right now as I speak. To the southwest I can see the canyon on the ranch where you and I and the dogs treed that lion that killed Old Red... My, my, Brother, how the memories flood my soul as I sit here now." My voice quivered uncontrollably.

In a voice that also strained from the shared emotion, Joe replied, "Oh man...Ross. I know the spot exactly...I wish I was there. I bet you wouldn't trade it for the world".

"That's the thing, Joe... I already have," I responded.

"Yeah, I guess you're right... We both have." We sat in silence, 1500 miles apart, but our thoughts and our hearts were side-by-side, one and the same.

Joe broke the silence, which if it could have been verbalized, would have spoken volumes. "You know, Ross, my son Colton asked me the other day if I was afraid of dying. I told him that I wasn't afraid of dying, I was afraid of not living... let me tell you, I'm not living. This is crazy brother. I work in my high-rise office, making a six-figure income. I live in a massive house with a swimming pool, drive a new Hummer. I've got more toys than you can shake a stick at, and I never have the time to enjoy life. I'd sell it all just to have a small place up there in Montana, where I could just forget about this dog-eat-dog world I'm living in now. Shoot, I haven't strung my bow in years, and I can't remember the last time I cast a fly. Heck, I don't even know where all that stuff is packed."

"I hear you, Brother. Maybe it's time you get out," I remarked.

"I am, Ross, real soon. I'm serious, too. Jill and I have talked about it, and by next summer when Colton starts high school, we're out of here... Hey, by the way, why are you in Montana and not back in Chicago."

I hesitated for a moment, trying to decide whether or not I should tell him, but then decided that maybe I should. It might be the last time I speak with him.

"Joe, I'm going into the Bob. I'm supposed to meet with Belden."

"Is he still alive?"

"It looks like it," I answered.

"Brother, you sound a little worried."

Trying not to reveal too much fear, I told him about the map, the letter, Wren, and the FBI.

"It sounds like you're in serious doo-doo," Joe commented.

"Yeah, it may be tough. Listen, Joe, I better go. I love ya, Brother."

"I love you too, Ross. You be careful and watch your top-knot." I smiled as I hung up the phone. Talking to Joe had made me feel a whole lot better, and helped me put some of my thoughts back into a better perspective. Talking to Joe always made me feel that way. I sat there, staring across the interstate, looking toward the home place, and memories of moments spent together with Joe began to resurface, as if they had just happened. Fishing trips, hunting expeditions, backpacking adventures, working the ranch together, wrestling in the front yard; my mind was full of memories, fond memories, of times we enjoyed together.

Joe, mama's baby, was always so full of life. Even in the midst of trouble, you could always count on Joe to somehow find a way to lift your spirits. Joe and I shared an unbendable and unbreakable relationship. I was the oldest and he, the youngest of five children, almost eight years between us. In a sense, I guess, I felt like I was his protector and guardian. It isn't that I love my sister or other two brothers any less, it's just that Joe and I shared so many of the same interests. Both of us were also deep thinkers and we could spend hours under a star-lit night, sitting around the campfire, philosophizing about any aspect of life that a person could imagine. Interestingly enough, there were very few subjects that we disagreed upon.

A truly powerful aspect of our close relationship was our shared passion for the wild outdoors. Joe's passion for hunting and fly-fishing was unequivocally as strong as mine, if not more so. I can close my eyes and see him as he approaches a fine hole of water in pursuit of a trout. His eyes scrutinizing the surface of the water for a clue or hint of a fish feeding near by; his shoulders and face lean forward, keeping low and out of sight. Fly rod in hand, he strips the line from the reel and slowly raises his rod and puts it in motion. After a few false casts, the fly would land on the water, soft as a feather. Just watching him cast, every movement, precise and fluent, is magnificent to behold. There were many times when I would just stop fishing to observe his mastery of the fly rod. He loved it. Anyone could tell. And yet again, I was saddened by the fact that I hadn't seen him in nearly two years, and I would be hard pressed to try to determine the last time we had fished together.

Memories are funny things. I really don't know for certain why specific memories will suddenly rise to the surface of our thinking, but one particular memory of Joe, leaped into my thoughts, and with it came a deeper understanding and perspective for the tight bond that had developed between us.

I had taken a few days off from working at the Gazette to spend Christmas with the family. My sister and her husband had flown in from Texas. Will was home from college for the break. Mark and Joe, still in high school, were also on their break.

Mark and Joe had been running their trap lines to make a little extra spending money. Furs and pelts were getting top dollar that year, and a good trapper could make a substantial profit. Income on the ranch had been extremely tight that year. The summer drought had cut into our hay crop, forcing Dad to sell nearly a hundred head of his cattle, and use most of that money to purchase enough hay to feed the rest of the livestock through the winter. Mark and Joe took it upon themselves to help out any way they could. Trapping was by far the most profitable means of doing so at the time. The season had only been open for a month and already they had netted a little more than four thousand dollars.

They already owned their traps, and made their own lures, and since their trap lines were all run on the ranch, they had no fuel expense. Other than a lot of sweat equity and legwork, something all of us were used to anyway, it was a profitable business.

It was the day before Christmas and a hard winter squall had blown in fierce and mean. Temperatures had plummeted below zero and the blowing wind and snow made visibility virtually impossible.

After we had all finished breakfast, Mark and Joe started getting dressed in their winter clothes to run their lines. Mama insisted that they had no business going out into the weather such as we were having, but Mark and Joe assured her that they would be just fine. Dad didn't say much one way or the other. I believe that he shared mom's feelings, but at the same time, he felt that it was time to let them make decisions on their own. It's that struggle that all parents eventually must face, holding on or letting go. I really wanted to go with them, but Dad needed Will and me to assist him with a couple of cows that needed some doctoring.

Targeting muskrat, beaver, raccoon and mink, Mark was running his trap line along the river. Joe was trapping the high country for bobcat, martin and fisher. It was just after noon when Mark returned from the line. Joe had not returned, but it usually took longer to run his line anyway. However, by 1:30 p.m., when he still hadn't arrived back at the house, everyone started getting worried. Mama was to the point of tears. The storm had worsened and darkness was only a few hours away.

Packing my gear, a rope, knife, pistol, ammo, matches, blanket, food and water, I donned my snowsuit and winter packs and headed for the door. Dad and Mark rode double on one snowmobile. Will and I rode double on the second. The third snowmobile was in the shop needing repair. As I got on behind Will, Dad informed us that Joe had been running his traps along the timberline and had a few set up the canyon. Once we made it to the old homestead, we split up from there. Mark and Will searched for Joe toward the south. Dad took the north side route, and I took the canyon. The snow was too deep and loose in the canyon to get around in on a snow machine, so I quickly climbed into my snowshoes and got ready to go. Before heading out, Dad paused; I could see the concern on his face. "Now listen boys, I want you back to the old homestead by dark. If you get there before I do, get a fire going in the fireplace. I'm sure we'll all need to warm up some when we get back."

"Yes, sir," we all answered in unison.

"What do we do when we find him?" Mark asked.

"You'll have to make that call on your own. It all depends on Joe's condition. Just remember the things I've taught you. Will, you and Mark need to stay together at all times. Do not split up for any reason. Ross, you're on your own." We all nodded our heads in agreement, our minds focused on the seriousness of the task ahead of us.

The blowing wind and snow stung the areas of my face that were not covered by my snow mask. Visibility was limited to twenty or thirty yards at the most. However, the wind had caused the deep snow to crust over, virtually creating a glassy, hard-packed surface to walk across, making it easy to slide and traverse along in my snowshoes, that is, until I reached the timberline. Once inside the timber, I was sheltered from the wind, but the snow was deep and soft, and without my snowshoes, it would have been unfeasible to try to travel anywhere.

If Joe had traveled up into the canyon, it was impossible to determine. The heavy snow had covered his tracks. I reasoned that I would have to think like a trapper and look for places that provided the best opportunity for Joe to make a good set.

Looking at my watch, it was just a little after 3:00 p.m. It would be dark in a couple of hours. It was already dim inside the timber. I tried yelling out for Joe a couple of times, but realized the futility of that effort, knowing he couldn't hear me over the howling winds. I pressed on. As a signal for help, I fired three shots in the air with my pistol, hoping maybe he could hear the gunshots, knowing that if he could, he would fire three more in return, giving me a possible fix on his location. I heard nothing.

By 4:30 p.m., I had not found any sign that would indicate that Joe had been up the canyon that day. I knew that I needed to turn around and head back to the old homestead. I had lingered long enough already that I knew it would be dark when I got there. Dad was worried enough already about Joe; he didn't need to be worrying about me as well. Taking one last look around, I turned toward the mouth of the canyon. To my left, I noticed a large pine limb leaning against the trunk of another pine. I knew that this was a martin set. Quickly shuffling my way over to the set, I noticed that the leaning branch and trap that was wired to it had very little snow covering it. Joe had been here today.

My hopes, which had all but dwindled to nothing, immediately boosted my adrenaline. I turned quickly, and started back up the canyon, darkness quickly swallowing up the day. A hundred yards up the canyon; I caught a glimpse of movement to my left. Still moving onward, I tried to focus my eyes through the swirling snow to identify the source. As I drew nearer, I discovered a large tom bobcat—his hind foot caught in a trap. Advancing closer to the cat, he hissed and snarled. The fact that the cat remained in the trap indicated that Joe had not made it this far, but it appeared that he had been at the last set, maybe a hundred yards away, which meant that he had to be somewhere in between the two sets.

Almost in a state of panic as the darkness began closing in around me, I scanned the area. Not more than 10 feet from where I was standing were Joe's snowshoes leaning against a small aspen tree, and only a few feet to the right, was Joe, lying in the snow, his wool jacket barely visible.

I rushed to him instantly. His body appeared lifeless. His lips were purple, his eyelids shut and covered with snow. The area surrounding his eyes was almost black while the rest of his face was pale and nearly as white as the snow around us. Brushing the snow from his face and coat, I removed my gloves to check his pulse, fearing the worst. At first, I felt nothing, but my fingers were so cold, that I couldn't feel much anyway. I shook him, calling out his name, trying to get some kind of response. Nothing. Unbuttoning his coat, I removed my toboggan and put my ear to this chest. I could hear a faint heartbeat. I tried to lift his body out of the snow, but his left leg was submerged in the deep snow and wedged between two logs, broken just a few inches above the ankle. Digging frantically, I managed to dislodge his leg and free him from the trap that would have killed him.

Dragging him up under a large spruce, I used one of my snowshoes as a shovel to dig out the snow. I had to get a fire going and do it quickly. I was sure he wouldn't last for long. Glancing at the bobcat in the trap, an idea came to mind. I pulled my pistol and dispatched him, then slit him open, removing his entrails in less time that it takes to tell. The inward heat of the cat's entrails felt almost too hot to bear against my cold fingers. Quickly, I unbuttoned Joe's shirt and placed the entrails on his chest and neck.

Gathering pine needles from beneath the tree, I rummaged around in my pack for my matches and a piece of pitch pine that I always carry in my pack for quick fire starting. The flame leaped as it touched the pitch. Adding twigs as quickly as possible, I had a good flame going, to which I began adding anything that appeared as if it would burn.

Pulling Joe closer to the fire, he exhaled a light groan.

"Hold on Joe; hang in there."

I wrapped him in the blanket I had carried and laid my own body across his, trying to transfer some of my body heat to his. While forcing his cold hands inside my shirt against my chest, I began rubbing and frisking his body at the same time in order to establish better circulation. He was still unconscious.

The heat of the fire was working. In the flickering glow of the dancing flames, I could see color returning to his lips and face. I added more fuel to the fire and turned his body around to expose the other side to the greater heat put off by the fire. It was then that I decided that I needed to examine the extent of his broken leg. I carefully removed his snow packs and rolled up his left wool pant leg. It was a compound fracture, the bone barely protruding above the skin. His feet felt like ice, so I removed his socks and rubbed them gently while holding them near the flame. Suddenly, Joe started moaning. While we were far from being safe and void of danger, I almost started crying. I knew he was going to be alright. Finally, he started mumbling. I really couldn't make out what he was saying, but it didn't matter. The most important thing was he was alive.

Holding his head up, I poured a little water from my jug that I had placed near the flame to thaw. It was not very warm, but it was wet, and Joe had dehydrated. He drank it all, so I packed it full of snow, and sat it by the flame again.

"Joe, can you hear me?" I asked.

"Yeah..." he muttered. "Is that you Ross?"

I looked over into is face where he could see me and a big smile came to his face. "Man, Brother, it's good to see you."

"You too, Joe."

I softly rolled my hands across his face, looking into his eyes, thankful that he was alive. I couldn't take it anymore. For more than three hours I had been operating on pure adrenalin, doing everything in my power to keep him from dying, and it was then that I realized for the first time just how much I loved my little brother. Tears welled up in my eyes.

"Ross, it's going to be all right." Joe whispered.

I chuckled to myself, amused by the irony of the statement. "Yeah, I know, and I sure am glad, Little Brother. Now listen, your leg is broken pretty bad, and it's going to really start hurting once you get more feeling in it. It's nearly 8:00 p.m. and a long time until daylight. Now, either we can sit here while I keep the fire going and wait until morning when Dad and the brothers arrive, or I can make a travois to drag your butt down to the old homestead. The snow is a little tough here in this canyon, but once we get below the timber, it's crusted and I can make good time. It can't be much more than three miles and certainly I can make that in a couple of hours."

"Ross, it's hurting pretty bad already. My concern is more about going into shock. I think we better get on out of here."

I could tell by the look on his face in the reflection of the firelight that he was in severe pain, and knowing Joe as well as I did, he wasn't one to let a person know if he was hurting. I handed him a bag of trail mix to munch on while I built a travois.   Placing Joe's packs and gloves near the fire to warm and adding more fuel to the flame, I grabbed my hatchet and proceeded to cut a couple of lodge pole pines, along with some good sturdy sticks to use as cross-members. Joe ate and watched me while I worked, wincing every now and then, as the pain shot through his leg. The travois wasn't fancy, but it was solid, and I felt certain it would hold together.

Laying it near his body, I heaved him on top of it. For certain, the movement had to be painful, but Joe was tough and didn't hiss at me too much. His socks and packs were warm and I could see the delight in his eyes as I slid them back on his feet.

"How cold do you think it is, Ross?"

"Oh, I'm guessing about thirty below, but the wind has died down, so it really doesn't feel too bad. Of course, I'm working and we're here by this fire, too."

Wrapping him as tightly as I could in the blanket and then strapping him to the travois, I shouldered my pack, which I had fastened to the travois.

"Joe, you've got to understand, that once I get started, I can't stop. I'm sure that I'll break a pretty big sweat really quick like, and if I stop and rest, it will freeze to me in a hurry. I know there's going to be some bumps along the way, but you'll just have to grin and bear it. Of course, I can just cut that bad leg off at the knee and make a wooden ski that we can attach to the stump." I teased.

Joe chuckled at the humor. "Don't make me laugh, Ross. It hurts. Just go. I can take it."

Setting out, I found out right away, that it was going to be a lot tougher than I thought. Even in my snowshoes, the extra weight on my shoulders forced me deeper into the waist-deep snow. Often I was forced to use my hands and arms to elevate my legs, one at a time, out of the snow. My thighs burned in agony. Sweat was gushing forth from my body, and I could tell that my long handles were soaked. My heart raced and pumped in my chest, like a sledgehammer beating against a rock. My lungs felt as if they were going to burst, the cold air strangling me with every breath.

The storm had long since passed, and the cloudy night sky had given way to the light of a million stars. It was nearly 10:00 p.m. by the time I reached the lower timberline. Far below, I could see a light. Dad had evidently hung a lantern from the porch of the old homestead.

"Joe, are you doing all right?" I asked.

"Yeah, Brother, I'm all right. From the sounds of it, I'm better off than you are," he replied.

"Well, I've dragged elk out of the woods that felt lighter than you do. I declare you feel like a thousand pounds. However, we've made it to the crusty stuff now, and I can see a light on at the homestead. We should be there soon."

The crusty snow, again, made the traveling so much easier. In no time, I was within a hundred yards from the house, when I hollered out. Dad was the first out the door, followed by Mark and Will. Immediately, they came running as hard as they could go. Dad got to us first, which surprised me. I didn't know he could run so fast. Grabbing the travois, the four of us ran to the old homestead, dragging Joe across the top of the snow. We stretched him out in front of the fireplace and proceeded to clean him up. When Mark unbuttoned Joe's shirt, he stood up with shock on his face and blurted out, "Dad, Joe's guts are hanging out."

I looked at the entrails and chuckled to myself. I quickly explained to everyone what it was and what I had done, and then Dad assessed the damage to Joe's leg.

Dad stated, "We're going to have to get him into the Billings hospital. Let's get him home and then get him in the truck. Ross, you're wet, so you'll need to get out of your long handles and pants and just wear your snowsuit. Joe, can you ride?"

"Yes, sir." Joe replied.

"Good," Dad continued. "It will be tight, but I think the Big Artic Cat will hold the three of you, unless you just want to stay here until morning and let me come and get you then."

"We're going!" Mark emphatically stated.

Will laughed. "Yeah, don't forget it's Christmas Eve—Santa Claus is coming tonight."

We all laughed.

That was a long time ago, but sitting here now, reflecting on the memory, it occurred to me, that perhaps it was this particular event that became the turning point in our relationship with each other. Joe knew that I had saved his life, and he expressed his gratitude on more than one occasion. My response was always the same, "You're my brother. That's what brothers do. You'd 've done the same for me." I have no doubt he would have.

From that day forward, Joe became more than a brother to me. He was my friend. Perhaps there is a time in the life of brothers when they don't view each other so much as boys, but they look at themselves and each other as men.

By the time Joe recovered from his broken leg, trapping season was over. I was finding myself returning home more often after the workweek at the Gazette was over, to spend more time with him. Many of our evenings were spent sitting around the kitchen table, tying flies and anxiously awaiting summer, when the dreams of large trout caught on the flies we tied, would become a reality.

Of course, the kitchen table wasn't just reserved for Joe and me. Many a long night was spent there as a family while Joe and I tied our flies. We never lacked for conversation. However, long after everyone else had gone to bed, Joe and I would visit and it was then that we would share our deepest dreams. From hunting to fishing…to dogs…to guns…to women. Usually in that order.

When Joe went off to college, I was astonished at how detrimentally lonely I became, but I also realized that it was because of the great love that had developed between us over the years and the absence of one another's presence that brought on this feeling of despair.

While attending college, Joe met Jill, a beautiful young lady from west Texas, the daughter of a rich oil tycoon from the Permian Basis. Joe married her just a few months before receiving his degree, and called me to personally ask if I would do the honors of serving as his best man. I told him that the honor was all mine.

After Joe's college graduation, Jill's father offered him a job in Midland, supporting an annual salary of more money than I would make in 10 years, doing the job I was doing. He took the job. Personally, I always felt that it was Jill's father's way of keeping his little daughter close to home, but I kept my opinion to myself.

Although we kept in touch, as so often is the case, time and distance did not allow the two of us to enjoy our passions together as we once had. He, like me, and so many other American men I knew, had got caught up in the rat-race of wanting more, so working more, and then wanting more, and working more. How is it that we allow ourselves to get so busy trying to make a living that we forget about living? I thought about that long and hard, especially as it related to Joe and me, and although our love for each other never feigned, I suppose that eventually, the unfilled voids we have in our lives, must be replaced with something else, even if we consider them to be of lesser value. Sitting alone in the truck, thinking about him, it was obvious that I missed him more than ever. One thing was for certain; I decided right then as I was pulling the truck back on to the interstate, when this situation is over, I would never live anywhere outside of Montana again, and from the sounds of things, Joe had it in his mind to be back within a year. The very thought of being able to spend time with him again was a pleasure for my mind to entertain.

In so many ways, Montana remained to be what America once was. Oh, modernization had made its mark on the state, but there were still places where a man could easily escape all of that. That was the life I once knew. One day I hoped to reacquaint myself with it again. It was the life that Clovis Belden had lived nearly all of his life, outside of his stretch in 'Nam. I took one last look toward home and felt terribly guilty, knowing that my parents were just a few miles away, but I wasn't going to stop and see them. My concern for their safety meant that I had to push aside my own emotions.

As I kept pushing westward, my thoughts kept drifting back to Wren. I really didn't know much about her, but there was no doubt that I found myself attracted to her. The softness of her sweet lips on mine created a memory that my mind enjoyed revisiting over and over again. I could close my eyes and see her in my thoughts. Obviously, her physical beauty was something I couldn't keep from thinking about. There was something more, though, than her physical features that reeled me in. She was smart, witty, and so "real", but even then, there was something about her that captivated my heart and soul like no other woman ever had done before. In my mind, this feeling did not make any sense, because in reality, I barely knew who she was, and yet what I was feeling inside was an emotion too strong to deny.

As I thought about Wren, I wondered if she was alright. Was she able to convince her colleagues that a burglar had been in the house? I sure hoped so. I hoped that one day I would get to see her again.

About four hours later I pulled into Augusta. Dialing my cell phone, I called Judy on her cell phone. She had picked up another one and used it to call only me, which means she didn't use it often. I had not spoken with her for more than a year, so I wasn't sure if she still had it.

"Judy?" I asked.

"Yes."

"This is Ross Tyler."

"Ross, how are you? Where are you?"

"I'm fine. Is it safe?"

"Yes."

"I'm in Augusta."

"Are you going into the Bob?" she asked.

"How did you know?"

"The FBI have been coming out every day for the last week. They've been asking a lot of questions about you. Right now, I'm in the north pasture feeding the cows. Two FBI agents are back at the house, sitting around, smoking cigarettes in their car. Listen Ross. Clovis is alive. I've known it for a long time. Nobody knows except Kelli and a friend of Clovis, although I'm certain that the FBI has a pretty good idea as well. I didn't tell you because Clovis informed me that it wasn't safe to do so."

"So, you've spoken to him?" I asked.

"No, not exactly, but we do communicate. I'll tell you more, later. Ross, you have got to get up there. He's got it in his mind to turn himself in. Ross, he doesn't stand a chance of proving his story."

"Has he told you why he killed Peterson?" I asked.

"Not really, but I believe it involves something he found out, something really big."

"What do you mean by something big?" I asked.

"I mean something that involves some people in very high places. I believe it's the reason the FBI won't give up."

"So what do you want me to do, Judy?" I asked again.

"Get to him, Ross. I know that he has made contact with you, and I know that you are headed to meet him now. Do NOT let him come down. Make him understand that we know he loves us, and we know he's concerned about Kelli and me, and that it's killing him to be apart from us, but let him know that we're doing fine, and we would rather he would come home later, alive, than to come home now and end up dead. They'll never let him make it to the law. They'll kill him first. Tell him... tell him, Ross, that I love him and I don't want to attend his funeral AGAIN." Judy started to cry.

"I'll do the best I can, Judy." I replied, not really knowing what to say. I had a lot more questions, but it obviously wasn't the right time to ask.

Judy gained her composure. "Ross," she continued, "the FBI are not the only folks trying to kill him. There's a group of killers hired by AFFA."

"Who or what is AFFA?" I asked.

"Alternative Fuel for America," she answered.

"I don't understand. What do they have to do with Peterson?"

"I don't know all the details, Ross. Somehow, I believe Clovis knows something, but he says that he can't prove it. He won't tell me, because he's afraid they'll try to get it out of me. That's why he wants you to meet him. He wants to tell you what he knows and then let you make it public. If you don't meet him by the 31st, he's coming down on his own. I figure the FBI will either follow you hoping that you'll lead them to him, or they'll kill you, because you're the one person who can expose them for whatever it is that they are trying to hide. Ross, you must get to him as soon as possible. And do not trust anyone you may meet on the trail."

"Do you think there are some already in the Bob waiting for me?"

"Yes, I know there are. Clovis has a cousin who works for the Forest Service and he told me that he saw some men go in there two days ago. He said that they didn't look like your normal nature lovers. Listen, Ross, I better get off the phone before those agents back at the house begin to wonder what is taking me so long to look after these cows. Hey, you be careful. When you get to Clovis, don't forget to tell him how much I love and miss him."

"I won't forget, Judy, and I'll be careful. I'm pretty good in the woods, too, you know."

Driving through town, I had just reached the other side, when a patrol car pulled in behind my truck with his lights on. I cursed to myself. I knew that I was thinking about the conversation I had just completed with Judy and was not paying attention to my speed. I pulled over on the shoulder of the road. As he pulled in behind me, I could see in my rear view mirror that he was running a check on my license plates. When he got out of his car, I rolled down my window, still watching him in my mirror as he approached. I saw his hand reach for the snap on his holster and withdraw his pistol.

"Crap!" I said aloud to myself.

"Mr. Tyler?" he asked.

"Yes."

"I'm going to have to ask you to step outside of your truck."

"Did I do something wrong?" I asked.

"You were going 40 mph in a 25 mph speed zone," he replied.

"Do you normally pull your gun on someone who drives a little too fast?" I asked.

"No, but, Mr. Tyler, it turns out that you are wanted by the FBI, and I was told to arrest you and bring you in."

I was sick inside. I wasn't sure just what to say or do. This was bad luck, I thought. Parts of me wanted to see if I could take the gun away and make a run for it, and the other part of me didn't want to get into more trouble. As it turned out, I didn't have to make a choice.

"Mr. Tyler, when I pulled you over, I did not know it was you. Clovis is a very dear friend of mine, and I never have believed that he's really dead. There were a few men in town a couple of days ago asking questions, and I get the feeling they don't believe it either. They wanted to know if you had been in town. Now, that I have just notified them, they've got other agents on their way. I'm really sorry."

I stood there for a minute, trying to figure out a way out of this mess. He was about 6' in height, about 200 pounds and looked to be in his mid-fifties. Noticing his nametag, I asked, "Mr. Smith, what can I do?" It was a question it seemed I had been asking a lot lately.

"Mr. Tyler, if I don't bring you in, I'll be in serious trouble, unless, of course, you should happen to get away."

"What are you proposing?"

"I'm proposing you take these cuffs and put them on my wrists. Hurry it up… you don't have a lot of time.

I pulled his arms behind his back and put the cuffs on his wrists and started to go.

"Hold up, Tyler. You've got to hit me," he stated.

"Sir?"

"You heard me. Hit me hard. No one is going to believe my story if it doesn't look real."

"Are you sure?" I asked.

"Do it now, and make it good."

"Okay, on the count of three," I said.

He braced himself, looking at me, ready for the punch he knew was coming.

"One…two…" I hit him, knocking him to the ground.

He got up spitting blood out his mouth. "Tyler, you hit like a mule. Dang. I think you broke a couple of my teeth." He winced in the pain of speaking. "Okay," he sputtered through the blood, "now get out of here. Tell Clovis that George Smith sends his best regards."

"I'll do it, George. I owe you one. Thanks."

"You bet, kid. You be careful out there."

I grabbed George's gun and stuffed it behind my belt and got into my truck and sped out of there, headed for Benchmark as fast as I could go.

CHAPTER SIXTEEN

In less than an hour, I had pulled in to the Benchmark trail-head. There were a few local trucks with horse trailers parked in the parking lot and three SUV rentals. I figured these carried the men who were looking for Clovis. No one was present. I parked the truck, grabbed my pack and pistol, and hit the trail running. I knew that they would never find Clovis. The thing that concerned me was getting caught or leading them to Clovis.

The one big advantage I had over everyone else is that I knew where I was supposed to meet Clovis. It would take me at least two days to get to Larch Hill Pass, but three days was more realistic. I had four.

The first four miles passed quickly. The trail split where the West Fork of the South Fork of the Sun River empties into the North Fork of the Sun River. I continued north. Most of the tracks I studied at the intersection indicated that the makers had taken the western route. Three sets, however, did move to the north in the direction I was headed. I could not determine if backpackers or the predators who wanted my hide made the tracks. I checked the clip on my .45, worked the action to put a round in the chamber, engaged the safety, strapped it around my waist and then proceeded up the trail.

By evening, completely soaked with sweat, I concluded that I had put nearly 12 miles behind me, seeing only one other person, a fisherman on the Sun, who never did notice my presence. Still, I had reached the confluence of Moose Creek and the North Fork of the Sun, and that was precisely as far as I had hoped to go. Moving off of the main trail into a secluded patch of pine and spruce to set up camp, I quickly hung up the clothes that I had been wearing all day to let them air out and dry. The evening chill had started to set in and my body temperature began to drop. It wasn't until I started to crawl into my sleeping bag that I realized that I hadn't eaten a bite all day long. I also realized that I was starting to smell rather ripe. A fire, I concluded, was not a safe choice, so I dug around in the contents that Wren had packed for me. It seemed like she had packed everything that I could possibly need: dry clothes, matches, first aid kit, a knife, ammunition, and a single burner gas stove. I found a bag of soup mix labeled Day One, took out a handful of various dried items including a small bag of trail mix and began munching on them, chasing each mouthful with a drink of water. Priming and lighting the single burner stove and boiling some water, I held my hands near the flame to break the chill that was quickly developing in my fingers as the daytime heat began giving way to the cool of night. I surely knew that I was back in Montana when the 75 degree daytime turned into 35 degree evenings. Reaching back into the bag, I noticed a folded note. Using my headlamp to see more clearly, I opened it up and read it.

Dear Ross,

I am assuming that if you find this note, you have made it safely to the Bob Marshall Wilderness. I have prepared an evening meal for 3 nights. In each one I have placed a small note just to encourage you a little and to let you know that I am thinking and praying for you. Please be careful. Watch your back trail.

Thinking of you,
Wren

I considered opening each bag and reading all of the notes, but it just didn't seem right. I would wait just as she had intended. I hoped that someday I would be able to show her my appreciation. As much as I needed to stay focused to the task at hand, she continually entered my thoughts, but I realized that I didn't mind. Thinking of her flashy smile, soul-searching eyes, and the way she looked at me kept me entertained, and the more I thought of her, the more I desired to see her again. I hoped that she was safe. The thought of Kirby came to mind. The brutal, sadistic personality that Wren had described suddenly sent a chill down my spine, and I quivered at the thought of Kirby exposing what Wren had done to help me escape. As I vigorously rubbed the palms of my hands against the goose-bumps of my arms, I knew then that the feeling I had for Wren was growing deeper every day.

The hot soup warmed me with every swallow, and I enjoyed holding the hot cup as much as I did eating the soup. Cupping it with both hands and holding it close to my chest I sat there in the darkness, pondering what the events of the next day might be. Somehow, the men who were looking for Clovis were aware of his general location. Either they hoped to reach him before I did or lay in wait and allow me to lead them to him. My gut feeling told me that they would wait and try to kill both of us at the same time.

The closer I progressed toward the Chinese Wall, the more careful I would have to be. That meant that tomorrow would be a day of extreme caution for me, for I intended to make it to the Wall. I did not intend on taking the well-beaten trail that most who visit the area take; instead, I would move through the deep dark timber along the creek, which would be rough and make for very slow travel. Whether or not I ascended Larch Hill Pass would depend on the time of day.

Lying there in the tent and contemplating my actions for tomorrow, while looking through the open flap of the fly, millions of stars illuminated the sky. It was like so many other nights I had enjoyed as a boy with my family and even later as a young man. Only then, unlike the present, my life was not overwhelmed with a conglomeration of garbage. Once, life had been simple and my cares were few. Oh, I thought to myself, if we only knew how good it really was, when it really *was* good. I reflected on a particular moment when my father, my brother Will, and I were hunting elk along the Missouri Breaks. Just like tonight, the stars shone brilliantly, and as we lay in our sleeping bags in our camp on a hill above the river bottom, we listened to the screams of bugling bull elk and the songs of coyotes all night long. Nothing else in the world seemed to matter. We lay soaking up the wonder and glory of heaven's radiance with our eyes, and listened to nature's orchestra in the valley below. No bills, no timelines, no obligations. Obviously, it is unrealistic to expect life to be void of these things all of the time, but every now and then, it's good to be able to experience moments when we don't feel so burdened or hard pressed by their reality.

Before drifting off to sleep, I decided to record the events on the mini-tape recorder Wren had left in my pack. Recording would be easier than trying to write and a whole lot faster. I must have fallen asleep rather quickly. I awoke to the squawking of a pinion jay, a bird that we called a "camp robber". The eastern sky was just beginning to illuminate the valley floor. Frost, although light, clung to the foliage and I was not anxious to crawl out of my sleeping bag, but I knew I had a long day ahead of me. Forcing myself to crawl out of the tent, my muscles were sore and stiff. My feet were killing me. I couldn't believe I had let myself get in such poor physical condition, at least compared to the way I had kept my body through the years of growing up. Stretching and finishing off the last of the trail mix that I had not eaten the night before, I packed my gear and slowly began penetrating my way through the timber.

The route that I had chosen to take was rough. The fallen timber, mostly spruce and pine, dead from both previous avalanches and beetle kills, densely covered the hillside, making it almost impossible to penetrate. Moss hung from the branches and the smell of skunk cabbage hovered strongly in the breezeless air. The density of the foliage dampened the sunlight. At times, I had to crawl through the tangled mess on my hands and knees. I was soaked in sweat and my hands were sticky with pinesap. It was the kind of habitat that moose preferred, and judging by the abundant droppings, both old and fresh scattered on the ground, they obviously used this area frequently. Occasionally, I found a trail the moose had made that would allow me to move at a little quicker pace. By noon, I figured that I had only moved 3 miles at the most.

On several occasions I was tempted to move away from the timber and take the beaten path, but this option would certainly lead to trouble. It was better to just take my own sweet time and be careful. Stopping to rest a spell near the edge of a creek, I located a service-berry patch and gorged myself with them. Mama used to make pies out of them that were out of this world, and the very thought of her taking one of them out of the oven with the steam rolling off of the dark purple berries made my mouth salivate.

A split second before the shot, I saw the glimmer of a rifle barrel about 150 yards up the hill and dove head first into the brush, the bullet striking only inches from my face. Grabbing my pack I ran through the brush back into the timber as fast as I could move. I could hear voices from up above.

"I think I got him!" someone shouted.

"Where?" another asked.

"Down there in the brush."

Stopping in the timber on a vantage point, I looked back where I could watch them as they cautiously crept down the mountainside to look for my body. For the first time, it really hit me just how serious a situation I was in. I had never been shot at before, and it made me fuming mad. The more I thought about it, the angrier I became. I gave some very serious thought to taking the fight to them, but decided that it may be better to wait. For certain, I was going to have to be more careful.

Taking careful measures to assure that I did not leave an easy trail to follow by avoiding the heavier-traveled, more obvious trails and stepping only on surfaces that would not leave distinguishable tracks, I hurried along. By mid-afternoon I stood at the base of the Wall. Ascending the pass now would be too dangerous, not knowing who may be lying in wait. Confident that I had eluded my pursuers and did not have any visual indication that they were still on my trail, again, I pitched my tent in the dark timber, this time in a patch of dried leaves from a plant that I could not identify. They were extremely loud and noisy when stepped upon, so this idea appealed to me in case someone or something should try to approach my camp during the night. Although I felt like I had chosen a well-hidden campsite, extra caution was in order.

Lighting the camp stove, I rummaged through the meals again that Wren had prepared. Finding the one labeled Day Two, I opened it up. It was freeze-dried roast beef and potatoes, a package of hot chocolate and another bag of trail mix. Another note accompanied the contents.

Dear Ross,

It would be my guess that tonight, you are camped some-where near the Chinese Wall. I will not take the time to tell you how I know that right now, but as I told you earlier, if we both sur-vive this thing, I'll fill in all the blanks. I hope that you have not run into trouble yet, but be warned, it will happen. The men who are after you aim to kill you and Clovis as well. If it comes down to you or them, don't show any kindness. They know that if you print the story that Clovis will share with you and that story can be proven, they will face capital punishment, so their lives depend on the death of both of you. I wanted to share more with you earlier, but decided to wait until now. Please, with all my heart, I ask you to be careful.

Wren

How did she know where I would be on the second night? I remembered her saying something about satellite photographs. Evidently, the FBI must have some photographs of Clovis on or near the Wall, but evidently, they do not know where he is hiding.

More and more I became aware that I was in this mess way over my head, but at the same time, I could not see a way out. It is difficult to explain, but I felt stuck in something that I really wasn't sure if my involvement was needed. After all, how much did I really know? I had a map that supposedly would lead me to Belden, but I did not have anything else that the FBI could use to prosecute him. Maybe there was something they were trying to hide. Maybe they were trying to satisfy the feeling of anger or revenge that President Watson harbored for the loss of his best friend Peterson, or maybe, they were trying to cover up something that they did not want the world to know about. Although I could only speculate at their motive, the cold, hard truth remained. I was in this thing for the long haul and to survive would require every ounce of caution and care that I could muster.

Taking fishing line from the survival kit, I wrapped it around the small trees that surrounded my tent, about 15 inches off the ground and hung a couple pans on the line. This would serve as a trip wire and alarm me if anything or anyone should try to approach my camp at night. By the time I had finished, darkness had enveloped the night, so I crawled into my tent and sleeping bag, rummaging through pockets for my mini-recorder to again record the events of the day. I had just got started when the sound of pots and pans clanging together brought me out of my bag in a single leap with my .45 in my hand.

"Mr. Tyler, this is FBI Agent Cordell, you are completely surrounded. Do not make an attempt to escape or you will be shot. Come out from your tent with your hands in the air. That's an order."

Helpless inside my tent, I had no choice but to do as I was ordered. "Mr. Cordell, I am dropping my weapon and coming out. Please, do not shoot."

Unzipping the tent fly, I tossed my pistol on the ground in front of the tent and crawled out on my knees with my hands held high in the air. Three bright flashlights shined their beams directly into my eyes making it impossible to distinguish the faces of the men who were holding them.

"Mr. Tyler, my name is Agent Cordell. This is Agent Adams and Agent Slyvenski. We're with the FBI. We are placing you under arrest for harboring information regarding the whereabouts of a certain Clovis R. Belden, a known federal criminal. Please, stand and put your hands behind your back."

I didn't know what to think. What were they planning on doing? Were they going to torture me? Did they have plans to execute me? Should I try to escape? I really didn't know. I was at a great disadvantage. I was not wearing my shoes and to try to escape into the darkness with nothing to defend myself or a light to help shine the way would be sure suicide. Lord, I was terrified. A million thoughts swirled through my mind. So this was it. This was how my short life was going to end. I was going to die for a man that I had never met, a man with whom I had shared only one telephone call almost 3 years ago. I would die without having the opportunity to say goodbye to my folks, or get to know Wren a little better. Fleeting thoughts of trying to escape kept entering my mind, but, rising to my feet, I did exactly as I was told. Agent Cordell walked me to a tree, pulled my arms behind my back and around the tree, and cinched the handcuffs on my wrists good and tight. I looked at Cordell, straight in the eye. His face was covered with scars, what appeared to be burns, and his tight, thin lips moved very little when he spoke. His beady eyes held absolutely no sign of compassion or mercy and I was sure that I would not receive any from him.

"Slyvenski, call the other men and tell them that we have Tyler," Cordell instructed.

Slyvenski made the call. I could hear both sides of the conversation in the stillness of the night.

"Agent Carol, we've got Tyler," Slyvenski stated.

"Good. Where are you?" Carol asked.

Slyvenski shined his light at his GPS and gave Carol the coordinates.

Carol replied, "That looks to be about 10 or 11 miles from here. It will probably be morning before we can make it that far."

"What do you want us to do with Tyler?" Slyvenski asked.

"Get as much information out of him as you can. I don't care how you do it, but make sure he's still alive and conscious when we get there," Carol stated.

I didn't like the sound of that one bit.

"Cordell, did you get all that?" Slyvenski asked.

"Yeah, I got it," Cordell answered and then turned toward me. "Well, Tyler, it looks like you have about 10 more hours to live. A lot can be done to a man in that amount of time."

"Adams, gather up some wood and let's get a fire going here," Cordell ordered. "It's going to be a long, cold night and besides, I want to see how Tyler likes the sensation of hot coals against his flesh."

To this point I had not stated a word. I knew that they were not going to let me live, but they wanted to know where I was supposed to meet Clovis. Pleading and begging for my life was not going to produce any mercy on their part.

"You so much as touch me, and I'll kill you Cordell," I stated, trying to sound confident but knowing I didn't stand a chance of harming anyone in my helpless condition.

Walking up to me, Cordell asked, "Is that so? We'll see about that." His right fist slammed into my gut, knocking the wind completely out of me, and then a left hook crashed down across the right side of my face. Gasping for air, I couldn't say a word.

All three men laughed as they stood there beside the fire that Adams was building. Staring at me, they watched me agonize helplessly in pain.

Cordell came to me again. "Now, you can either tell us where you're supposed to meet Belden and we'll just wait here until Carol shows up with the other men and let him kill you quickly, or we can make it hurt really bad. Either way, you're a dead man. So what will it be?"

"I'm not telling you anything... 'cause I don't know anything!" I stated defiantly.

Grabbing a stick with a searing hot end from the fire, he walked to me and held it to my face. Grabbing my shirt and ripping it off, he said, "Okay, so you want to be tough, do you?"

I tried to grit my teeth and take the pain as he shoved the glowing stick into my naval, but I screamed at the top of my lungs. Pulling myself tighter against the tree, I quickly raised my legs and kicked him square in the solar plexus, knocking him to the ground. Gasping for air, Slyvenski jumped up and cut a rope from the tent and tied my legs to the tree. Cordell was cussing me every second. Grabbing another hot stick from the fire, he approached me again. "Tyler, where are you supposed to meet Belden?"

"Who's Belden?" I sarcastically asked. He shoved the glowing end of the stick deep into my armpit. Struggling and squirming, I screamed in agony, biting my lip to try to endure the misery. The smell of singed hair and burned flesh from branding calves never bothered me, but the odor of my own sizzling flesh made me want to vomit. Gasping for air, my right eye nearly swollen shut, blood dripping from my nose and face, I finally relented.

"Okay. I'll talk," I gasped, trying to catch my breath. "But since we have a lot of time, would it be too much to ask you why Belden killed Peterson? I mean, I really don't know, and I'd like to at least die knowing what I died for. I swear, I'll tell you where I'm supposed to meet him."

Cordell looked at Slyvenski and Adams. "What the hell, we're going to kill him anyway," Adams remarked. Slyvenski just shrugged his shoulders as if he didn't care either.

"Alright," Cordell replied, "but put some more wood on the fire." He ordered to Adams. "It's a long story."

Standing there, I could taste the sweat and blood running down my face. Surprisingly, the burns didn't hurt too much, which meant that they were third degree burns, which often destroy not only the skin, but the nerve endings as well.

Cordell and Slyvenski sat down by the fire as Adams gathered more wood. Cordell started, "Well, Tyler, it's like this. It's all about money. As you well know, gasoline prices in the United States are at an all time high. The cost of foreign oil continues to rise, and consequently, we have been forced to investigate alternative fuel resources. AFFA, Alternative Fuel for America, has proven that they can produce ethanol from corn and within a couple of years, cut America's fuel prices in half, maybe more. The problem involved with producing ethanol is that it takes an incredible amount of water to produce a gallon of ethanol. Watson opposed every bill that went to Congress, because of the high demands of water for ethanol production, and of course, since most of the members of Congress practically worship the ground that Watson walks on, they would never override his veto. Peterson, however, felt that the need to supply America with a cleaner and more cost efficient fuel should be top priority. Peterson also believed, that since the members of Congress liked him as well, that if he were ever President, they would follow his lead. AFFA's feelings were mutual. AFFA also believed that for every year they were held back on ethanol production, they were losing billions of dollars. So..."

"So why not see to it that the President has a little accident." I stated, cutting off Cordell in mid-sentence as the assassination attempt was starting to paint a clearer picture in my mind.

"That's right," Cordell answered.

"So what happened?" I asked.

Cordell continued, "AFFA approached Peterson about the idea of being President. At first, Peterson didn't quite get the picture, but then they explained that they wanted him to be the next President of the United States as soon as possible, meaning that Watson needed to be removed from the picture, permanently. They were confident that Watson would win the next election again.

Peterson was incredulous about the idea of seeing his best friend murdered. Peterson also told them security was much too tight around Watson for a successful assassination attempt to take place. AFFA said, 'That's why we would like for you to do it. You're the only one whom he really trusts.' Peterson got madder than hell. I mean, he really lost his temper and was about to have them arrested. However, when AFFA offered him 25 million dollars and a week to consider it, Peterson came back a few days later with an affirmative answer."

"So how did the FBI get involved?" I asked.

"A leak," Cordell answered. "Somehow, several of our agents found out and instead of spilling the beans to Watson, we went to AFFA and bribed them for money, a lot of money, to keep it quiet. There are only about a dozen of us who are up here chasing you and Belden around in these God-forsaken mountains, doing it to protect our necks. The others are doing it 'for God and country' and all that other idealistic crap."

Listening attentively, I kept trying to buy more time, although the idea of rescue was hopeless. "Alright, so how was Peterson supposed to kill Watson?" I asked.

Clearing his throat and stoking up the fire with the same stick that he had used to burn me, he started again. "Well, I'm sure you know how well Watson and Peterson loved hunting and fishing together. Peterson did his homework for a fly fishing trip just south west of us here, as you well know, and he offered Newsome half a million dollars to assist him in finding a place where Watson could have an 'accident'. Newsome knew of a place along the North Fork where it could happen. Watson was going to step around a rock that protruded into the trail while Newsome assisted. Peterson would go next. The plan for Peterson, as soon as he stepped around the rock behind Watson, where both of them would be out of sight for a few seconds, was to grab Watson by the collar and simply jerk him off the trail, letting him fall off into the canyon below." Pausing for a minute, Cordell just sat there shaking his head. "Somehow, at least we think, your Mr. Belden found out about it and managed to single-handedly put a stop to it."

"How did Belden find out?" I asked.

"We don't know," Cordell answered, "and in truth, we really don't know how much he knows, but we're going find out, real soon."

"How did you find out Belden was still alive? I mean, most of the world thinks he's bear crap, and they've forgotten all about him... and Peterson for that matter."

"Well, the evidence looked like he had been killed by a grizzly, but when we do an investigation and we don't find a body or any evidence of one, we keep on looking. Nothing showed up until about 6 months ago, in spite of all the surveillance we had put out on him. To top it off, we couldn't believe that a man could survive the winters up here anyway. We heard rumors that maybe some friends were allowing him to stay with them, but that never panned out. Then we got a tip from a sporting goods/grocery store owner from over near Kalispell, that every month some guy would come in and buy all kinds of groceries, ammunition, fishing equipment, a generator, fuel, and so on. The store owner did not know his name, but we kept a look out for him anyway. He never came back into the store. So, we decided to use our eye in the sky again. We managed to get a couple of pretty good photographs of your boy. Yeah, we know he's alive and so does AFFA. If we don't kill him and you as well, as I'm sure you have figured out, we'll face 'the chair'. I don't plan on letting that happen." He stirred the coals with a long stick. "So, that about sums it up, Tyler. Now, why don't you politely tell us where you're supposed to meet Belden?"

I looked him square in the eye. "Cordell, when hell freezes over."

Slyvenski and Adams just shook their heads. I guess they knew how sadistically cruel Cordell could be. Cordell grabbed his red hot stick again and walked over to me. The hatred in his eyes burned cold.

"Tyler, you may live till morning, but you won't see it, because I am going to burn your eyes out."

A powerful man, he pressed his hand on my forehead and held my head tight so I couldn't move. He raised the stick and started to move it slowly toward my left eyeball when suddenly he collapsed to the ground like a ton of bricks. Blood, bone and brains were splattered on my face. I looked down to see that he was obviously dead. Adams and Slyvenski jumped to their feet, both of them dropping dead to the ground the second they stood up.

Adams squirmed a little on the ground and something hit him again, putting all movement to an end. I heard nothing—no gunshots, no movement in the timber. The crackling of the fire, the trickling, gurgling sound of the creek in the valley below and my heavy breathing were the only sounds to be heard in the calm, dark night.

Standing there for what seemed an eternity, I remained quiet and motionless. Then, like a ghost, he was there. "You're a little early." Belden stated in his deep, soft voice. He moved around in front of me where I could see him.

Dressed in camouflaged wool, his hair long and pulled back in a pony tail, his beard, a speckled, peppered gray, hanging down below his chest, and an AR-15 slung over his shoulder, he looked at me and smiled, his teeth reflecting the fire light. He was not as large as I thought he would be. Although I had done the homework and research on the man and knew that he was rather small in stature, I suppose that subconsciously I had created a mental image of Belden to be a giant.

"Good to see you, Tyler," he stated with a grin.

"It's even better to see you, Mr. Belden."

"Just call me Clovis, Tyler," he replied. "Now let me help you get off this tree."

As Clovis rolled Cordell over to search his body for the keys to the handcuffs, I could barely make out what was left of Cordell's face. Truthfully, it made me so queasy I thought I might throw up, and so I did.

"It will be alright, son." Clovis said. "I'm going to take care of you, but first we have got to get you out of here."

Quickly, he untied the rope from around my feet and then gently unlocked the cuffs from around my wrists. As soon as the pressure came off of the cuffs, I started to fall forward, but he caught me and helped me gently to the ground. Digging through my pack, he found my shirt and jacket and helped me into them. Sitting there I heard a loud audible click. Clovis turned quickly toward the sound.

"What was that?" he asked.

I smiled. I had completely forgotten about my recorder. With any luck, perhaps it recorded all of the conversation that Cordell and I had shared about the assassination attempt.

"That," I smiled, "may be your ticket to acquittal. Look in that tent and see if you can find my tape recorder."

Clovis grabbed the flashlight that Adams had been carrying and crawled into and out of the tent, bringing with him my water bottle, a towel, and my recorder. Helping me sit up against the tree, he handed me the recorder and began, ever so gently, washing my face with the cool water and towel.

"I'll have to wait until we get home to treat those burns, Tyler."

"Home?" I asked.

"Yeah, home, the place where I've been living for the last three years."

While gritting my teeth and trying to endure the pain as Clovis did his best to clean the wound on my head, I rewound the tape on the recorder and hit play. Fast forwarding the tape through the first two days of notes that I had recorded, I punched play again. My screaming and the yelling made Clovis stop dressing my wounds. In curiosity he sat back against the tree with me and listened to every detail. Tears began to flood his eyes until he finally put his head in his hands and sobbed bitterly.

"Clovis, are you alright?" I asked.

"I'm sorry, son, but I've lived up here for almost three years because I had no way to prove why I killed Peterson. I knew I would face capital punishment if I was ever caught, but more than anything I wanted to clear my name. This is the first ray of hope with any teeth to it that I've had at all."

"So how did you find out about it?" I asked.

"You mean, about Newsome and Peterson's plans for killing Watson?" Clovis looked at me and said, "I'll tell you tomorrow. Right now, we've got to get you some place safe."

Helping me to my feet, I took a look at Slyvenski and Adams, both of them dead, both of them shot through the head just as Cordell.

"Where were you when you shot these men?" I asked. "It took you quite awhile to get to me."

"Oh, about 300 yards up there on that hill," pointing into the darkness. "I wanted to get closer, but I was watching them through this night-vision scope, and I was afraid I would be too late, so I flopped down on the ground and squeezed them off. The fire light was tough on my eyes through that scope, but it was also the fire that caught my attention and led me here."

"That's some mighty fine shooting," I stated.

Clovis just looked at me. "Tyler, I've killed a lot of men, and even though it was during war time, I've never taken pleasure in it, but shooting, well, it's what I do best. I'm just glad I was able to be here."

"You and I both."

"Do you have any idea how many more are up here?" Clovis asked.

"No, I'm not sure how many, but I do know that there are more FBI agents moving this way now. I heard Slyvenski give them the coordinates on the phone. They figured it would be morning before they made it."

"What about AFFA's group of idiots?"

"I don't have a clue," I answered.

"Well, we're a long way from being out of the woods yet," Clovis replied. "Do you think you can make a couple of miles?"

"Yeah, I think so," I answered.

"Okay, follow me."

"What about the bodies?" I asked.

Looking at the bodies, Clovis answered, "Let their buddies deal with them. Either that, or the bears and wolves can eat them. They're as dead as they'll ever be."

CHAPTER SEVENTEEN

In a state of shock or something similar to it, I held on to Clovis's coat as we moved up the mountain toward the Chinese Wall. He helped me climb nearly 20 feet or so up the cliff in the darkness, before we stopped at the small entrance to the cave. In the distance, the forlorn howling of a wolf broke the silence. I felt like crying, and it made me feel lonely as well, but I smiled in spite of it all. Yes, I felt lonely, but I was alive. I had Clovis to thank for that. With a little luck, I hoped to be able to return the favor.

Entering the cave, Clovis helped me to lie down on a bed of mountain goat hides and in seconds I was asleep. I slept hard and when I awoke, I was surprised to find myself in such a large room. I could smell something cooking and my stomach growled with hunger. Looking around the room, I felt as if I were in a large guest room at a dude ranch. Antlers and furs were hung on the rock walls. Log furniture made of aspen and pine, book shelves with a library of literature, a table, a bed, and the entire floor was covered in animal skins. Clovis was standing next to a large camp stove and noticed that I was awake.

"How do you like your eggs?" he asked.

"Scrambled is just fine," I answered.

"This is quite a place you have here Clovis," I commented.

"Thank you, Tyler," Clovis replied as he motioned me to join him at the table. "Eat this, and then I'm going to doctor up those wounds."

I was sore and stiff and my right eye was swollen almost completely shut. My naval was charred a nasty, red and black color, and I could barely move my left arm for the burn in my armpit.

Clovis observed my wincing to the pain. "Tyler, I'm going to have to stitch up that cut on your head, and the dead tissue on those burns is going to have to be removed so they can heal from the inside out, otherwise they'll get infected. It will take you a week or so to recover enough to get you out of here; you're in no condition to travel right now."

"What are you suggesting?" I asked.

"Well, I want you to drink this. Put it in your coffee," he replied handing me a small bottle of clear liquid.

"What is it?" I asked.

"It's an anesthetic mixed with some stuff that will knock you out. I'm not a plastic surgeon, but I know enough about burns and cuts to get you fixed up, and I've got everything I need to fix it up right."

"Alright," I replied, "I guess I don't have much of a choice. When do you want to get started?"

"I suppose we can wait a couple of hours if you wish. You can drink this stuff later. It takes about 30 minutes to kick in. Let's talk a little first, if that's alright with you."

"Sounds good to me," I replied.

We both sat there eating breakfast and drinking the coffee. He asked me about my trip from Chicago, and I explained some of the trouble I ran into with FBI Agent Jones in Nebraska and how Officer George Smith had pulled me over outside of Augusta, and how he allowed me to cuff him and hit him to make it appear that I had escaped arrest.

"How is ol' George?" Clovis asked.

"He sends his best regards. He told me that he never did believe you were dead," I answered.

After pausing for a few minutes to drink our coffee, Clovis continued, "I assume you found the note and the map alright, back in Chicago?"

"Yes, I found the note and the map. Who put them there?"

"Kendall," Clovis stated. "I'll tell you more about that later. What happened after you found them?"

I explained the details and events and about being followed to a local night club and meeting Wren and how she helped me get out of Chicago alive.

"It sounds like you're kind of fond of this Wren woman," he chuckled. "I notice how your eyes light up when you mention her name."

"Well, I can't get her off my mind, Clovis. I really don't know a whole lot about her, but I think about her constantly."

"Tell me about her," Clovis inquired.

"Oh man, she's gorgeous. She seems so real and fresh and intelligent. Her smile draws me to her like a honey bee to a columbine, and her eyes, I swear, can look right through me and read the very thoughts of my soul."

Clovis laughed aloud, his eyes glistening, "Sonny boy, it sounds like you're hooked. That's good. A good woman is hard to find, and if you're fortunate enough to find one, you better hold on to her. Now, I'm not telling you what to do, but when we get out of here, I'd suggest you look her up."

With a twinkle in his eye, he said, "Tell me about Judy."

I went into as much detail as I could remember about the time I had spent with Judy and the conversations we shared. Clovis's deep, piercing brown eyes grew soft and full of tears. He hung on every word. Obviously, he loved Judy with every fiber of his heart, more than life itself.

"I miss her so much. She and Kelli are the one reason I've got to get out of here. I cannot take this isolation anymore."

"Clovis, I need to talk to you about that. Judy made me swear that I would."

Clovis leaned forward, intent on hearing what I had to say, "Okay, shoot."

"Well," I started, "Judy wanted me to make sure that you understand how much she and Kelli love you, and they both understand how difficult it must be to live up here away from them, because it's difficult for them too, but both of them agree that they would rather you stay here and remain alive than for you to try to come out, where you know and they know you'll end up dead."

Clovis stared at me, his eyes squinting, the wrinkles furrowed deep in the dark, weathered skin of his forehead, speechless, obviously contemplating what I had just shared with him. For a long moment, he said nothing. Finally, he responded, "I'll have to give this some more thought." The tone of his voice indicated that this topic of conversation was finished.

Looking around the cavern, I changed the subject. "Clovis, how did you make it through the winters up here?"

Clovis smiled, "Shoot, Tyler, other than the loneliness and desire for the companionship of my wife and daughter, I have lived like a king. Let me show you. We got up from the table and he walked me to the far end of the cavern, where an elk hide, serving as a door, hung over a large crevice in the wall. Stepping into the crevice, we walked into another cavernous room. Lighting an oil lamp, Clovis pointed to the floor. A hot spring, about 8 feet in diameter, bubbled. I couldn't believe it.

Chuckling to myself, I asked, "How warm is it?"

"It stays a constant 104 degrees and keeps the room in here about 75 degrees year round. During the winter, I open up the door and the heat escapes into the front cavern and keeps it plenty warm. It's perfect for taking a bath or soaking sore muscles although it does have a light sulfur odor to it." He stooped and stirred the water with his hand. "Hey, let's get in it. It would help relieve your soreness and soften the skin around your burns. We can talk some more in here."

We both stripped down to nothing and stepped into the water. In the light of the small room, I noticed the scars on Clovis's naked body; obviously they were the wounds he had received from the war. Although he was not large in stature, he was lean and muscular, and it did not appear that he had an ounce of fat anywhere on his body.

At first, the sulfur water felt a little too hot, but in no time, we were both comfortable. It was the closest thing to a bath that I had taken in more than a week.

"Clovis, tell me about Peterson and how you managed to find out about his scheme and plan to kill President Watson."

Clovis sighed and thought for a moment. "It really was nothing more than fate, I guess. Sometimes I wonder if God had something to do with it, but I don't know. It all started one morning when I was chasing a bull down stream on the North Fork River. He was with a group of cows, and I kept calling to him and putting the pressure on, like I was another bull trying to steal his harem. I talked to that bull for most of the day, but he stuck close to his cows and steadily moved them away. Finally, that afternoon, that bull had taken all of me that he was going to take, and he came to my call looking for a fight. I arrowed him at less than 10 yards. I gave him a little time before I picked up the blood trail that appeared to be moving upstream through the brush along the river. I found him piled up about 30 yards on the west side of the river later that evening. I had just finished field-dressing him when I heard some voices. Slipping through the willows and brush toward the creek, I noticed two men fishing on the river. It appeared to me that one of them was Vice President Peterson, but at first I couldn't tell. He was carrying a heavy backpack and I thought it strange to be fishing with something so cumbersome on his back. The other was Newsome. I had seen him up here before. He made more money outfitting than he did working cattle on his ranch. Anyway, as they approached closer, I heard Newsome ask Peterson if he had the money, and Peterson opened the pack and showed it to Newsome. Newsome shouldered the pack and told Peterson to stay put for a minute. He then walked into the brush, less than five feet from me and proceeded to hide the pack under a rock overhang on a little bluff just off the river. He came back out and told Peterson that he would come back and retrieve it when it was all over. That's when I heard the details for the assassination. Shoot, they couldn't have been more than six to seven yards from me. I couldn't believe what I was hearing. Both of them went over the details several times, I guess in order to assure that their plan and strategy was well understood. Finally, they started back toward their camp."

"What did you decide to do?" I asked, already knowing much of the answer.

"I thought about it really hard. At first, I thought about going up to the camp and warning Watson, but I was sure that no one would believe me, and even if they did, Peterson would most likely deny it and try again later. I didn't have a way to communicate to anyone outside of The Bob, so I took the money and hid it in a hollow log near an elk wallow that I hunt frequently, and then I located the place where the assassination was supposed to take place. I left my llamas back at my base camp and spent the night just a few hundred yards upriver. That morning, I climbed up to the top of the cliff and watched through my binoculars as Watson, Peterson, Newsome and the Secret Service agents moved up the river. It appeared that everything was going according to Peterson's plans. When they crossed over to the east side of the river, I tucked into a well-hidden crevice and waited. I watched as they came up the trail and approached the large rock that protruded into the trail. Watson cleared the rock first and then Peterson. Just as Peterson cleared the rock he reached out to grab Watson. That's when I let him have the arrow. If I had waited only one more second, Peterson would have killed Watson. That's how close it was. I wasn't counting on Newsome falling too. The other thing, if that arrow had passed completely through, I doubt that anyone would have known that Peterson's death was not accidental. It's safe to assume that in an autopsy the wound would have appeared to be a stick or other sharp object. So, for almost three years, I've been living the life of a fugitive."

The story was incredible. I could hardly wait to bring it to the press, not for selfish reasons, knowing I would get a lot of publicity, but more for Clovis.

"Clovis, I've got to ask you. If you had it to do all over again, would you?"

"Yes, without a doubt." Clovis paused for a few seconds and then elaborated on his answer to my question. "Oh, Tyler, I have thought of it many times. If I had not taken that shot and killed Peterson, I'd be home with Judy and Kelli, but you know, I believe we live in the greatest country in the world, and our way of life allows me to enjoy certain privileges and rights that I could never enjoy if I lived in another country. The only reason I am able to do that is because there have been men and women who stood for what they knew was right, even if it meant losing everything. Tolerance for the evil that men do will lead us to our destruction quicker than anything I know. Yea, sure I've thought about the fact that if I had just let it all slide, I would not be in this mess I'm in now, but then I'd just as well be a mushroom. I'm not sure that I could have lived with myself, knowing that I could have saved the President's life but chose not to."

I sat there thinking about that for a minute. Clovis was a man of principle—a patriot—a man with qualities rarely seen in the look-out-for-number-one world in which we live. I could clearly see that he was a man who stood for what he believed in.

"How long was it before Judy knew that you were not really dead?" I asked.

"About a month," Clovis responded. "It took me awhile to elude all those men; they were really putting the pressure on me. That's why I faked my death with the grizzly the morning after my conversation with you and came here to hide. I knew that no one knew about this place because I never have found one sign of human existence here. After things settled down, I hiked out of here about 50 miles toward home. If you noticed, our cabin is built back in a canyon and on the west side is a large bluff about 150 yards from the house. When I finally made it back to the ranch, I climbed that bluff. I knew the house and surrounding area would have hidden cameras, so I dared not get any closer to the house. I wrote a small note on the shaft of one of my arrows and launched it off the bluff into our front yard early one morning and waited for Judy to get up and do the chores. I sat there for about an hour watching and waiting when she finally stepped out of the house. At first, she walked right by it, but then she stopped and looked back at the arrow sticking in the yard. I'll never forget watching her through my binoculars. She picked it up and examined it closely, and then I could see her reading the note I had written on the shaft. Looking up toward the bluff, I waved my hand at her. She jumped with joy. Lord, I'll never forget that moment."

Tears streamed down Clovis's face. Observing the expression of Clovis's emotions forced a lump in my own throat. "This man's love for his wife," I thought to myself, "is perhaps deeper than any love I have ever witnessed before in my life."

A long moment of silence followed. I could tell Clovis was too heartbroken to speak. Finally, breaking the silence, Clovis began, "Tyler, there are only a few things in life worth clinging to. Oh, a straight-shooting bow or gun, or a great feeling fly rod in your hands are treasures a man enjoys during their seasons, but the things that really matter, the things that you should never let go of, are the things that you really can't hold in your hands. For instance, the first time your baby smiles, or calls you 'Daddy', or takes that first step, or rides her bike without training wheels, or gets on the bus to go to school for the first time. Lord, how I miss my Kelli." He looked away to wipe his eyes, and then looked me straight in the eye. "Let me tell you though, in this life, the most precious gift of all that a man can ever receive is the love of a good woman. I'm talking about the kind of love that takes a lifetime to grow. You learn that that kind of love is made up of all the little things that come to mean so much to you, like the smile on her face when you bring her a small bouquet of wildflowers, or the frown on her face when she fusses at you for leaving your clothes scattered on the floor, or the way she wraps her arm around your chest in bed at night and puts her cold feet next to yours to try to get warm. It's working together, playing together, laughing together, and crying together; it's these things that make life worth living, Tyler. It's these things that keep me doing my best to stay alive. I'm afraid that very few men ever experience the kind of love that Judy and I have known. It seems they get all caught up in chasing after the dollar. America has painted a picture of happiness and framed it with gold. Money can't buy happiness. Happiness comes only when we give our most precious possession to someone else, and that's our heart. Judy and I share that kind of love."

Without intending to or at least I don't believe he did, Clovis had stepped all over my toes. The fact remained that I had let myself get caught in the same snare as so many other young American men. Money and wealth had become the focus of my life, always believing that somehow, someday, somewhere, I would have enough to really enjoy life, and yet the truth of the matter was that life was passing by me right now. Always in my mind, I kept thinking that if I could save up enough money and make a few wise investments, then when I retire, I'll do all the things I have always dreamed of doing. More and more I was beginning to understand that this type of mindset, although so prevalent in my own mind and among my peers, is faulty reasoning. After all, it does seem pretty arrogant to believe that we'll live long enough to see retirement, and then if we do, who's to say that our knees will be strong enough to carry us to those places we desire to go? Clovis was indeed pricking the issues that I had been wrestling in my own life.

"Clovis, it's obvious that you love Judy very much, and based on the times I've spent with Judy, there's no doubt that her feelings for you are mutual. I mean, it just seems to me that they don't make women like that anymore. Where does a man find love like that in our day and age?" I asked.

Clovis gave a sort of grin, and then he squinted his eyes and pointed his finger at me like a father who might be lecturing his son. "Tyler, listen to me close. I do not claim to have a complete understanding about women. Shoot, I doubt that any man ever will. However, what I am fixin' to tell you is something you need to remember for as long as you live. You can read all the books you want to about improving your marriage and your relationship, but I promise you, if you practice what I'm telling you, you'll not only save a pile of money buying those books or visiting marriage counselors, you'll find the deepest and most fulfilling love you'll ever know."

I sat up in the pool a little straighter, listening closely. Already I found myself being drawn to the simple and sensible wisdom Clovis had to share. He did not speak like some kind of arrogant know-it-all, but as one who had learned a few things along the course of life.

"First of all," he continued, "a love like Judy and I share is not something you find, but rather, it is something you grow. That's important to remember. Most precious things take time. Second of all, and hear me now, if you want to have a good wife, you have got to be a good husband. I know that sounds so simple, but I'm tellin' ya, if you want a woman that loves you and adores you and appreciates you and respects you more than anyone or anything, well then, you need to be a husband that loves her and adores her and appreciates her and respects her more than anyone or anything. You reap what you sow—plain and simple."

Pausing for a minute, Clovis apologized, "I'm sorry, Tyler. I didn't mean to go preaching at you. I guess I've had a whole lot of time to think up here, and I'm just talking out loud, but seriously, Tyler, think about what I am telling you. Life goes by quickly, so it's much too short to live it in such a way that you spend whatever there is that remains, entangled in the thorns of regret. Decide what's really important, Tyler, and then pour your soul into it." He turned away, stretching his legs in the hot pool. "Say, you ready to get out of this pool and let me doctor those wounds?"

CHAPTER EIGHTEEN

I woke up feeling like I had a hangover. My head felt like a football that had been kicked by a mule. The cavern room was spinning in circles, and I felt the urge to vomit. I tried to lean to the side, but didn't make it and puked all over my chest. Clovis came to my aid and began washing me off.

"How long have I been lying here?" I asked.

"Almost four days. You took on a really bad fever and sure got me worried, boy," Clovis responded. "Your wounds are healing up nicely though, and once we get some food in you, you'll be ready to get out of here in a day or two."

He helped me sit upright as I slowly took my time getting to my feet. Feeling my head with my fingers, I could tell that Clovis had stitched and bandaged the wound.

"That cut took 14 stitches, Tyler. I doubt a surgeon from the Mayo Clinic could have done any better," Clovis proudly commented as he smiled at me while taking a sip from his coffee cup. "Here, I have some elk bouillon made for you. Drink it up. It's got some herbs in it, too, that will perk you up really fast."

Sipping the bouillon, I asked, "Have you heard or seen anything of the others?" referring to the FBI.

"Well, there's six less FBI agents we have to contend with and one less Secret Service Agent, by the name of Carol. I decided to go prowling one night while you were sleeping so peacefully."

"Where did you find them? How did you kill them?" I asked curiously.

Clovis pulled a hunting knife from his scabbard and showed it to me. I just stared at him in disbelief, although I knew he was telling me the truth. I kept wondering how a man with so much love and passion for life, whose gentle voice and hands and soft eyes, would give you the impression that he meant no harm to anyone yet could be such an incredible adversary to his enemies.

"With your knife?" I asked.

"They had me surrounded, Tyler, and made me throw down my gun. They didn't know I was carrying my blade. They thought it would be funny to hang me by my feet and gut me open. I had other plans." Clovis looked at me hard for a minute, reading my thoughts I was sure.

"Clovis, I've got to ask you something."

"Yes." Clovis cut me off short before I could finish my question. "Yes, I have killed a lot of men over the last three years." Pausing, looking at the walls around us, his mind obviously some place else, he looked back again at me and asked, "Tyler, are you aware that there is a one million dollar bounty on my head?"

"No, I was not aware of that," I answered.

"Well, there is. Do you have any idea how many money hungry fools have come in here to The Bob looking to kill me or capture me and collect on that bounty? A bunch!!! Most of them I have been able to avoid, but there have been some who were very good at what they do and very persistent. The FBI and AFFA have the money to hire the best, so I've had a few close calls."

Obviously, I knew Clovis could not let those who sought to kill him leave the Bob Marshall alive for fear of his existence and location becoming public knowledge. I wanted to ask him what he did with the remains of those he killed, but I felt it would be better to leave it alone. Looking at me, it seemed as if Clovis knew exactly what I was pondering in my mind, and replied, "I'd rather not discuss it any further. Now, come on, let's see if you can get up and make it to the table."

I knew Clovis was not going to share any more details. Even though I tried to imagine myself in his shoes, it was inconceivable in my mind. I couldn't find it in myself to judge or condemn him in any way for the death he had brought to so many. A man will do what he has to do to stay alive, especially if he knows that someone else is depending on him.

I slowly walked to the table. Looking at my burns, I was surprised to see how clean and well they were healing. All of the charred tissue was gone, so I asked Clovis how he had managed to clean the wounds so well.

"Maggots," Clovis answered.

"Maggots?" I asked in disbelief.

"Yeah, I learned it while I was in 'Nam. They used them all the time to treat burnt victims during the war. I found a dead mule deer buck down in the canyon, a lion kill, and gathered up about a quart of maggots. I put them on your burns and they ate up all the dead tissue. I didn't even have to use a scalpel. A few herbs mixed in with some pine pitch to create a salve, and I doubt that you'll have much for scars."

Glancing at his book shelf, I noticed THE BIOGRAPHY OF PRESIDENT ANTHONY WATSON, written by Peterson.

"You know," I said, "I never have read this book. Is it any good?"

"Man, it's great," Clovis replied enthusiastically. "Watson is a brilliant man and Peterson is or was a marvelous writer. You have to read it. You still need a couple of days to recuperate."

Grabbing the book from the shelf, I dropped it on the floor, knocking the paper cover off the hardback. Picking it up, I read a written message on the inside. I couldn't believe what I was reading.

To Newsome,

Tomorrow, this country will have a new Commander in Chief. Thanks for making it possible.

Sincerely,
President Peterson

It made no sense to me to think that Peterson would write something like this where it may one day be found. Was he so confident, believing that no one would ever find out? Certainly, he could not have been that stupid. Perhaps I would never know.

"Clovis, have you ever read this?" I asked, indicating the writing on the inside of the cover.

Clovis slowly took the book from my extended hand and read the lines. Shaking his head in disbelief, he stood their staring at it, trying to absorb the idea, that for almost three years he had lived as a fugitive of the law, his name probably already being printed in history books, and here, right underneath his nose, was probably enough evidence to have acquitted him from the crime.

For a moment, I thought he was going to get angry, but finally, he handed the book back to me and said, "Well, you can't do anything about the past. Yesterday is gone for good. However, between the tape you recorded and this written dedication by Peterson, I should be able to keep myself out of prison."

"Clovis, you aren't going to prison. As long as we can get this information to the press, you'll be all right. The hard part is going to be getting out of here without getting killed." Our eyes met and held for a moment, "How do you do that anyway?" I asked.

"Do what?

"You know, you always maintain a positive outlook on things. You always have a way of looking at things from an optimistic perspective. You don't get mad; you don't throw a fit or use foul language. You make lemonade when life gives you a lemon."

Clovis laughed and said, "Tyler, I'm not perfect; I've got plenty of faults. Just ask my Judy about that, but the way I see things, it's all a matter of faith. The rain falls on the good and the bad, and either you believe the Lord will see you through the tough times or you don't. It's as simple as that. I've traveled too many rough roads in my life to believe that I've made it this far on my own. Now, granted, the Lord doesn't always work on my schedule, but I figure he knows a whole lot more than I do, so he must have his reasons for doing the things he does." Clovis turned back toward the coffee pot and poured himself another hot cup. "Now read that book, Tyler. You'll like it. I've got a recorder over here and I'm going to make another copy of that tape of yours, just to be safe. Maybe, I'll make two."

Looking around at the inside of the cavern, the place Clovis had called home for so long, I asked, "Clovis, how did you get all of this stuff up here. Shoot, you've got a T.V., VCR, video tapes, radio, generator, guns, blankets, all kinds of stuff?"

"I had it flown in. A good friend of mine, a government trapper, makes a drop about once a month. I make him a list for the next month and send letters I've written to Judy back home with him."

"Does anyone know he makes those drops?"

"Only he and Judy and I, as far as I know," He answered. "His name is Tommy Holder. He told me that he was sure that the FBI was on to him in Kalispell where he normally picked up the supplies, so he just started doing his shopping elsewhere."

"So, he actually lands that plane of his?" I asked. "Where does he do that?"

"Helicopter, actually. He makes night drops on a flat spot on top of the Wall, about two miles from here, but you have to hike three miles north to Larch Hill Pass to get on top, and then back south 5 miles to get there. I had to disassemble that generator into three parts and make three trips to get it here, but it sure has been nice to have

"When is he supposed to make his next drop?" I asked.

Glancing at his watch to confirm the date, he said, "In four days."

"How much room does he have on that bird?" I asked.

Clovis looked at me and smiled, as he began to understand what idea I was spinning around in my head. "Enough," he answered.

"I'm thinking we go and meet him. No one will expect us to fly out of here. All we have to do is contact a reporter for Channel 2 News out of Great Falls and let them run this tape and interview us publicly, or better yet, I have a reporter friend that works for CNN. Yeah, that would be good. Once it goes public, we take it to the law. No one will dare touch us then. I'm sure that Watson will see to it that an all-out, full-scale investigation is conducted and that you'll receive the tightest protection until the investigation is complete."

Clovis sighed deeply. He looked at me through tear-filled eyes holding my stare. "For almost three years I've been on the dodge. I gave up everything and everybody I loved for one decisive action, to save a man who doesn't even know that I saved his life. The idea of being a free man is almost more than I can fathom. I want it more than anything I have ever wanted. I owe you Tyler. You're giving me my life back."

"Don't thank me yet, Clovis. We aren't out of the woods yet, literally. Besides, I wouldn't be standing here today if you hadn't come along and saved my skin down there in that canyon."

CHAPTER NINETEEN

For the next two days, I hung around the inside of the cavern, reading the book, taking time to exercise and regain my strength. Occasionally, Clovis slipped out to see if anyone was looking for us. He spent one morning springing all of his snares, dead-falls and other traps he set for capturing food. He wasn't going to need them anymore.

At supper I noticed his longbow standing in the corner along with a quiver full of arrows.

"Is that the bow you built?" I asked.

"It's one of them," he replied, handing it to me along with a couple of arrows to inspect.

"This is beautiful," I commented. The woodwork was exquisite. I could see how his drawknife had meticulously followed the rings of the wood, leaving the natural curve and shape in the bow. The arrows were nothing fancy, but I noticed that the shafts were barreled and the fletching was flawless.

"You're a real craftsman, Clovis."

"Thank you, Tyler. I really enjoy building these things, but as you well know, hunting with a weapon such as this is about as good as it gets. Almost everything I've killed up here has been with that bow. I seldom use this gun. Even though it has a suppressor on it that won't betray my presence, I prefer the challenge of hunting up close and personal." Waving his arm around the room, he continued, "I guess I'll have to leave all of this and come back and get it one day after we're out of here."

"I'll help you," I replied.

Standing at the entrance to the cave looking out across the Moose Creek drainage to the mountains beyond, my thoughts turned to Wren. I couldn't seem to get the girl out of my head. Would I ever see her again? Was she doing alright? What was it that she saw in me? Clovis stepped to my side at the entrance, evidently reading my thoughts.

"Let her be the reason you get out of here alive, Tyler. You'll find that staying alive for the sake of someone else will keep you alive a whole lot longer than just trying to live for yourself. Besides, if you don't mind my saying so, I think you might make a pretty good son-in-law."

Turning to Clovis, I asked, "What? What do you mean by son-in-law?"

Clovis laughed out loud in his deep, low voice. Tears filled his eyes, and he could hardly catch his breath. I didn't understand his amusement. Finally, he put his arm around my shoulder and looked me close in the eyes.

"Sonny boy," he chuckled. "Wren is my daughter. That's right, Kelli Wren Belden."

I was astounded. I didn't know what to say. Clovis was stricken with laughter, but as he laughed and smiled, for the first time I noticed the resemblance of his eyes and Wren's. They both had those brown, soft, captivating eyes. Poking at him in the ribs, I asked, "Why didn't you tell me earlier? I can't believe you held out on me like that."

"Tyler, I had to get to know you a little bit. Wren writes about you all the time and sends me letters just like her mama does. She thinks you hung the moon. Now, don't you go telling her that I told you all of that."

Taken aback, I was still speechless. This was too ironic for me to grasp. Clovis continued, "You see, Tyler, Kelli missed her old man and decided she was going to try to find a way to get me out of these mountains. To do that, she was going to have to find a way to help me prove my innocence. I would not tell her the reason why I shot Peterson because I was afraid for her safety. There are some pretty mean people in this world that can make you reveal everything you know, one way or the other. If she didn't know, then perhaps she would remain safe. I also never revealed where I was hiding, obviously for the same reason. The FBI questioned her continually for several months and kept a close eye on her, but she led them to believe that she didn't want anything to do with me anymore. In time, they left her alone. However, she did her home-work and figured a few things out for herself. She managed to get on with AFFA, and before long she was in the middle of things, which of course, means that somehow she hooked up with the sur-veillance crew that was constantly watching you. No one there knows she is my daughter; at least that's what she says. I continu-ally find that difficult to believe. I just hope for her sake that she is right. She had a complete identity change, which I funded with some of the cash that I confiscated from Newsome, but still I won-der whether or not they really know. AFFA has always believed that I am still living and that if I ever decided to reveal myself in public again, I would contact you. They were right about that. They also believed that I would never do so until I had proof to acquit myself. Until now, I didn't have it. I was going to get out anyway. I'm tired of living up here. Judy and Kelli pleaded with me not to do it, but a man can only take so much. When you love someone as much as I love them, life isn't much worth living if you've got to do it alone."

Clovis paused for a minute. He continued, "So, anyway, I let Judy and Kelli know that I wanted to come home, but I needed to tell you my story before I came out. Knowing that it would be nearly impossible to get to you, I arranged for you to meet me, via the folks that work in your office."

"How exactly were you able to make those contacts, and how did you make that phone call to me at my office in Chicago?" I asked.

"Tommy Holder, you know, the government trapper that we're supposed to meet in a couple of days? Well, he has some contacts and helped me set it up. He also let me use his phone to make that call. I made it short so it couldn't be traced. I didn't want anyone to know except you where this place is. Even Tommy doesn't know. As I said, the place where he lands his chopper is a fair piece from here. I also knew, through Wren, that your office, car, and home were under very tight surveillance. So, when you got my call and the information revealing where to meet me, the team at AFFA picked it up. Wren knew they would, that's why she purchased the truck and set things up for your escape before hand. She wasn't sure just how to get the map to you without being noticed, but she knew that she could trust Kendall to get it done. She's one sharp cookie."

"There's something else, Tyler. Has your father ever mentioned my name?"

"No, not exactly," I answered. "Well, I mean he spoke of you after you killed Peterson. Why do you ask?"

"Has your dad ever mentioned how he got that scar on his shoulder?"

"Yeah, he told me he got shot during the Vietnam War, but that's it. He wouldn't talk about the war, and he refused to allow us to ask him questions about it. How do you know about that scar anyway?"

"Tyler, I know this is almost too much to believe and the coincidence of all of this is mind boggling to me, but we're more closely tied together than just the story you're writing about me."

"What do you mean?" I asked.

"Your daddy is one heck of a man. He was in 'Nam several years before I got there. He flew a medevac helicopter during the war. Your father would go into some of the hottest combat zones to get the wounded out and back to the M.A.S.H units. His reputation preceded him long before I ever got there. I can't tell you the number of men he managed to bring back out of those jungles and rice patties, who wouldn't be living today if it weren't for him... and I'm one of them."

"My father saved your life?" This was simply incredible. "Clovis, first you tell me that the woman, who saved my life, is your daughter. Now, you tell me that my father saved your life during the war. Either you're lying to me or you've got a wild and vivid imagination."

"It's the truth, Tyler. Fall of 1969, I got sent on a mission. I had my assignment to take out two North Vietnamese colonels. Things got a little spooky. I made the hits and was working on getting out of there, running through the jungle on a trail, and I practically ran over this woman who was returning from the rice fields. I could have killed her, but I didn't. She started screaming at the top of her lungs and within seconds about 50 Viet Cong were hot on my tail. I ran harder than I had ever run, but I could tell that they were gaining on me. I came to a rice patty and had no choice but to try to run across it. Not quite halfway across it, I tripped and fell and twisted my ankle. Getting up, I kept on running, but I was losing ground. Suddenly, I heard this chopper right over my head and I looked up and it's your father. He lands that bird and tells me to 'get in' with the Viet Cong in sight and getting closer by the second. As he started to lift that bird off the ground, gunfire was spitting everywhere, but he got us out of there. I didn't even know he was hit until we were miles away. I noticed blood staining his shirt. The bullet ripped through his back, exited through his shoulder, and lodged in the windshield of the chopper."

Clovis paused for a minute, evidently reliving the events in his mind. "Yeah, your old papa saved my life and the lives of a lot of men... So, you didn't know that?"

"No. That's the first thing I ever knew about Dad and the war. Shoot, I didn't even know he flew a chopper."

"So, I'm assuming you don't know about the Purple Heart or the Congressional Medal of Honor either?" I shook my head. "Well, maybe it wasn't my place to tell you, so why don't you just keep it to yourself if you don't mind?"

"Alright, Clovis. My lips are sealed, but it sure explains a few things that I have always wondered about."

"Like what, exactly?" Clovis asked.

"Well, when I was a little boy, Dad left. Mom told us that he was working on a job that took him a long way from home and wouldn't be back for a really long time. Sometimes at night, I would hear her crying. I just thought she was lonely and missing Dad and I guess she was, but now, I realize that she was worried too. Later on, when Dad was home, on several occasions there were some folks who called and wanted to interview Dad. I never did know what for. He always declined. Another time, when I was just a little boy, we were in Billings, getting groceries at K-Mart. In the parking lot were a bunch of folks protesting the war and saying that our soldiers were a bunch of baby killers. Man, I remember it like it was yesterday. Dad told my brothers and me to stay right where we were. He stepped over to the crowd and told everyone that they needed to go home. Some of them started mocking him, asking him what he intended to do about it if they didn't go home. Dad cleaned up about half a dozen of them in less time than it takes to tell. My brothers and I were shocked. Needless to say, they left. When Dad walked back over to where we were standing, he knelt down to us and said, 'Now boys, usually I don't encourage fighting. There'll be times, many times, when you'll be confronted with conflict, and most of the time, you need to just walk away from it. However, there are some things worth fighting or dying for. This was one of those times. No one walks all over this country in front of me. Now, don't you dare say anything to your mama about what you've seen here today. She'll skin me alive for misbehaving in front of you boys.' We never did."

"That's him, Tyler. He was a heck of a soldier… You know, I've seen him a couple other times since the war, too—one time in Miles City at a cattle auction and another time at a Cattlemen's Convention in Billings. He's a good man. I owe my life to him."

Looking to the east across the mountains, Clovis started again, changing the subject. "The thing that's got me worried, Tyler, is the fact that we haven't run into any of the bad boys from AFFA up here yet. Wren tells me that AFFA has a mole inside with the FBI that keeps them informed, so I know that AFFA has to know that the FBI is up here, so I'm wondering why we've seen neither hide nor hair of any of their bunch yet? Something's not right, I'm telling ya."

As darkness fell upon the canyon below, a light rain began to fall. It was August, and winter would be along soon. Summers don't seem to last long in Montana, especially at this elevation. The events of the last 10 days were all starting to come together. Clovis and I stood in silence as the rain and darkness swallowed up the view of the canyon floor below us.

"Say, why don't we put on a fresh pot of coffee, eat a bite, and let me tell you a little about my daughter," Clovis suggested.

"Sounds good to me. I'm starved," I responded as we both turned back inside the cavern.

Elk steak with sautéed wild onions sprinkled with roasted pinion nuts, baked Blue Grouse, dehydrated potatoes and peas, steamed wild cabbage, served with coffee and homemade chokecherry wine made for a delicious supper. We both ate until we were stuffed. Clovis talked into the late hours of the night, clear into early morning telling me about Kelli, whom I knew as Wren. He was proud of his daughter and loved her dearly. My ears never grew tired of hearing the stories of her past, and my desire to see her again was second only to seeing her and Clovis reunited after all these years.

Kelli had grown up her whole life on her father's ranch. She could stretch wire, drive post, bale hay, brand calves, ride, rope, and operate every farm implement on the ranch as well as any man. During the summer months, she would get up at the crack of dawn and work until dark along the side of her mother and father. The rest of the year, she would rise every morning to help her father with the chores, which included feeding the cattle in the sub-zero temperatures of winter, before she went off to school. Her interests were much the same as her father's. She loved hunting, fishing and riding her horse in the mountains. Clovis told me "Kelli is the best 'son' I could ever ask for."

Chosen as the most likely to succeed in her class and also the valedictorian of her class, it was obvious to anyone who knew her that she was a disciplined and hardworking individual. Along with her intelligence, she was an extremely attractive young lady, and was nominated homecoming queen her senior year in high school.

The quality Kelli possessed that was the most attractive was her splendid personality—always smiling, always willing to help others, never considering herself better than anyone else. People found themselves drawn to her, like a bear to a honey tree, and they found themselves feeling like they were a better person by spending time in her presence.

Clovis did admit to me that she was strong-willed and had a stubborn streak about her that was nearly unbreakable. He stated, "Once she makes up her mind about something, you can forget about trying to change it." He chuckled, "She gets that honest."

Clovis looked at me with soft and searching eyes, as if he were trying to read my thoughts, then he reached inside his shirt pocket and withdrew a letter, slowly and carefully opening it. "Tyler, I pulled this letter from the box where I keep all of the letters that Judy and Kelli send me, and debated with myself real hard about whether I should share it with you, but you've got to promise me that you'll never tell Kelli that I read it to you." I shook my head to affirm my promise. He cleared his throat, looked at me once, and then began.

Dear Father,

It's March now and this month marks two years since I came aboard with AFFA. The weather has been wet and cold and it's plain to see why Chicago is called 'The Windy City', but every time I feel like complaining about this weather, I think of you and the difficulties you must face trying to survive the winters in the high country. I don't know how you do it. I sure hope you are doing well.

As I've written before in numerous letters, I have really developed a deep fondness and respect for Ross Tyler. It's apparent to me now that the admiration you have held for him, as a writer, for all these years, was not just because of his beautiful and exquisite writing, but also because of the man you could read about between the lines. Even the other members of our surveillance team occasionally express their respect and praise for Ross's character. He's just not your typical modern day man.

Watching him every day as we do, I would have never believed that a person could learn so much about another individual without actually having a real-time conversation with him. I have found, however, that you can really learn the truth about a person's character, if you're able to observe him without him knowing it. What a person does when no one is watching, or, as in this case, when he doesn't know that you're watching, reveals the type of person he really is inside.

Last month, Ross had stopped by the grocery store, as he does every Thursday, and after carrying his groceries to the car, he realized that the teller had given him too much change at the register. Putting his groceries in his car, he reentered the store, went to the back of the long line and patiently waited to return the change. Shoot, it couldn't have been more than fifty or sixty cents if it was that much. Father, who does that?

Just a few days ago, he got in a heated argument with his boss. His boss wanted him to print a story that did not exactly reveal the whole truth about the matter and both of them knew it. Ross refused. He told his boss that he would never purposely print a lie for anyone including him. Not now or ever. His boss threatened to fire him and Ross told him to do what he had to do. Evidently, he got over it, because an hour later he came back to Ross's office and apologized and praised him for his integrity.

Oh, and last week, Ross was stuck in a traffic jam. Ahead of him was a black woman, also in the traffic jam, whose daughter began having a seizure. The woman, jumped out of the car and began screaming for help, but no one came. It was snowing outside and I suppose that no one cared to get out and help, then all of a sudden, Ross shows up, looks at the girl, takes her in his arms and runs as fast as he can for more than a mile in the snow and sleet to the nearest hospital. Of course, when he returned, his car had been towed off and he had to pay for the impound fee.

Ross is a strong man. He's confident, sure, steady, stable, and honest. He has a certain air about him that makes you believe he's real and genuine. He's proud, but certainly not arrogant. I've noticed, too, that he never compromises his morals or beliefs, and while he is careful about whom he'll choose to trust, you get the feeling that you can always trust in him. He reminds me a lot of you.

There is one other thing that I find kind of humorous. Ross, no matter how hard he tries, just cannot find a way of fitting in to the city life. Oh, he's put his cowboy hat, boots and wranglers away in the closet and dresses like a big-city reporter, but even after all this time, he has not been able to conform. The more I watch him, the more obvious it appears to me. Sometimes I don't know whether to laugh at him or cry for him. I remember as a girl, you used to tell me, "You can take a man out of the mountains, but you can't take the mountains out of the man." I never really understood exactly what that meant until now.

I could go on, Father, but the point I'm trying to make is I do believe I have found a man with whom I could spend the rest of my life, but here I am in a situation where I can't even introduce myself. Every time he goes out on a date with some girl I get all

torn up inside. First, I get jealous and then I get scared, afraid that
he might start having feelings for her. I don't know, Father, maybe
I'm just crazy. I mean, think about it— is it even possible to fall in
love with someone you've never shared a conversation with? I
can't get him off my mind. Of course, keeping tabs on him is part
of my daily assignment, but, well, you know what I mean. Other
men ask me out on a date at least twice a week, but I haven't gone
out in more than six months now, because Ross is the only man I
am interested in. I have never felt like this before about anyone.

Father, I'm going to close for now. I want you to know how
grateful I am to have a father like you, who listens to me and cares
for me and loves me the way that you do. I really don't know of
another woman who shares a relationship with her father as close
or as deep as we do. I miss you so much.

Love,
Kelli

"Well, Tyler," Clovis commented, "There it is. Take it for
what it's worth. I do believe that my little girl has fallen in love
with you."

I looked into his eyes and tried to determine why he had made
the choice to read that letter to me. Did he want me to know how
his daughter felt about me? Was it his way of assuring me that I
met his approval for his daughter? I really didn't know why and
thought about asking him, but I decided to let it pass. He must
have read my mind, because he started again. "Tyler, we live in a
world where it seems that everybody is consumed with selfishness.
They look out for themselves and step on anyone that happens to
get in the way. We raised Kelli different than that. It's rather obvious that physically she is a very attractive young lady and I'm sure
that if she desired, she could act like a snob and still get her way
with things, but she doesn't. Her mama and I have instilled in her
the attitude of kindness and compassion to all people, and that's the
one characteristic that I believe most people find attractive.

" Now, I say all of that to say this, it isn't often that you run
into a man that carries those same attributes, but I believe, and

apparently so does Kelli, that you're that kind of man. So, man to man, I just want you to know up front, that my daughter isn't the only individual that holds a deep admiration for you."

I was a little taken aback and didn't know just what to say.

"Don't say anything," Clovis replied. "I just wanted you to know how I felt, and it's just my opinion, but I think that the good things that need to be said are too often left unsaid."

"Well, thank you, Clovis, I really appreciate it. More than you know."

Changing the subject, Clovis stated, "Tell me about your brothers, Tyler. I've been doing all the talking. I've heard you mention them on several occasions."

"We're tight, Clovis. Every one of us loves the outdoors. Hunting and fishing have been a part of our life for as long as we can remember. We owe Dad and Mom for that. Even my sister loves to hunt and fish. Thing is we saw how tough it was for Dad to punch out a living on the ranch, and by the time we graduated from high school, we were ready to go somewhere else where we could make a decent living, and all of us do. The ironic thing about all of it is that every single one of us wishes we were back in Montana. Even after all of these years, we can't seem to make a phone call to each other without the subject of returning to Montana coming up in our conversation. I guess it will never happen though. My brothers are all married with kids and jobs and debts. I'm the only one who isn't tied down yet, and I'm the oldest." The more I pondered the distance, the more it gnawed at my heart. "I sure wish they were here. They're pretty tough boys and all of them can shoot. I don't know that we're in the same category as you, but when we put the crosshairs on our target, you can bet it's a done deal."

"I hope I get to meet them some day," Clovis replied. "They sound like fine young men." With eyes that whispered understanding, he finished his drink, "Hey, let's go sit in the hot spring and make sure that we're good and loose for the hike out of here."

Moving into the room with the hot sulfur spring, we undressed and sat down in the warm water. Again, the hot bath soothed our aching bodies.

"What are your plans, Clovis?" I asked. "I mean, about getting out of here?"

"Tomorrow night, we'll travel under the cover of darkness. You just follow me. Tomorrow, we'll sleep in and get as much rest as possible, and then spend the day getting things ready. You'll need to pack as lightly as possible, but take the necessities, take the book and the cassette. I've got a copy of the cassette as well. Also, take a little food, and an extra set of dry clothes, knife, matches, and this here gun."

Clovis pulled an old lever-action .30-30 Winchester from out of a scabbard and handed me a couple boxes of ammunition.

"Take that and your .45. I hope you don't need them, but I have a feeling that something's up. It's been too quiet around here the last few days, and we still haven't heard a word or seen anything of those folks from AFFA. I don't like it."

"What do you make of it?" I asked.

"I don't know. I just don't know. I've been down in this canyon every day and have not found a track of anyone. I've watched it with my binoculars and spotting scope and all I've seen is wildlife. I've watched them, but they haven't given any indication of threat or fear, so I just don't know. However, tomorrow night we're getting out of here, and we're going to meet Holder on The Wall."

Sleep should have come easy at such a late hour and a stomach full of food and wine, but I dreamed the whole night long, tossing and turning, occasionally waking and thinking about the day ahead of us and trying to play out every possible scenario. Clovis knew these mountains, and he had been in many difficult situations before, so when he said that something didn't quite feel just right, I wasn't going to second guess his feelings. The uncertainty got the best of me and left me restless. Finally, somewhere among all the anxiety and worry, I fell asleep.

I awoke again to the smell of breakfast cooking. Clovis was preparing another one of his fine meals. Getting up and stepping outside the cave entrance to relieve myself, I was happy to see that the rain had dissipated and morning had already made a good start.

Clovis was not as talkative as he normally was. Something was bothering him; I let it be for a while. We talked very little at breakfast, and after eating we both started packing our packs and cleaning our guns. Finally, Clovis broke the silence.

"You see that rock wedged up there in the ceiling," pointing as he spoke. "If something should happen to me, the rest of Newsome's money is hidden behind that rock. Take it to Kelli and Judy if you don't mind."

"I'll get it done, that is, if nothing happens to me either," I replied. "What's eating you, Clovis?"

Clovis looked at me and then stared at the wall, not really seeing either, but rather trying to focus on something he was contemplating in his mind.

"It's like I told you last night. Something ain't right. If those animals are trying to kill us and they're not pursuing us, then it must mean that they are waiting for us, and that must mean that they think they have a pretty good idea what we're going to do. But how could they?"

"I don't know, Clovis. I'm feeling pretty restless, too. I'm not sure if it's a gut feeling like you're having or if your feelings are rubbing off on me, but I could hardly sleep last night."

"Well, we'll just have to be really careful. We're the hunted here... and there is something else I think you need to know."

"What's that?" I asked.

"Did Kelli ever introduce you to a man named Kirby Nations? He's about my size and about my age," Clovis asked.

"No, I already knew Kirby. I met him a couple years ago at the nightclub. We used to visit some when I'd stop by. However, he never gave me any idea or indication that his presence at the club was directly related to me. It wasn't until Wren told me about AFFA and his involvement that I knew anything about him. Why do you ask?"

Clovis closed his eyes for a minute, leaned back in his chair, as if thinking about another time and another place, and then he continued, "Tyler, I went to Nam in the summer of 1969. Right away, I was put into a special unit where I was trained to be an assassin for Uncle Sam. Most of the training I received came almost naturally to me. I won't deny it, I found a lot of pleasure and satisfaction not in the killing itself, but in the challenge to kill without being killed, and of course, killing an enemy while at war made killing easier to mentally accept. Out of the dozen men that I trained with, only two of us survived the war and returned home. I was one and Kirby Nations was the other."

"Judging by the sound and tone of your voice, Clovis, I sense that there is not a lot of love loss between you and Nations?"

"No, definitely not. Both of us had the same kind of training, and both of us took to it like we were born for that kind of work, but Nations was a brutal savage. During the second year of service, both of us were given assignments, and our targets were not really that far apart. Our rendezvous destination where we were to be evacuated was at the same location. Well, the Viet Cong had put a pretty large bounty on our heads and Nations was determined to collect the price they had on mine. As you can see, he never did collect, but he sure gave it a few good shots…

"You mean, he tried to kill you in order to collect the bounty that was on your head?" I asked.

"Yes, sir. Nations is crazy. I remember on another occasion I witnessed Nations slaughter a whole family of Vietnamese…South Vietnamese. When I asked him about it, his comment was something like 'kill 'em all let God sort 'em out later.' I'm tellin' ya the man is utterly ruthless. On another occasion he falsified some information about an assignment that was given to me that put me in a position that made me vulnerable to the cross hairs on his scope. Fortunately, I figured out his little scheme and was able to divert the plans enough to keep myself from getting killed. When he returned home from the war, I heard he became a professional mercenary. After I killed Peterson, and Kelli hooked up with AFFA, Kirby Nations also became part of the group. I'm guessing he wants to finish what he started so long ago."

"Does Wren know?" I asked.

"No. She knows he's a dangerous man, but she doesn't know that Nations and I have a history. At least I don't think she does."

Pulling out his knife, Clovis stroked it smoothly on a whetstone, testing the edge until it peeled the hair off of his arm. Loading his gun and checking it again several times, he put two more full clips into his pockets and another 50 rounds in his pack. From

the backside of his waist, he pulled out a .45 automatic and scrutinized the action and barrel. In no time, we were ready to go,
checking and double-checking everything we had. Now, all we
had to do was patiently wait for the darkness of night.

CHAPTER TWENTY

For hours we waited, pacing the floor, with very little to say. Clovis was worried and so was I. Both of us were ready to get on the trail. The uncertainty of what lies ahead, is quite often more difficult to endure than the actual events the situation may unveil. For certain, the uncertainty was making both of us restless.

Slowly, but ever so surely, the sun began to set in the west and the shadows of evening began to engulf the canyon floor below us. We stood at the entrance to the cavern looking down into the canyon, as an ominous wind blew through the pines, whistling a lonesome song. Clovis sighed deeply before he spoke.

"This has been my home, Tyler, for almost 3 years. It seems like an eternity. I love these mountains. It's one of the few places that remain unspoiled. However, a man gets pretty lonely in places like this when he hungers for companionship and realizes that he can't have it. I miss Judy and Kelli. I miss the home place and the comfort of going out on my porch after supper and watching the sunset. I miss sitting on the swing and talking with Judy clear into the late hours of the night and listening to the wind blow through our little valley. I can't even begin to enumerate all the little things I have found myself longing for. It sure makes you realize just how much you take for granted." He paused for several minutes while I stood there listening in silence, then he began again, "You know, between the war in 'Nam and this battle I'm fighting now, I've lost 6 years of my marriage." It was obvious by the gloomy look on his face and the tone in his voice that Clovis was feeling down. "Sorry, Tyler, I don't normally get down. I guess I'm just ready for it to be all over with."

"Then let's get it done," I said excitedly.

Clovis smiled and slapped me on the back. "You don't see an anchor tied to my rear. I'm with you. Let's get our stuff and get out of here."

Carefully, we scaled the 20 feet down the cliff face until we were on solid ground. The night was dark and it was difficult to see more than a few feet in any direction. Clovis whispered, "We'll just take our time. It only takes about 4 to 5 hours to get there, but I would rather travel in the darkness and wait in the timber until Holder flies in with his chopper than to risk traveling during the light of day and take a chance of being spotted. Now, just follow me."

Clovis moved like a ghost. He didn't seem to ever trip over anything or make a sound. I, on the other hand, was as clumsy as a newborn calf. Several times Clovis turned to rebuke me with his finger held to his lips and whispering shhh... Finally, he stopped and said, "Tyler, let me teach you a little trick about walking in the deep, dark night. You're trying to let your eyes do all the walking. Step lightly and feel with your foot extended, testing not only for what is in front of you, but what your foot is stepping on before you put your weight down."

It took about a mile or so before I started to get the hang of it, but eventually I was making progress without stumbling so often. As an avid hunter, I have always been pretty good at walking softly, but compared to Clovis, I was a novice. I could not ascertain if his skills were really that much better than mine, or if I had lost the touch from lack of use over the past three years.

The climb up Larch Hill Pass was tough on my legs and lungs. The trail was steep, making our ascension painstakingly slow. Every few feet I had to stop and catch my breath. Clovis wasn't even breathing hard. "What are you, Belden," I asked, "part mountain goat?"

Clovis laughed, "Living up here for all this time will do that to you."

Once we made it to the summit of the Chinese Wall, the going was relatively flat and made the walking easy. Two miles or so south from the Pass, Clovis stopped and walked to the edge of the cliff.

"Do you know how to rappel, Tyler?"

"Yeah, I do alright."

"Good. Look here."

Clovis bent down and grabbed a rope that was well hidden in the brush and lifted a nearby rock and pointed. "Under this rock is a harness in a plastic bag. This rope drops down directly over the entrance to the cavern we've been staying in. If you get in trouble up here on the Wall, don't try to run all the way back up to the pass. Most likely it will be guarded anyway. Come here and rappel down to the cavern. If no one sees you go off the side, they'll never find you. Hopefully, you won't have to do it, but it's a good thing to know if the need arises."

I made a mental note of it and we got back to the trail. An hour or so later, Clovis stopped again. "This is it. This is where Holder lands his bird. He'll be here about an hour before first light."

Glancing at my watch, I figured that first light was at least three more hours. "What do we do until then?" I asked.

"We wait, over there in the timber." Clovis answered. "Come on, I've got a great little place where we can build a fire that won't be seen."

Once inside the timber, Clovis led me to a rock overhang that we proceeded to crawl up under. Clovis turned on his flashlight, gathered some twigs and sticks and had a fire going in no time. There was not enough room to stand up, but plenty of room to sit back against the rock wall under the overhang and be quite comfortable. The warm reflection and heat of the fire was exactly what we needed.

"Let me show you something," Clovis said, pointing his flashlight at the rock walls where etchings of animals and other symbols and figures were painted.

"Who made those?" I asked. "Was it the Nez Perce or Blackfoot?"

"Could have been, but I think they were made long before they came along. I just don't know."

As my eyes observed the work of hands from someone who had lived, God only knew how long ago, the question entered my mind, "What kind of mark on this world will I leave behind?"

My thoughts were interrupted when Clovis asked, "What are you going to do when you get out of here, Tyler?"

"Well, I've been studying on that a little. Assuming we both get out of here alive, I'm hoping that you are pardoned. I really believe you will be. Then, if you don't mind, I'd like to tell your story, but not for a paper, but as a novel."

"Go for it. I really won't mind. Let me tell you something else. If you do it right, there's a good chance it will do well."

"I'm counting on it, Clovis, and since it's about you, I'll cut you in on a high percentage of the sales profit."

Clovis thought about it for a minute and then said, "No. I have a better idea. If it does well, you can keep my share on one condition."

"What's that?" I asked.

"If your brothers really want to come back to Montana as bad as you say they do, then why don't you expand your father's ranch and make it possible for them? At least make them the offer."

"You've got a deal," I commented as I extended to shake his hand, which felt like grabbing a handful of steel.

"What other plans have you got?" Clovis asked.

"What is this, 20 questions?" I knew what he was getting at. "Yes, I'm going to find your daughter. I'm going to chase her until she drops, and if she's as much the woman as I think she is and you tell me she is, I'm going to slap a big ring on her finger and marry her and give you all kinds of grandchildren to keep you and Judy busy. How's that?"

Clovis laughed and roared out loud, losing his breath and choking until tears came out of his eyes and rolled down his cheeks into his beard. Looking at his beard, I asked, "How long have you been growing that thing?"

"Ever since I left to come up here hunting," he answered. "Judy hates the thing and would never let me grow one. I doubt she'll recognize me when she sees me."

The hours passed quickly and conversation was light and easy. Clovis did not seem as nervous as he had been earlier. Maybe talking about his family had helped remove the idea of unforeseen danger from his mind. Somewhere in the early hours of morning, I had fallen asleep and slept hard until Clovis nudged me.

"Tyler, it's about an hour before dawn."

I stoked up the hot coals of the fire a little to break the morning chill. "Warm up real good, Tyler. I still have a feeling something isn't quite right."

Waiting there by the fire, I dug into my pack and pulled out a bag of trail mix. Inside was another note from Wren.

Dear Ross,

I hope that you are safe and that you have found Clovis. Please try to   convince him to stay. Without any proof of his intentions for killing Peterson, he'll get the chair for sure. Please be careful.

Wren

I showed the note to Clovis. "Won't she be surprised?" he said. "Not only am I going to get out of here, but I've also got proof that will make me a free man."

"That's right," I added.

Munching on my trail mix and sharing it with Clovis, a few short minutes passed when we both heard the thumping, drumming sound of a helicopter.

"That's him. Let's go."

Burying the fire in dirt and grabbing our packs, we crawled out from underneath the rock overhang and headed toward the meadow where Holder was supposed to meet us. The early morning was still dark, but a faint hint of light on the eastern horizon meant that dawn was near. Hearing the chopper, we continued advancing through the timber toward the small meadow where Holder would land the chopper. Clovis studied the clearing to make sure the coast was clear. Holder started to land, his runners just touching the ground, when suddenly he pulled up. From out of the timber on the southwest side of the meadow, gunfire erupted. Several automatic weapons blasted as he lifted toward the sky. Black smoke began to spill out of the fuselage, and the motor, spitting and sputtering, was on the verge of dying. Holder was doing everything to keep the chopper under control, but it veered to the east, over the cliffs and off into the canyon floor below. A loud crash and explosion followed only seconds later.

Clovis stared in disbelief. Biting his lip and brushing his hand across his brow, he removed his hat and stood silently. Finally, he spoke, "I've known Holder for a long time. We met at college in Great Falls years and years ago."

A loud voice on a megaphone captured our attention. "Belden, you had better come out. We have something you might want. Tyler, the same goes for you."

Neither Belden nor I could see anyone. We just held still. "Belden, I'm warning you. Either show yourself, or we'll kill your wife and daughter."

Both of us swallowed hard. "I think they're over there in that patch of timber, about 200 yards from here," Clovis stated, pointing his finger.

"What are we going to do?" I asked.

"I'm thinking. They believe that we are here, but they don't know it for sure. They won't kill my girls until they're sure we're here, because that's the only leverage they have against us, but they also won't let any of us live if they catch us, so a trade-off won't work either. I have got to see if I can locate them and see how many there are. Stay here. I'll be back in one hour. If I'm not, you high-tail it back to that rope I showed you last night and stay put."

"And do what?" I asked.

"Son, listen to me. If I'm not back in an hour, then that means I've been caught. If I'm caught, they'll kill all three of us. If I get the chance, I'll tell them that you never showed up, that I haven't seen you. There's no way that they can know. Wait a few days, travel by night like I showed you, and tell my story. At least I'll die knowing my name was cleared."

Clovis checked his gun to make sure that it was loaded and that the action was free of any dirt or debris. Disappearing in his ghost-like fashion to which I had already grown accustomed, he was gone. I checked my watch. It was 6:45 a.m. Again, a voice rang out over the megaphone. "Tyler, Belden. You had better come out." Obviously, the team from AFFA had figured out Wren's true identity. I didn't like it in the least and I sure didn't like sitting there on my butt, chewing my fingernails and waiting for Clovis to return. The minutes slowly passed. The eastern sun slowly melted away the light morning fog that had settled on the Wall. Seven forty-five rolled by and I decided to give Clovis another ten minutes, but he didn't show. I turned north, back toward the timber where Clovis had showed me the rope.

I hadn't gone 10 steps when I heard a "Pssst. Over here." Holding the Winchester at hip level and looking, I couldn't see anyone at first. "It's me. Don't shoot." Hidden behind some dead-fall, my youngest brother slowly stood up.

"Joe Tyler, what are you doing here? How did you get here?"

Joe came over and threw his arms around me, squeezing me like the long-lost brother that I had become. "Ross, it's great to see you. You look like crap. Looks like you stuck your face in a meat grinder."

"Thanks, Joe, now how did you get here and how did you find out," I asked again.

"Wren called. Told us you were in trouble. She said she had a recent satellite photo that showed you were on the wall, so we came a-running."

"Who's we?"

"All three of us, Ross. Haven't we Tyler brothers always stood together when times got tough?"

"You mean Mark and Will are here, too?" I asked.

"Yeah, they're here. Now listen up. We're wasting time. I ran into Clovis a few minutes ago. He about slit my throat before I was able to tell him who I was. Crap, I don't know where he came from. I heard the gunfire and came running as fast as I could, and the next thing I know, I'm lying on the ground with a blade to my throat. Evidently, he believed me when I told him I was your brother. He said that I resembled you too much to be lying. Anyway, I explained to Clovis what I'm fixing to tell you."

"I'm listening, go ahead."

"There are nine of them, Ross. They have got a little camp set up down in a draw. My guess is they've been waiting for that chopper to come in and have spent the last couple of days there. Mark and Will are posted on a little knoll on the south side and have them in their sights, but it's too touchy to make a move just yet. Judy and Wren are tied up to a lodge-pole pine on the west side of their camp. One guy, I noticed, has been messing with Wren a little, but I don't think he's done anything but aggravate her. The other guys won't let him do anything else. I inched in close last night under the cover of darkness and tried to listen to their conversation. They're getting a little impatient. I don't think they like the idea of being up here. One guy, I think they call him Kirby, swears to God that he's going to find Clovis and skin him alive. Do you know him?"

"Yeah, I know him, but Clovis and Kirby have a history that goes all the way back to Vietnam. He's bad news, Joe."

"Clovis told me that they really don't know if you're here or not, so that could provide an advantage to us. Now, I know where they are, and I told Clovis where to find them. He wants us to stay put for about an hour more and if we don't see or hear from him then we are to move and get into position to shoot, but we are not to fire until necessary, and he said, when we do, 'make it count'. I've already got the perfect place. When we get there, I'll radio Mark and Will and let them know we are in position. Oh, and Dad said he would be here by this evening."

"Dad!" I exclaimed. "What's Dad doing up here?"

"Right now, Ross, he's taking care of some business. That's all he told me, so I don't really know what that means. I always knew something was up with that old man that we never knew about. Shoot, I didn't even know that he could fly a helicopter. He borrowed old man Denny's bird. You know the auctioneer who flew all over the country to the cattle auctions."

"How's Dad doing?" I asked

"He's doing great. I haven't seen him in such high spirits in who knows how long. It's like all of a sudden he has a purpose in life, or at least it seems he's found a new one."

Trying to absorb the complexity of our present situation and all of the external factors that came into play, I found it difficult to stay focused on the task at hand. My main concern at the moment was for Judy and Wren, because their situation presented the highest degree of peril or danger. However, as much as I was happy to know that my brothers and father had come to help, it also meant that the likelihood of tragedy was greatly multiplied. The idea of one of them getting hurt or killed on my behalf was almost more than I could bring myself to think about. Even though we lived miles apart from one another, and did not get to see each other that often, we had always been a close family. I feared for their safety. Joe must have recognized that my thoughts were wandering.

"What's eating you, Brother?" he asked.

Sighing deeply, I replied, "Oh, I just hate to think of one of ya'll getting hurt because of me and the mess I've gotten myself into."

"Shoot, Ross, wouldn't you do the same for one of us?"

"Of course I would. You know that. I'd give my life for any one of you boys."

"Well, we feel the same way about you, Ross," Joe reasoned. "All of us recognize the fact that we might not live to tell about this day, but that's the risk we're willing and ready to face. I mean, look at me Ross. I'm here in Montana, standing on top of the Continental Divide. Right now, I feel more alive than I have in years. Smell the air, Brother. Do you have any idea how long it's been since my lungs have been inflated with thin, clean mountain air? Yes, sir, it's good to be home. If I die today, I will have died a happy man. If I live through today, I'm headed back to Texas and selling just about everything I own as quickly as I can and coming home to Montana to stay. My Lord, Ross, how in the world did we allow ourselves to succumb to the temptation of a better life, and leave Montana?"

"I don't know, Joe," I answered, and squeezed his shoulder. "I guess we just didn't really know how good we had it when it really was good. I do now, and you can rest assured, I'm here to stay."

Looking at his watch, Joe said, "I don't think Belden is coming back. Let's go. Follow me."

Running quickly and quietly, I followed behind Joe through the timber since he knew where the AFFA men were camped. The day was warming up, and it did not take either of us long to develop a good sweat. Finally, stopping to catch our breath, Joe pointed to the top of a rock outcropping and said, "Let's get to that little point. We'll be able to see everything from there and no one will be able to see us."

Crouching down and staying low we hurried toward the top, belly-crawling the last few yards. As we neared the crest of the point, we peeked over the rocks. Fumbling in my pack for my binoculars, I focused on the camp in the draw about 500 yards below. It was a grassy, well-shaded place. Immediately I identified Tank and Hog who were sitting in the grass talking to one another. The other men I had never seen before, and I could not locate Kirby, which made me inwardly nervous. From what Belden had told me, Kirby was every bit the woodsman and marksman that Belden was, but ruthless. Joe spotted Wren and Judy first through his binoculars as we both peered over the rocks into the camp below.

"They've moved 'em," Joe stated.

"Where are they?" I asked without taking my eyes from my binoculars.

"Look to the west of camp. Do you see that little grove of quakies?"

"Yeah, I see it."

"OK. Look south from there in the shade of that lodge pole pine."

"Got em".

Lying there, we watched the men in the camp. Nothing of any importance seemed to be taking place. They appeared as if they were just sitting around waiting for something to happen. Joe and I decided we would just wait there along with them and see what developed. For the moment we felt that we were in as good a place as any. We had absolutely no idea what Clovis was up to.

Through the binoculars it appeared that Judy and Wren were sitting back-to-back against the lodge pole pine tree, arms tied behind them, but in no apparent immediate danger. Although we obviously could not hear what they were saying, we could see that they were talking to one another.

"Joe, where's Mark and Will from here?" I asked.

Joe pointed south. "You see that rise over there about half a mile. They are somewhere over there."

Joe looked at me straight in the eye and asked, "So, did he do it?"

"I assume you're asking about Belden and if he killed Peterson?" I asked in return, and then answered, "Well, yes, that's pretty obvious, but you won't believe the reason why."

"Tell me."

I told the story as Belden related it to me, and then I told Joe how Agents Cordell, Adams, and Slyvenski caught me and how Clovis had saved my life.

"You say you've got a cassette tape of Cordell's conversation with you that will explain why Peterson was going to kill Watson? Have you got more than one copy?"

"Yes, I do...here." Digging around in my pack, I pulled out an extra copy and gave one to Joe. "Take this and hide it on you somewhere. You have a copy, I have two more copies and the original, and Clovis has a couple of copies. Somebody ought to be able to get out of here and put one of these in the hands of someone who can help."

Joe just couldn't seem to get over the idea that Peterson would sell out Watson for 25 million and the Presidency. "You know, Ross, there are just some things that money can't buy. No amount of it. Friendship ought to be one of them."

"I hear you, Brother," I replied. "You can't put a price on the bond of love between two friends."

Before returning my eyes to my binoculars, I looked at Joe first, "I love ya, Brother. Thanks for coming."

"I love y..."

I never heard the shot. Little Joe just lurched forward toward me a bit with a soft guttural grunt. Blood stained the front of his shirt, the red mass growing larger by the second.

"Joe!" I screamed, reaching for him, pulling him down into the scrub brush below us to better conceal ourselves from the shooter, wherever he was. Ripping open his shirt to see the extent of the wound, his left hand gripping the sleeve of my right arm, I knew by the sight of the damage made by the bullet, that it was hopeless. I pulled him to me, cradling his head in the crook of my arm.

"Joe," I pleaded. "Hold on, Brother. Oh, God... Don't go, Joe. Please, please don't go."

Joe's eyes glazed as they stared into mine, his grip tightening on my arm. Mustering the strength to speak, he lightly coughed, a trickle of blood flowing from the corner of his mouth.

"Ross...oh, God, Ross, I never thought it would end like this."

"I'm sorry, Joe."

"Oh, Ross, life is good. Things just should have been different...Tell Jill and the boys I love 'em...Tell Dad and Mom I...

One last and final breath and Joe lay lifeless in my arms. My little brother, who only moments earlier had told me that he was willing to lay down his life for me if necessary, had just proved to be a man of his word. My heart was broken. It still is broken.

Reaching for Joe's two-way radio, I stayed low, still not knowing where the shot had come from, but I felt confident that I was well hidden from all directions. Tears blurred my vision and several times I tried to make a call to Mark and Will but couldn't find the inner strength to do so. How was I going to tell them that our little brother was dead? I kept hoping that this was just a bad dream and that soon I would wake up, but I knew it wasn't. The reality of the danger of my present situation was confirmed when I raised my head slowly above the brush and a bullet grazed the side of my left temple. Dropping down into the brush again, I now had a basic idea of the direction from where the shot had come. Lying beside Joe's body, already beginning to cool, I whispered into the radio.

"Mark, Will, can you hear me?"

"Hey, Brother, it's good to hear your voice. What's up?" Mark asked.

"Bad news, Boys...real bad." I couldn't bring myself to finish.

"What's the matter, Ross?"

I paused, and finally stated, "Joe's dead."

The silence was deafening. Although I could not visually see my brothers, I knew them well enough that I could mentally picture what they were doing now. No doubt, they were experiencing perhaps the greatest grief that they had ever known.

After waiting for several minutes, Will spoke up on the radio in a voice that had grown hoarse from crying, "Ross, what happened?"

"Somebody shot him and just took a shot at me." I replied. "Right now, I'm in a tight spot, but I feel pretty well hidden from view."

"Ross," Mark added, "how are we going to tell Dad about Joe?"

"You don't have to." Dad's voice came in loud and clear on the radio. "I've heard you boys' entire conversation." Dad paused and we waited for him to speak again.

"Now listen to me, boys. I loved Joe and it's going to break your mama's heart when she learns the news, but there ain't nothin' we can do about that now, except keepin' ourselves from gettin' shot, too. Ross?"

"Yes, Pa," I answered.

"I'm on the west side of the Divide, about 500 yards from their camp below. I ran into Clovis about half an hour ago. He told me that a man named Kirby is with this bunch of scum. Do you know him?"

"Yes, sir, I do"

"Well, chances are, he's the one who shot Joe and took a shot at you. I'm surprised he missed."

"Well, Pa, he didn't really. The bullet grazed the side of my temple, just above my ear, but hasn't even drawn blood... Say, you sound like you know him?"

"Oh, yeah, I know him. I met him in Vietnam years ago. I never did like him very much. He's the worst kind of scum, and he is a very dangerous man. Just imagine a man with all the ability of Clovis, but with an evil heart, and that's the kind of man Kirby is. I mean the worst kind of evil. Ross, listen, son, you have got to stay put. Kirby has the patience of Job, and he'll wait until you come out in the open. Nightfall is still a long time comin' and even if you wait until then, he's likely to have a night vision scope. Promise me you'll stay put until one of us radio's you and lets you know it's clear."

"Yes, sir. Have you got a plan?" I asked.

"You bet. Clovis and I discussed it. He's going to try to eliminate Kirby from the scene first, so we're to stay put until I hear from him. I gave him the radio that I brought for you, Ross. Mark and Will, are you still listening?"

"Yes, sir," they both replied.

"Okay, Boys, if I don't hear from him by 3:00, which is just a little less than three hours from now, we'll decide what we need to do next. Let's stay in contact on the half hour. Ross, keep your head down and stay low."

"Yes, sir. Hey, Dad…What should I do with Joe?"

A long moment of silence followed. I waited. Mark and Will waited. Finally, I started to ask again, "Dad…?"

"I hear you son…" obviously spoken through a voice that couldn't hide the sorrow and grief he was experiencing. "…We'll have to leave him there for now. You boys be careful and keep your eyes open down there in their camp. I realize that none of you have ever killed a man before, but this is one time that you can't hesitate for even a second or you'll end up dead, too."

Mark spoke up, "Don't you worry about it, Dad. We'll kill 'em all."

CHAPTER TWENTY-ONE

Low in the scrub-brush I lay still. I buried Joe with leaves and twigs and tried to hide his body knowing that if the shooter advanced toward my position and was able to see Joe, he would identify my relative location as well. The touch of Joe's cold, lifeless body tore at my heart and soul. I could not restrain the tears that kept clouding my vision. How does a person live with the idea that someone he loved would love him enough to give his life for him? The more I dwelt on the question, the more my sorrow turned to anger. I was mad, fighting mad. I recalled a verse in the bible that said, "Vengeance is mine, saith the Lord." Well, today, I was sure hoping that the Lord didn't mind allowing me to be his instrument of death, judgment, and damnation.

I decided to take Joe's .308 rifle that he had brought along and to leave the .30-30 that Clovis had let me borrow. I then proceeded to burrow my way back deeper into the brush. The idea of being trapped and unable to move did not sit well with me, but I didn't like the idea of being dead either. At 12:30 p.m., Dad checked in on the radio. From his position and Mark and Will's position, they told me that everything in the enemy camp seemed pretty quiet. Wren and Judy were still tied to the lodge-pole pine tree and occasionally they were brought a little food and water. Of course, I was not able to look into the camp from my position, being pinned down as I was just below the crest of the hill that overlooked their camp.

None of us could figure out what these men were waiting for. Finally, somehow, some way, Dad came up with an assumption that Kirby had persuaded the rest of the AFFA men to allow him the first crack at killing Clovis, one on one, the best against the best, just like the good ol' days. It sounded logical and the more that I thought about it, the more I convinced myself that Clovis had probably expected this very thing to happen.

Through the under brush, I kept my eyes open, wondering where the shooter might be. With my binoculars I meticulously scanned the area from which I believed the two bullets had been fired. Nothing. For two hours I continued to watch and to wait, speaking with my father and brothers every 30 minutes. Nothing of the situation had changed for them nor had it changed for me. We continued to wait. My patience was wearing thin, and I was chompin' at the bit to get out of there. Clovis finally made contact with us on the radio to assess the situation. We told him about Joe.

At first, Clovis did not say anything. I'm sure that it ripped at his heart to think that a life had been lost while trying to save his. Finally he spoke to all of us, "Guys, I am so sorry. I don't know what to say. I feel like Joe's death is completely my fault. If it weren't for me, he wouldn't have even been up here."

"Clovis," Dad responded, "You're a man of principle. I'm a man of principle. I've raised my boys to be men of principle. We do what's right because it's the right thing to do—even if it costs us our lives."

A deep feeling of inner pride for my father swelled up in my chest. Men like him and Clovis were hard to find in our day and age. The mold from which they were cast had been broken and never had the reality of that truth been made as vividly clear as it did on that day. Joe had come all the way from Texas to help me, his older brother, because it was the right thing to do. He died for that decision. Mark and Will came all the way from Tennessee to help me, their older brother, because they felt it was the right thing to do. Dad was here, because I was his son, and that's what dads do. They stand, they fight, and they defend and perhaps even die for what they believe is right. I said a silent prayer that no more bloodshed would come, at least neither to my family nor of Clovis, Judy or Wren. As far as those who had, because of their greed, set themselves against us, I hoped a lot of blood would be shed, and I intended to do a lot of spilling of it myself.

Raising my eyes to my binoculars again, scanning the surrounding area for the umpteenth time, I noticed a small bachelor group of muley bucks grazing together in a distant meadow approximately 500-600 yards away. They all still wore velvet and one old buck in particular grabbed my attention. His heavy rack protruded with sticker points in all directions. His body was massive and his Roman nose wore the scars of many battles. He was the kind of buck a man dreams about, and even in the midst of the present danger I was in, I still thought that it was interesting that I could appreciate such a fine animal.

Watching this small group of bucks through my glasses, I noticed that all of a sudden, their heads jerked to attention. Their eyes focused in the same direction, and their ears pointed forward alarmed by something that I was unable to identify. Bringing the radio to my lips, I whispered, "Clovis, can you read me?"

"Yes, Tyler, what is it?"

"Look northwest, about 11:00 o'clock from my position at the meadow just above that large dead pine."

"All right."

"Do you see those bucks fixing to bolt?" I asked.

"Yea, I see 'em," Clovis confirmed.

"My guess is Kirby's what they're looking at down there in that brush."

"Yea, I'd say you were right. Listen, Tyler, Kirby has you pinned down pretty tight from what it appears to me. The patch of brush you're hiding in can't be any more than 50 yards wide and 60 maybe 70 yards long. The nearest cover from there is a good 125 yards. If somehow I can distract Kirby for a little bit you might be able to make a run for it. We have got to get Judy and Wren out of their camp, and it's going to take all of us to do it. I just disposed of one piece of trash who was standing guard on the south side of their camp. I'm slipping up on another right now. The dumb fool is sleeping."

Although I was unable to see what Clovis was doing, I knew that he was just across the meadow below my position and somewhere on the side of the adjacent ridge. Kirby had to be somewhere between us.

The bucks had bolted off, running in their pogo-stick gait. Something, no doubt had spooked them. I was convinced it was Kirby.

CHAPTER TWENTY-TWO

Many of the details of the events that followed were shared with me post-facto. Though the details are vividly clear, I still battle with believing they unfolded the way they did.

Crouched down in the brush under sniper fire, it was impossible for me to know every thing that was going on around me. I continued to stay in touch with Dad and my brothers as they informed me of the present situation in the camp of the AFFA men. According to them, Judy and Wren had been untied from the tree and allowed to stretch and take care of nature's business. Most of the men were napping or playing cards. Mark and Will, whose position was a little closer to the AFFA camp than Dad's position, assessed that the AFFA men were heavily armed, but seemed to display the appearance of boredom and impatience. We still wondered what they were waiting on. We felt pretty confident that they were waiting on Kirby to kill Clovis, but we could not know that for certain. I suddenly realized that if Kirby were successful, Wren and Judy would no longer be needed. They were only being held hostage as a bargaining chip against Clovis if the need were to arise. The thought of them being killed, only kindled the anger that was running its course through my veins. Feeling helpless and unable to do anything at the moment didn't help a whole lot either.

It was 4:30 p.m., and I had not heard from Clovis for half an hour. Again, I waited. My patience was running thin, and my eyes were growing weary of staring through my binoculars trying to locate movement or identify anything that might reveal the presence of my brother's murderer. It was difficult for me to believe that anyone could conceal himself so effectively in cover that appeared so thin. The crest of the Chinese Wall does not have a lot of vegetation for the most part. It is extremely rugged, made up of granite and limestone rock, piercing its naked back into the empty sky, and yet, trying my hardest, I could not locate the presence of anyone.

The brush where I lay waiting was only about two to three feet high. I really did not have the luxury of sitting up, afraid that I might expose a part of myself, and risk getting shot. Finally, Clovis came in over the radio.

"Okay, Boys, listen to me now. What you are about to see from your position will not be what it appears so do not fire. Tyler, you keep your eyes focused on the area where those muley bucks were looking and be ready to shoot."

All of us got the message and confirmed it on our radios. I swabbed the lens of my binoculars and scope and checked the chamber to make sure I was locked and loaded, and then began glassing again. What happened next, I would have never believed if I had not seen it with my own eyes, and even then, at the time, I wasn't sure exactly what was taking place.

An unfamiliar voice yelled out from the west. My eyes quickly searched the direction that my ears had heard. Standing dangerously close to the edge of the cliff on the west side of the Chinese Wall, nearly 800 yards out or so, a little down-hill from my location, and less than 500 yards from the AFFA camp, Clovis stood at gun point about 10 steps in front of a man that I could not recognize at that distance. A lump developed in my throat when the unidentified man began to yell.

"Hey, everyone, I've got Belden!" he shouted, hoping, I suppose, that his voice would be heard back in the camp.

At that distance, I knew that I could not make the shot and it was too risky to try. Certainly, even if I could hit the man, I would have to kill him instantly. Even wounded, he would still be likely to hit Clovis who was only a step away from falling more than a thousand feet to his death. Still, in the back of my mind, I remembered that Clovis had warned us not to shoot, and that things would not appear, as they seemed. What did that mean? Did it still apply? Had he been captured since our last conversation? Glanc-

ing quickly to my left at the location where I believed Kirby was
still hiding, I noticed movement. I raised Joe's rifle to my cheek
and looked through the scope, but I was too late. Kirby had shifted
his position and took the shot at Clovis, rolling him over off the
cliff into oblivion. My heart sank in despair. All of my hopes and
aspirations of seeing Clovis pardoned from the crime that hung
upon his name had just been put to an end. Anger boiled in me like
a Yellowstone geyser. I could not clearly see Kirby in his hiding,
but I knew his general location. I fired three quick rounds into the
area hoping to flush him out into the open, but obviously not hitting anywhere close. He stood up in defiance and threw a shot in
my direction, the bullet hitting dangerously close in the brush to
my right. I was out-gunned, and he knew it. He stood there with
his rifle slung over his shoulder and both hands on his hips, mocking me. I felt certain he wanted me to take another shot so that he
could better pinpoint my location. I withheld. Finally, he shot me
the bird and began walking toward the cliff where he had just killed
Clovis. The unidentified man had disappeared. I just stared in disbelief as Kirby walked away.

Will's voice came over the radio, "Ross, are you all right?" he
asked.

"Yeah, I'm all right, but Kirby just killed Clovis." I replied,
having a hard time spitting the words out of my mouth. "Dad, are
you listening?"

"Yeah, son, I'm listening. I saw the whole thing too. Kirby
didn't even give him a chance. I think he wanted to make sure that
he was the one to kill Clovis and was not about to let anyone else
share in that pleasure. Dang, Clovis was a good man."

"What are we going to do?" Will asked.

Dad replied again. "We're going to wait for a few minutes.
Ross, I know that you cannot see down into the camp right now, but
Mark and Will and I can. Those shots you fired have got the men
in camp stirred up, and I can tell that they're not sure what is going
on up here. I do believe the element of surprise may well be to our
greatest advantage. I do not believe that they know that we are
here. Just remember that Kirby is still out there, Ross."

"I can see Kirby down on the cliff looking over the edge
where he shot Belden. You're out of range, so if you're going to get

out of there, you better do it now. I suggest you run back north into the timber and then swing to the west and drop back south toward his location. I'm guessing he's going to be headed back to this camp in a little bit. He knows you're still alive, but he doesn't know that Mark, Will or I are here. Let's wait until nightfall and see if we can stir things up a little then. I really doubt that they'll hurt Wren or Judy until they get their hands on you."

"Okay, Pop. I'm out of here. Let's keep in touch... Hey, Pa..."

"Yeah, son, what is it?"

"I'm sorry about Joe. It's my fault that he's gone." My voice cracked and tears flooded my eyes.

"No, son, it's not your fault. Joe came here because he loved you, Ross, and love... well, Son, sometimes love costs us dearly. We'll all miss Joe, your mama especially, but let's make sure that the rest of us get back home alive and in one piece."

I could tell by the sound of his voice that Dad was struggling to be strong because he knew that the situation demanded it, and he didn't want to lose any more of his sons. However, even if he was right, I still felt responsible for Little Joe's death.

Turning off the radio for the time being and stuffing it into my pack, I wiped the tears from my eyes while slowly stretching my legs. I took one last look at the mound of leaves and twigs that covered Joe, and I made a promise to his lifeless body that I would kill the man that killed him and Clovis.

Breaking out from the brush, I ran to the timber as fast as I could go. Although there is very little timber on the Chinese Wall, here was certainly enough to hide and conceal my movements. Judging by the position sun, I had just a little more than an hour and a half of daylight left until darkness fell over the Divide. Once in the shadows of the timber, I turned west toward the edge of the Wall, then immediately started making my way south toward the last spot that I had seen Kirby. As I neared the edge of the timber, I looked out across the open, boulder-strewn area before me. He was near. I could sense it. The hair stood up on the back of my neck. That sixth sense that tells you that danger is lurking ever so close was as strong, perhaps stronger, than I had ever felt it before. Not since the time when Vance and I had spent all night worried about that grizzly, actually just a few short miles from here, had I felt the feeling like I was feeling it now. I meticulously scrutinized the area with my eyes, examining each and every possible hiding place, searching for any clue that might reveal his location, when a voice from behind startled me.

"You got a light?" Kirby asked. I knew it was Kirby by the sound of his voice. He had asked me that same question many times back in Chicago in the bar where I first met him and visited with him on occasion.

"Hey, Kirby," I said, "How's it going?"

"Drop the gun, Tyler, and turn around... slowly." I squatted and laid the rifle on the ground. It had been Joe's favorite rifle, so I did not want to harm it or scuff it up.

"Now stand and slowly turn around with your hands behind your head."

I did as I was told. "Take off your pack and drop it to the ground beside your rifle and move over there," he said, pointing with the business end of his sniper rifle. Again, I did exactly as I was told.

Our eyes met and we held each other's stare for a long, drawn-out minute. I am sure that the hatred and pure disdain I felt for the man was obviously noticeable in my face and eyes as the wrath in my blood boiled through veins. Kirby, who smiled sadistically at me, knowing that he held all of the aces, chuckled out loud and then sarcastically declared, "Tyler, you are a fool. You got lucky back there in Chicago when you escaped. I still have a hard time believing you did it. But your luck is fixing to run out, just like it did for Clovis, and just like it is going to run out for that witch and her mama, after I'm finished with you."

"What ya' got in mind, Kirby?" I asked.

"Oh, I've been thinking about it a little bit. Part of me says I just need to shoot you and get it over with like I did Clovis, but you know, that just seemed so easy and impersonal. I really wanted to take his scalp as a souvenir, but I'm not going to hike all those miles just to get to the bottom of that cliff where his body lies, so I'm thinking about lifting yours instead, except I think I want to do it while you're still alive so you can feel the pain."

"Just how do you propose to do that?" I asked tauntingly. "You're kinda getting up there in years." I was trying to be calm and show no fear, knowing that if he were half the man that Clovis was, he would be a very dangerous adversary. However, taunting him and picking a fight, hoping that he would accept the challenge, provided more hope for survival than facing the end of the barrel on that rifle he kept pointed at me.

Kirby just laughed aloud. "Are you suggesting that I might have trouble whipping the likes of you?" He asked, laughing even louder. "Why, son, even on my worst day, I could whoop you without breaking a sweat."

I could tell that I had touched the right nerve. He was thirsty for blood, and he wanted to see my life trickle slowly away before his eyes.

"Well then, let's see what you're made of, Old Man. Put that pee-shooter over there with my brother's gun and let's get it over with." I was having a hard time believing the words that were coming out of my mouth; however, I realized that this was my only chance. The thought that Judy and Wren depended upon me stirred an emotion inside of me that I can only describe as "deadly". I knew what I had to do. Then the memory of Little Joe's face, as I held his dying body in my arms, elevated my adrenaline to a level I hope I will never experience again.

Kirby moved slowly to my pack and gun and laid his down.

"This is going to be fun," he sneered.

Methodically approaching me, he reached behind him and pulled a large knife from a sheath that he obviously kept hidden but easily accessible. Flipping the knife in his hands, he caught it by the blade and extended it to me, handle first.

"Take this blade boy. You might have a chance."

We glared at each other. I knew that as soon as I reached for it, the fight was on. Still staring into his eyes, trying to determine his next move, I didn't budge. He was about my size, maybe a few inches shorter, and though he was about 25 years my senior, he was obviously in very good physical condition. He was broad at the shoulders and narrow at the waist. I was hoping as I continued to glare at him that he would grow nervous or anxious, just enough to give me a little bit of an edge, but he acted as if he were bored.

Slowly, I extended my hand with the palm up, suggesting that he place the knife in my hand, and then I reached for it quickly.

Quicker than lightening, just as I had taken a hold of the handle, he had thrown me with a judo throw over his back and shoulder. It was a throw my father had practiced with me for years. Breaking the fall and coming quickly to my feet, crouched low with the knife still in my hand Kirby looked at me and smiled.

"You're pretty fast there, boy...but you won't be fast enough."

Kirby waded in, carefully watching, light and quick on his feet. He was sure and confident. Feinting with a left punch, he kicked me with his right foot along the left side of my ribs, taking away most of my breath. I sliced with the knife at his mid-section, missing, but catching the top of his right thigh on the return swing, laying it open and deep.

His anger kindled, he attacked me with full force. Kicking and punching and knocking me to the ground, he took the knife from my right hand and then moved in to finish me off. Upon hitting the ground, a sharp pain shot through my lower back, instantly reminding me that I had stuffed my .45 behind my belt and had forgotten all about it. As he reached for my shirt with his left, the blade in his right, ready to finish the job, he sneered with a chuckle.

"Well, Tyler, you can't say that I didn't give you a chance. Now, I'm going to show you what real pain is all about."

Straddling me, he squatted down on one knee and grabbed a handful of my hair as he raised the knife to my scalp. Before his blade could break the skin of my forehead, I pulled the pistol and fired twice into his midsection. For a moment, he knelt above me and stared into my eyes. I pushed his crumbling body backward, off of me.

"I don't believe it, Tyler... You've killed me," as he stared at the bloodstains on his shirt rapidly increasing in size.

I snatched the knife from his hand, stuffing my gun back into my belt. "That's right, Kirby. You're a dead man. But before you go, this is for my little brother Joe and for Clovis." I jumped on top of him with my right knee in his sternum. Grabbing him by his long gray hair that he always wore in a ponytail, I pulled it straight up and sank the blade into the scalp all the way to the bone of his forehead, making a quick circular cut around the top of his skull. Kirby screamed at the top of his lungs as blood gushed down his face and the side of his ears.

"Your killing days are over, Kirby. I'll leave your body for the bears and the wolves and I'm sure that the devil will have a nice warm place for your soul." Grabbing his ponytail and wrapping it around my fist, I pushed him to the ground, stepped on his face and yanked off his scalp, which popped loudly much like a wet plunger being pulled from a bathroom floor.

Still alive, he looked up, a bloody mess of exposed veins and skull, and he pleaded, "Finish me, Tyler."

With no more remorse than killing a snake, I shot him again. Although I do not consider myself a violent man, looking back, even to this day, I have no regrets.

Picking up my pack, I stuffed Kirby's bloody scalp inside and then grabbed Joe's rifle. Looking at it closely I decided to leave it there and retrieve it later, opting to take Kirby's sniper rifle, equipped with a suppressor. I knew it could come in handy. The magazine was full as was the chamber. I shouldered it a couple of times and quickly familiarized myself with the placement of the safety and the eye relief to the scope. With only about half an hour toward dark, I started toward the AFFA camp.

Reaching the spot where I had watched Clovis fall from the cliff, I peered over the edge, and could barely make out his lifeless form lying among the rocky rubble below. Pulling the radio from my pack and turning on the power, I called dad and my brothers.

"Where have you been, Ross?" Dad asked in a whisper, the sound of relief ringing in his voice.

"Kirby's dead, Dad. We don't have to worry about him any longer. I'll tell you more about it later. Why are you whispering?" I asked.

"Ross, Mark, Will and I are only about 60 yards out from their camp. We're hidden behind some boulders on the south side. These boys in camp are getting nervous. I don't think they are going to wait much longer. They've heard the shooting, but they are uncertain of the results. It's pretty obvious that they are waiting on Kirby to return before they have their way with the girls."

"Have you got any suggestions?" I asked.

"We're trying to wait until dark. There are only six of them left. There are four of us. With the element of surprise to our advantage, I'm sure that we can take them, but I don't know if we can do it without harm coming to the girls. It's pretty risky."

Nearing the upper rim of the camp, peering down at the men below, I could see that Judy and Wren were sitting on a log near the fire with their arms tied behind their backs. The men appeared to be arguing about something.

"Okay, Dad. I'm directly across from you about 120 yards from the camp below. The sun will be down in about 5 minutes. When it sinks below the horizon, I'm going to try to move in a little closer."

"Be careful, Ross. We've got you covered."

Glowing orange like a lake of fire, the sun quickly began to sink into the western horizon. The thought of judgment day came to mind as I moved quickly to within 30 yards of their camp. One of the men grabbed Wren and yanked her up, screaming at her and slapping her across the face, pulling a pistol and placing the muzzle to her forehead. Tears were streaming down her face, and Judy was pleading to take her life instead. With the few trees scattered around the camp, most of which were between them and me, I could not find an unobstructed path to get a clean shot. Uncertain what to do at the moment, I yelled.

"Hey, I'm the one you really want."

Guns were quickly pulled by the remaining men and pointed in the direction of my voice.

"Tyler, is that you?"

"Yeah, it's me, Tank."

"Come down here or we'll waste these two ladies right here and now."

"Is that you, Hogg?" I asked, knowing full well that it was.

"That's right, Tyler, you little prick."

"Well, here's the deal, boys: I know that you plan on killing all of us anyway. After all, you can't have anyone left living that might spill the truth. If I come down, then all you have to do is kill all of us."

"Yea, but if you don't come out, we're going to skin these two ladies alive, Tyler, that is, after we've had a little fun with them," Tank replied.

"You won't, Tank. My cross hairs are right between your eyes even as we speak right now. Besides, if you kill them, you still haven't caught me, and I've got enough proof to make sure that everyone of you gets the electric chair."

Tank, Hogg and the rest of the men were nervous. They didn't like the idea that they were sitting ducks.

The man holding the gun to Wren's head spoke up. "I'll kill her, Tyler. I mean it," he said, while pulling the hammer back on his pistol.

"Let's make a deal," I shouted.

"I'm listening," Tank replied.

"You let the women go in exchange for me. I'm the one who's got the hard evidence against you boys. All they have is hearsay. Besides, if you let them go, certainly you guys can find them again."

"What about Clovis?" Hogg asked. "He's still out there somewhere."

"Clovis is dead. Kirby killed him," I blurted out like a fool, not thinking about the impact such news would have on Judy and Wren, who immediately began sobbing.

Hogg immediately stepped over and slapped Judy and told her to shut up.

"Touch her again, Hogg, and I'll drop you where you stand."

Tank was contemplating the situation. He knew he was a dead man if he wasn't careful.

"Let 'em go, Tank," I yelled.

"I'll tell you what, Tyler. I'm in a tough spot. How do I know that you won't run off if I let them go?"

"You're right about one thing, Tank. You *are* in a tough spot, because if you don't let them go I'm going to make sure that I kill you first. Let them go, and you can have me."

The AFFA men kept trying to locate my presence in the dark, while the campfire made it easy for me to see them.

"Looks like a standoff, Tyler. No deal tonight."

A wolf howled just outside of camp. It was a long and mournful cry, followed by yips and cackles, the sounds made by a coyote. My mind told me that something wasn't right about what my ears were hearing, but it didn't register. I could see the faces of Wren and Judy, who looked at one another and casually smiled. What was that all about? I asked myself.

Suddenly, it hit me. Clovis was out there in the darkness and very near. They knew that sound. But, how could Clovis be alive?

I saw Kirby shoot him. I saw him fall from the cliff. I looked off the edge and saw his lifeless body more than a thousand feet below. The sound came again. Undeniably, it had to be him. A wolf makes the sound of a wolf. A coyote makes the sound of a coyote. They cannot imitate one another, I reasoned. These AFFA men were city slickers; they wouldn't know the difference, even though the lonesome cry was causing nervousness among them. What was Clovis trying to say? Was he just letting us know that he was near?

I thought about it really hard. "Okay, Tank. Let's make a swap. Let one of the girls go. You choose which one. Then, I'll come in and you can let the other go."

The men discussed it for a few seconds and Tank replied. "Sounds fair enough, Tyler. We're cutting the old lady loose. Then you come in, and we'll let Wren go."

The men cut the ropes on Judy.

"Give her a flashlight, Tank," I hollered. "I don't want her stumbling around out there in the dark." One of the men gave Judy a light. "Judy," I yelled, "do you know where Marias Pass is?"

"Yes, Ross. I know the way."

"Good. Head in that direction and don't stop running. Be careful." I knew that Mark and Will and Dad would intercept her and keep her safe.

"Tank, give her a few minutes, and then I'll come in."

I knew that my brothers and my dad were close, waiting with their guns ready to drop the hammer when and if the time came, and I hoped the sound of the wolf was really Clovis somewhere in the darkness nearby. My greatest fear was that if the shooting started, Wren might get caught in the crossfire. On the other hand, if Tank let her go…oh, what was I thinking? He wasn't about to do that.

After a couple of minutes, Tank grew impatient. "Come on in, Tyler. The old hag is gone."

From the darkness, I stepped into the glow of the campfire holding the rifle in front of me in a non-threatening manner, every man's gun bearing down on me as they circled around me.

"Let her go, Tank," I demanded.

Tank laughed hysterically. "Not in this life, which, for the two of you, is going to be really short. As soon as Kirby gets back, he's going to make both of you regret the day you were ever born."

"Kirby's dead, Tank!" I said matter-of-factly.

"Yea, right." Tank responded. "If he's dead, then just how did he die?"

"I killed him."

"You!!! Ha!!! You ain't nothin' but a little twerp. You're just a two-bit reporter who couldn't whip his way out of a wet paper bag. I cannot begin to tell you how many times I just wanted to take you outside of that bar back in Chicago and teach you a good lesson or two."

"So, you don't believe me, eh? Let me show you something." I started to shed my pack from my back, making all the men nervous. I could hear the loud audible clicks of hammers on their pistols being pulled back.

"Easy now, I'm not going to do anything foolish." The wolf/coyote sounded off again, but everybody's eyes were on my pack. I looked at Wren, the first time that I had made eye contact with her since stepping into the open, and prayed that she would understand that Judgment Day was about to begin.

Fumbling around in my pack, I pulled Kirby's bloody scalp from the pack and tossed it to the ground. All eyes stared in disbelief. Someone cursed, and the gunfire erupted. Flames blazed from rifle muzzles, flashing like angry lightening bolts on a hot, rainy summer night, lighting up the darkness on the outer perimeter of the camp. The thunder

of muzzle blasts echoed off the canyon walls below.

The AFFA men, bewildered and confused, with nowhere to run, were soaking up the lead as the bullets riddled their bodies. Faster than it takes time to tell, all six of the AFFA men lay dead or dying on the ground. Hogg had taken 4 rounds and fell into the fire. Tank was still breathing, trying to mutter something, but breathed his last before he could utter a word.

I looked into the eyes of Wren, who stood there with her hands still tied behind her back and tears streaming down her cheeks, the campfire light flickering on the moist streaks. Walking up to her, looking into her eyes and wiping the tears away, I stepped behind her and untied the ropes that bound her hands.

"Hey, girl, you sure are a sight for sore eyes," I stated, trying to sound casual. As soon as the rope was released from her wrists and dropped to the ground, Wren turned to me and threw both of her arms around my neck, burying her face into my chest holding me like she was never going to let go. Sobbing and crying, drained from the exhaustion and mental anguish that she had endured, she wept, shaking and trembling from head to toe. I held her close assuring her that everything was going to be all right, kissing the top of her head, and trying to comfort her in the best way I knew how.

From out of the darkness the sound of someone clearing his throat broke the silence as Wren and I stood there in each other's arms. We both turned toward the direction of the sound. Clovis stepped forward from out of the shadows into the light of the lanterns that hung or sat around the camp. At first I couldn't believe my eyes. I had personally watched Kirby shoot Clovis and with my own eyes watched him fall from the cliff. I had even later stood in the very place where Clovis had been shot and looked down upon his body lying in the rocks nearly a thousand feet below, and yet, here he was, standing very much alive. Of course, it only took an instant, after looking at the clothes that he now wore, to realize that the man I witnessed shot and fallen from the cliff was not Clovis at all. Clovis had forced him to change clothes with him, hoping that Kirby would mistake the identity of the two men, which is exactly what he did.

"Daddy, oh, Daddy!" Wren yelled as she ran to his arms. I stood there and stared, trying in some small way to contemplate the magnitude of this emotional moment. For more than three years, Wren had longed for this day. The amount of hardship that Clovis had endured to stay alive for the past three years would be impossible to measure. I watched with pure delight and joy in my heart as I witnessed this beautiful reunion. Clovis, while holding Wren in a strong embrace, opened his eyes, looked into mine, smiled, and then winked at me. His eyes then looked past me, and I turned to see Judy walking toward us from out of the darkness with Dad, Mark, and Will. Clovis, moving quickly from his daughter's arms into the arms of Judy, grabbed her and kissed her passionately.

Dad moved toward me without saying a word. Perhaps words were not adequate enough to describe what he felt. Throwing his arms around me he held me harder and longer than any other moment I could recall in my memory. Mark and Will moved to him and helped Dad take a seat on a nearby log, the whole while tears flooding our eyes and streaming down our cheeks. Dad kept mumbling something through his quivering lips, but we couldn't ascertain exactly what he was trying to say. His grief had become a weight he could no longer bear.

Wren moved to my side, sliding her arm around my waist, "Ross, what has happened?"

I looked at her, deep into her eyes, biting my lip, striving to muster the strength to utter what my mind and heart still did not want to accept. "Joe's dead, Wren. Kirby killed him."

Wren gasped, holding her fingers to her mouth. Dad's weeping increased, his body trembling and shaking even more. Mark, Will and I could not contain the grief that we, too, experienced at the loss of Joe. Witnessing the reunion of Clovis with Judy and Wren was one of the most joyful moments my eyes have ever beheld, but in my own heart, I grieved in deeper sorrow for the loss of Joe than any other pain I had experienced before. The wailing of unconstrained anguish spilling forth from my father and my two brothers as we mourned the death of Joe defeated the happiness and delight of seeing Clovis and his wife and daughter finally brought back together. Perhaps we are not made with the capacity of harboring great loads of both happiness and sorrow at the same time.

CHAPTER TWENTY-THREE

Clovis, after visiting with Judy and Wren, finally moved toward us. Looking at my father, Clovis extended his hand. "Tyler, this is the second time that you have been there when I needed you in a bad way. I am terribly sorry to hear about your son."

Dad stood and shook his hand, looking Clovis straight in the eye, saying what words could never say and perhaps what only comrades of war could ever understand. Finally, he spoke. "I appreciate that Clovis. Joe was a good man... Now, we better try to get out of here and find us another place to set up camp for tonight. This place isn't exactly fit for these two fine ladies of yours. Too much blood and the smell of burnt hair and flesh are a little nauseating."

"We don't have any sleeping bags other than those that these here AFFA boys have so conveniently left in their tents. Somehow, though, just the idea of sleeping in the same bag as these guys turns my stomach."

"I feel the same, Ross," Wren replied.

"Well," Dad interrupted, "it's about an eight mile hike back to the chopper. It's dark, and we still don't know if we have eliminated all of the danger that's here in the Bob. Problem too, we'll have to make two trips out of it because it can only carry four of us plus me at one time."

I looked at Clovis. "Hey, Clovis, what about that large rock outcropping back there where you showed me the Indian writing on the walls? I know that there's not enough room to stand up, but there's plenty of room for us to spread out and catch a little sleep before sunrise."

"Yes, sir," Clovis answered. "That's a great idea. We can build a fire in there and stay very comfortable. We won't need sleeping bags, and the fire will not be visible from the outside."

"Dad, what are we going to do about Joe?" Will asked.

"I'm really not sure."

"Dad," Mark spoke up, "Will and I have been talking, and we are thinking that you need to get the girls and Clovis and Tyler back as soon as possible. We will stay behind and watch over Joe to make sure that the bears or wolves don't mess with him, then you can come back for us, and we can take him home and bury him properly."

It was a sensitive subject, but one that needed to be addressed, so Dad agreed to the plan. Meanwhile, we gathered our stuff together and headed back toward the rocks. It was 9:13 p.m.

Within the hour, we were inside the outcropping of rocks and had a fire going. Very little conversation took place. Wren pulled herself close to me, smiled, closed her eyes and fell asleep in my arms, assuming that I didn't mind, which of course I did not. Within minutes, the heat was reflecting off of the large stones, and the little room, if you could call it that, felt like an oven, warm and comfortable. Dad and Clovis spent about half an hour collecting enough firewood to keep the fire burning through the night.

Long after everyone had fallen asleep, I sat there staring into the glow of the flickering fire. Dad's snoring, which had always annoyed me through the years, was a welcome sound to my ears, and I chuckled and thanked God for bringing him and Mark and Will to my rescue. I burned inside at the loss of Joe, and found it practically impossible to accept the fact that Joe was gone. He was the closest friend I had ever known. I remembered a bible verse that I heard when I was a teen-ager that said, "There is a friend that sticketh closer than a brother." What a fortunate man I had been. My friend was my brother. I felt so undeserving of the sacrifice that he had made for me, his life for mine. Yet, I also knew, that I would not have survived if they all had chosen to remain at home. I thought of Mama, alone at home, worried sick I was sure. What a sad day it would be when she received the news about Joe.

I continued to sit there with my back against the rock and Wren's head on my lap. Try as I may, sleep would not come. Occasionally, I stoked the fire. The shadows of the firelight dancing against the sides of the rocks revealing the artwork of the Native Americans who lived here, perhaps thousands of years ago, caused me to ponder their way of life. Were the problems that they encountered as complex as the problems we face in the 21st century? I seriously doubted it, but felt sure, their problems, whatever they might have been, were just as real to them as mine are to me.

Mark awoke from his sleep and moved over to sit by my side, opposite of Wren. For a moment, he just sat there with his legs crunched up to his chest, his hands locked together in front of his shins and his face buried between his knees, rocking back and forth. Mark doesn't say a whole lot, but when he does, it's a pretty safe bet that he has thought it through.

"Ross, I can't believe that Joe is dead. I mean, it's tearing my heart out. I miss him already."

"I know, Brother. I don't believe I have ever hurt as much as I do now...Not ever."

"Hey, I've been thinking. Do you remember Joe's favorite stretch of the Stillwater River and how, if you couldn't find him, that's the one place you could be sure he'd be?"

"Oh yeah, I remember it well," I replied. "We fished there often if you recall."

"I suggest that we bury Joe high upon the bank above the river where his body can rest overlooking that stretch of river."

I thought about it for a minute. "I think that's a great idea, Mark. I'm all for it."

We sat in silence for a long moment, staring into the flickering fire while those around us continued to sleep. Mark finally broke the silence again. "Ross, I've never killed a man before today. I really don't feel bad about it, and I'm not sure if I should or not. I am wondering about the consequences with the law?"

"I don't think there'll be any, Mark. It was all in self-defense," I answered.

Again, we sat there pondering the events of the day. This time I started the conversation. "Mark, what are your plans for the future? Are you planning on staying in Tennessee?"

Mark looked at me and chuckled. Obviously, this was a subject to which he had given a lot of thought and consideration. "Funny you should ask that. Will and I have been talking for months about moving back to Montana. Both of our wives are ready for a change in lifestyle. We've got some money saved up and have already put our house on the market. Will doesn't have much, but he's out of debt and just as ready to go as I am. Both of us talked to Dad about it on the way here to The Bob, and he has agreed to divide the ranch up equally among us boys as long as we work the place together and provide for him and mom until they're gone. I do believe that he really wants us to come home, and I know mom does... How about you?"

"You bet. I don't ever plan on leaving again, and I regret the day that I did. A man is a fool to think that money is going to bring him contentment. I went to Chicago because the money was good. Shoot, it was great, but I haven't wet a fly in so long, and I can't even tell you when the last time I went hunting. Until I came back here, I had forgotten what it meant to breathe clean air...Yes, sir, as soon as we get this mess with Clovis straightened out, I'm coming back home to stay."

"What are your plans, Ross, concerning Clovis and trying to clear his name?"

"Well, Mark, the first thing I plan on doing is going public in a big way. I've got a good contact that works with CNN. His name is Kyle Sooner. He's from up-state New York and loves to hunt and fish. I guess that's the major thing that we share in common, although we still haven't had the chance to do either of those things together. We do run into each other from time to time and usually grab lunch or something to catch up on what's going on in each other's life. He's like me, single and busy and wishing he had more time to get away from the rat race. As soon as I can get to a phone, I'm going to give him a call."

"Dang, Ross, I wish you would have said so earlier. I picked up a satellite phone from those boys that we took care of down there in the camp. Let me get it."

Mark rummaged around in his pack and pulled the phone out.

"Are you sure that this guy is someone you can trust?" Mark asked.

"Yeah, I think so. He's never given me a reason to think otherwise, and he's got a pretty good reputation for being a straight-shooter from what I hear."

I took the phone and quietly crawled outside of the rocks and made the call. I never forgot Kyle's emergency number, and I was glad that I had it memorized now. The phone rang almost instantly and was answered on the first ring.

"Hello."

"Kyle...Ross Tyler. How are you?"

"Ross, I'm fine. How are you? What's up?"

"I've got him, and I've got hard evidence."

Kyle did not speak for a minute. "I'm assuming you are telling me that you've found Belden and that you've got proof to clear his name?"

"Yes." I answered. "Where are you?"

"I'm half way across the Atlantic, on my way to Paris, and then to Berlin. Are you sure that you've got what you say you've got?"

"Kyle, you know I wouldn't be calling if I didn't."

"Of course not," Kyle answered. I overheard him tell the pilot to turn the private jet around. "Listen, Tyler, we are headed back to Toronto. We'll refuel there and come to you. Where do we need to meet you?"

"Meet us at Malmstrom, Kyle. And hey, if you have any connections, we may need some protection."

"You got it. I'll see you there some time before noon tomorrow."

The fire popped loudly, causing Clovis to stir in his sleep and then woke up.

"Did I hear you talking on a phone, Tyler?" Clovis asked.

"Yes, sir, I called Kyle Sooner from CNN. He's going to meet us at Malmstrom tomorrow around noon."

"Oh, crap. Get everybody up. We've got to get out of here," Clovis stated anxiously.

"What do you mean? What's the matter?"

"Tyler, every time a phone call is made on a satellite phone, not only is the message capable of being intercepted by Homeland Security, but it transmits the global coordinates from where the message was sent. You know that most of the men that we have killed today are just a part of the clean-up crew for the 'big boys'. There's still more of them out there."

In less than two minutes, everyone was awake, guns checked, the fire put out, and Clovis began explaining his plan.

"I apologize, everyone. I was just trying to expedite the situation. I didn't realize that making that call would put us all in jeopardy."

"It's not your fault, Tyler. Things go wrong sometimes and when they do, you've got to be ready. I should have told you. If you remember when I called you the first time three years ago, when you were working for the Billings Gazette, I knew that the FBI would pick up the coordinates on my exact location. When I found that fresh grizzly kill, I knew that was my one chance to make it look like I had been turned into bear crap. Calling you that night on a satellite phone was my way of letting them know exactly where I was. Right before dusk as I was looking for a place to hide out for the night, I came upon a fresh grizzly kill, that's when I got the idea of creating a scene that would appear as if I had been killed and devoured by the grizzly. Of course, I needed to make sure that I led my pursuers to my exact location. The truth is, although I'm sure that the bear was probably somewhere close, I never did see it. Now, don't worry about that call, we'll be alright."

Clovis had such a gentle way of smoothing things out. Everyone knew I had made a mistake, but no one cast any blame. Wren moved to my side and put her arms around my waist and assured me that everything would be all right.

"Here's the plan," Clovis stated. "We are going to head back north and rappel down into the place that I have called home for the last three years. It will be a little time consuming, but we must do it before dawn so that we won't be seen."

"Do you really think someone will come?" Judy asked.

Dad answered first, "Oh, they'll come and they'll be here sooner than later."

CHAPTER TWENTY-FOUR

Due to the weariness of the long day and the fact that we were traveling in the dark, it took us the better part of two hours to reach the rope that stretched down to Clovis's cave. We thought about trying to continue north to Larch Hill pass and then dropping back south on the east side of the Chinese Wall to reach our destination, but we determined that we could not make it before daylight, and we could not risk being seen.

Finally, arriving at the rope, Clovis lifted the stone that concealed the harness and carabineers.

"Kelli, you're first. Judy, you're next, and then the rest of us will follow. I'll go last." Clovis proclaimed.

Wren strapped on her harness and was ready to rappel in no time at all. It was obvious that she was very familiar and experienced with rappelling. After one final check to make sure that all the buckles on her harness were fastened securely, she looked me in the eye and smiled. Her white teeth sparkled in the glow of the late summer moon. She stretched forth her face and gently kissed my lips. "Be careful," I said. Stepping out into the darkness, she disappeared into the ebony night. Approximately 10 minutes later, Wren gave three quick jerks on the rope from below to let us know that she had arrived. Pulling up the harness, Judy was next. Glancing at my watch, it was now 4:30 a.m. Time passed quickly. It took us 20-25 minutes per person to retrieve the rope, get into the harness, rappel the cliff, and retrieve the rope back up again. Mark and Will followed Judy. They had rappelled quite a lot while they served in the National Guard, and they continued to do it for recreation with their families in Tennessee. I was uncertain about Dad's ability so I asked if he knew how to rappel. He just looked at me, chuckled, and said, "Son, I could rappel this upside down in my sleep."

"Dad," I said, "if we get out of here alive, I hope you'll tell me a few things about yourself, the war, and whatever you have kept hidden for all these years."

"Son, if we get out of here alive, I'll tell you anything that you want to know." And with that, he disappeared into the darkness off the edge of the cliff.

The sound of choppers broke the silence of the predawn sunrise while Clovis and I were hoisting up the harness after Dad's descent. Looking at each other, we quickened the pace; hand over hand, pulling as fast as we could go. Floodlights from three choppers were scanning the area to the south where we had been sleeping, obviously led by the coordinates of the satellite phone. Two appeared to land in the immediate vicinity while the other circled the area, shining its bright lights on the ground below. A voice rang out from a loud speaker.

"Tyler, Belden, this is the FBI. We know that you are up here. Turn yourselves in and there will be no harm. There is no way off of this mountain. Do not, I repeat, do not make us resort to using force. You are heavily out-gunned."

Clovis looked at me and said, "Tyler, get into that harness and get down there to my girls and your family in that cave. There's not enough time for both of us to get down there."

"I'm not going without you, Belden," I rebutted.

"Tyler, this is no time to argue. It's getting light and they'll spot us for sure up here on this naked mountain. Now, I've been avoiding trouble for nearly three years, and I know every nook and cranny around here. Besides, one can hide a whole lot easier than two. I'll catch up with you tonight, and we'll leave this place in the dark."

I didn't like it, but what he had to say made more sense than my stubborn pride. I quickly climbed into the harness, wished him luck, and bailed off the side. Upon arrival to the entrance of the cave, everyone was waiting.

"What's going on up there?" Wren asked. I explained what Clovis had decided to do, knowing full well that it was going to cause a lot of worry for Judy and Wren.

For hours we sat and waited. Comments were made about the living quarters that Clovis had turned the cave into, and, much like me, everyone was amazed at the comfort and coziness of the place. I showed them the hot springs in the back room, and we made ourselves as much at home as we possibly could, eating food that Clovis had left behind and stuffing our packs with food that we might need later.

High above us we could hear the helicopters buzzing up and down the top of the wall in search of Clovis. Twice they buzzed right by the entrance of the cave, but did not see the opening that was hidden by the pine that grew at the entrance. We waited impatiently, pacing the floor, asking questions, wondering what was happening above us. The fact that we had not heard any gunfire brought us a little serenity, but the uncertainty of Clovis's well being was difficult to bear. Time seemed to be at a standstill, every minute seeming like an hour. To top it off, the feeling of helplessness was taking its toll on our patience, especially on Dad. Finally, I said to him, "Why don't you tell us a little about the war and what you did there and how you came to know Clovis."

At first, Dad declined, but then he changed his mind, perhaps thinking that telling a few stories might make time pass by a little faster. All of us gathered around and listened intently while we sipped coffee and snacked on trail-mix. Sharing stories with us, the likes of which we had never heard, and some of Clovis that were just as new to the ears of Judy and Wren, Dad held us captivated for hours. A deep sense of pride, a new kind of pride, swelled up in my heart as I listened to my father. All through the day, I thought of how much I wish Joe could have been there to learn about Dad and what he would never know. I found it very difficult to believe that Joe was gone. The sorrow and grief that I was feeling for his loss must have been noticeable. Wren, who had been sitting beside me, holding my hand, reached up and wiped the tears that were rolling down my cheek and then kissed me where her soft fingers had just been. She didn't say anything. She didn't have to.

Looking at my watch, I couldn't believe that it was almost 6 p.m. Stepping to the entrance of the cave, the east side of the cliffs was already casting shadows on the valley floor below. Darkness would be upon us soon, and hopefully Clovis would come to us. The choppers had quit buzzing around for the last two hours and that worried us, but then they started searching again, so we felt certain that they had not found Clovis. Still, we waited and waited.

Darkness fell heavy upon The Bob. Cloud cover had obscured the starry night. We tried to rest and sleep, but to no avail. The anticipation of Clovis's arrival made it impossible. At 10:00 p.m., Judy started to get really upset, and began thinking the worst, but her fears were relieved when suddenly without a sound, Clovis appeared at the entrance. The reunion of Clovis and his wife and daughter was almost as passionate to witness, as it had been the first time, only the day before.

Clovis explained that he did not have time to hoist the rope back up the cliff and get into the harness. His position left him too exposed and he would have been spotted for certain, which would also reveal where the rest of us were hidden. So, he chose to hide from the choppers and instead of traveling north to Larch Hill Pass as he guessed the FBI would believe he would travel; he moved south to the same slide he had used to escape off of the wall three years earlier. It was slow and tedious work because cover was sparse. The bare nakedness of the terrain had forced Clovis to spend most of the day crawling on his belly, moving snail-like, so as not to be spotted by the choppers that continually buzzed overhead, back and forth along the Divide. He felt confident that he had made it unseen.

"What kind of plans have you got now?" Dad asked.

"Well, it's about 20 miles to Benchmark from here. I'm thinking we can stay to the timber and travel tonight in the cover of darkness. Depending upon how far we make it, we may be able to travel a little tomorrow… if we move slowly and stay in the shadows of the trees. If we're not spotted we could be out of the Bob by tomorrow afternoon."

"Then what do we do?" Will asked. "It's still another 20 miles or so to Augusta, and we're not sure that it will be safe to go there."

"Bob Tidwell," Clovis replied, "is a friend of mine whose ranch borders the Bob Marshall. We can use his phone and maybe Tyler can contact his friend from CNN. Of course, I'm open to other suggestions, but that's the best that I have right now."

Nobody else had a better plan and so the long hellish night began. Trying to traverse through black timber during daylight hours is challenging enough for anyone, but at night without the aid of flashlights, which we dared not use for fear of being spotted, was enough to try the patience of all of us, except for Clovis and Dad of course. Dad said it was like being back in the jungles of 'Nam again. I just shook my head in disbelief at the transformation that had come over my father in the past 48 hours. The hard working cattleman that I had grown up knowing was showing a face of his character that none of his sons had witnessed before. Mark and Will and I whispered to each other about it from time to time along the path that we traveled. In its own way, the fact that this man, who was more than 20 years older than me, was making us look like novices in the woods, inspired us to keep going even when we were exhausted. Judy and Wren were doing fair, but Judy was growing weary. In spite of all the stumbles and falls, we trudged on through the night and were nearing the North Fork of the Sun River, not far from the place that I had camped the first night in The Bob, just a week earlier. Other than a lot of scrapes and bruises, we had faired well.

As the morning dawn began to break and the eastern horizon glistened to the birth of a new day, we paused to rest. Clovis turned and looked at the rest of us, taking off his hat and holding it at his waist in both hands. "Tyler, Boys, I don't know what your religious convictions are, but Lord willing, today I am stepping out of this wilderness, and come what may, one way or the other, the truth is going to be told. Right now, I want us all to take a few moments and speak to God and ask him to continue to be with us on this journey."

Removing our hats, we bowed our heads, something I hadn't done a whole lot of in my life, but was finding myself doing much more often in the last few days. At first, there was silence, and I thought that perhaps we were all expected to say our own silent prayer, and then Clovis started with a prayer that I will never forget.

"Oh, God, we know that you are the Creator of all that is good and we see your hand in the beauty of your creation round about us. For nearly three years you have kept me from harm's way, and I know that my life has been spared by your powerful might. I tremble, O God, in your presence, and for the times that I have sinned and transgressed against your will, I plead forgiveness, and pray that you will not hold the charges of my iniquity against me or any other.

I thank you, O God, for the unending grace that you have showered upon my life and upon my family. We grieve at the loss of Joe Tyler, who, Lord, in an effort to help bring me home to my family was so untimely removed from his own. I am forever humbled and indebted for the sacrifice that he has made. In this time of loss, we do not know what to say, except to ask that you provide us with comfort and relieve us from our sorrow... For bringing us this far, we praise your name and are eternally thankful. Now, O God, I beseech you and plead with you, as I have so many times before, that you remain with us throughout the remainder of our journey. May it transpire without bloodshed. Please, deliver us safely from the evil that men do. I pray these things this day in your presence as humbly as I know how, by the power and the name of your Son Jesus. Amen."

Not a single eye among us was dry. This was it. This was the moment when we would make our last run, our last effort, to bring the truth of the assassination of Vice President Peterson to the eye of the world. We had not been followed as far as we knew. We had heard choppers in the distance, but we felt confident that they continued to search for us along the Continental Divide. It was approximately 12 miles to Bob Tidwell's ranch, just south of Gibson's Reservoir, and then perhaps we would be safe.

We all ate a little for breakfast and then forded the river, taking a few minutes to soak our aching feet and wash and clean the dried blood from the many scratches and scrapes accumulated during the night's travel. Wren looked like a breath of spring in spite of all that she had been through. Her splendor moved me. Her poise, her figure, her smile, her eyes, and especially her tender and yet firm disposition held my heart captive. What she saw in me, I didn't know, but it didn't matter. I was glad.

Although still difficult to maneuver through the thick timber and blow-downs, it sure beat doing it under the cover of darkness. We made good time and within a few hours we were at the border of the Bob Marshall and the Tidwell Ranch. Clovis pointed to the ranch house below, about a mile or so away.

"There it is. We'll stay close to the cover of this tree line and then we'll scope it out with our binoculars when we reach that point," he said, pointing to a knoll about half the distance from the ranch.

As we approached the top of the knoll that held very little cover, we crawled on our bellies and looked down into the ranch headquarters below. We were uncertain if danger awaited us there, but we were certain that it was not a time to become careless. Through our binoculars we could see an older cowboy working cattle in the corrals. Clovis identified the man as Bob Tidwell.

"Clovis, there's something I've been meaning to say to you. You know, with the long history of malice between you and Kirby, it just seems to me that you should have been the one to kill him and not me. Do you understand what I am trying to say?" I asked.

"Tyler, when I was in Nam, I killed because it was my duty. Up here, I have killed simply as a means of survival. I have never killed out of vengeance."

After a lengthy discussion, we determined that Clovis and I would cautiously approach the ranch, while the others remained hidden in the timber. Slowly making our way down the hillside, we were almost to the corral when Tidwell's Border collie caught wind of us and came out barking. Tidwell turned to identify the source of his dog's attention and immediately spotted us. He stepped to the door way of the barn where he lifted a double-barrel shotgun to his hip.

"If you guys are friendly, you're welcome to come in, but if you're looking for trouble, then I'm ready to give it to you."

"Bob, I'm Clovis Belden, and this here is Ross Tyler from down near Columbus."

Stepping closer for a better look, Tidwell asked, "Belden, is that really you?"

"Yes, sir, Bob. May we come on in?" Clovis asked.

Clovis shook hands with Bob and then introduced me. "You're the reporter from the *Gazette* that followed the assassination story a few years back, ain't ya?"

"Yes, sir. That's me."

Looking at Belden, Tidwell just shook his head and stated, "I always figured you were still alive somehow. I didn't recognize you at first with that beard, but dang you look fit. Why don't you guys come in for a cup of coffee? I'll get Linda to put on a fresh pot."

"Thanks Bob, but we really can't stay that long and I need to tell you, we've got the FBI looking for us, so the longer we stay, the greater the risk of putting you and Linda in danger. All we really need to do is make a phone call, and then we'll get out of here."

Bob led us into the house, and I called Kyle Sooner.

"Where are you, Tyler?" Kyle asked.

"Kyle, I'm not that far from you, but I need to know what your plans are? We've got the FBI on our tail. I do not know who's 'dirty' and whose not."

"Tyler, I want to put you and Clovis on national news, live. Once the truth is exposed, you'll be untouchable. Do you still have the hard evidence that you told me about yesterday?"

"Yes, I do."

"Then tell me where we need to meet."

"Kyle. Who's with you? I need to know," I stated emphatically.

"Just me and my two cameramen. I did not try to make contact with anyone else because I got worried about the lines of communication and who might pick up on it."

Tidwell whispered to me and told me that it was perfectly alright if they wanted to come to his ranch. Kyle said they would be there in about 45 minutes.

"Bob, my two girls and Tyler's pap and two brothers are up there on that hill. Can they come on down?" Clovis asked.

"You bet! Bring them in."

CHAPTER TWENTY-FIVE

Sooner and his crew were at the ranch in a little under 40 minutes. Kyle leaped from the helicopter running toward all of us, who were now standing by the barn. Shaking hands quickly with me, he said, "Tyler, we've got to do this fast. I have a friend who works for the FBI. He just called me and said that he overheard communication from the men who are looking for you and they are headed this way. I have no idea how they would know. Let's get in the barn and get started in there."

Dad, Mark and Will helped clear off a place in the loft upstairs in the barn. Judy and Wren assisted Clovis and me by dusting off our clothes, straightening our hair and just giving us a good going over. Bob Tidwell stood outside the barn door where he could keep an eye out for possible trouble and watch the live broadcast at the same time. Cameras were set up and in no time, Kyle was ready to roll.

"Good afternoon Americans. My name is Kyle Sooner, reporting live for CNN. Today, we meet for the first time in an unnamed barn, in an unknown place, with a man whose name I am sure you will remember well. Standing beside me is Clovis Belden, believed to be the man who assassinated Vice President Peterson almost 3 years ago, and allegedly was killed and consumed by a grizzly bear in the Bob Marshall Wilderness..."

Kyle recapped the story and then asked Clovis to tell the world what actually happened. Clovis went into explicit detail as he recalled the events. After Clovis had explained the events of the assassination, Kyle turned to me and asked me to explain my involvement, which I gladly did. When I got to the part about being captured by some dirty FBI agents, I revealed the tape that had recorded the conversation of Agent Cordell and me before he was killed. We played it for the entire nation to hear. As the recording was playing, we began hearing choppers flying in from the distance, headed our way. A feeling of terror and panic began to spread over us.

With nowhere to run, Tidwell suggested that we hide behind the hay bales at the end of the barn loft, and given the situation, it seemed the best alternative.

Kyle and his camera crew stepped outside of the barn and pretended to be talking to Tidwell, asking him if he had made any contact with Tyler or Belden, in an effort to cover up their real intentions for being there. The choppers had landed in a field adjacent to the barn, and approximately 20-25 men approached the barn. We could see them coming our way through the cracks in the wall.

Wren, Judy, Clovis, Dad, Mark, Will and I stayed hidden behind the hay concealed from visibility, but capable of hearing the commotion outside. When the FBI men approached Tidwell, Sooner and his crew, I heard a familiar voice.

"Mr. Tidwell, Sooner," Jones spoke to Sooner as if they had met before, which I guess shouldn't have been a surprise to me. "I am FBI Agent Jonathan Jones. Mr. Tidwell, we have reason to believe that you may be harboring a couple of men that are wanted for questioning by the United States Government. Now, please understand that we do not intend for any harm to come to Mr. Belden. Not more than five minutes ago, I was notified by my commanding officer to bring in Mr. Belden and Mr. Tyler without a scratch. My orders came from the President of the United States himself. Although I have not seen it with my own eyes, my understanding is, that Mr. Sooner and his camera crew here, just went live on public television with a story that obviously requires a deeper and more thorough investigation."

From behind the hay bales, we all heard the entire conversation. I looked at Clovis and said, "I'm going out. I may be wrong, but I believe Agent Jones is telling the truth. He may be a knucklehead, but I don't believe he's a liar."

"Jones," I shouted, "I'm coming out."

All of the agents, Tidwell, and Sooner stood at the barn entrance, watching as I descended the ladder from the loft. No one had drawn a gun. They just stood smiling and shaking their head. This moment had been a long time coming.

Dusting the hay off of my shirt and out of my hair I walked over to Jones. His face was a multicolored mixture of blue, black, and yellow, his wounds healing nicely. I extended my hand to shake his, which was in a cast.

"Tyler," he said, "I have orders to take you and Belden in. We have orders to make sure that you arrive at the Pentagon unharmed. As far as your families are concerned, President Watson extends a personal invitation to all of them, and they are welcome to join us."

"Belden, did you hear that?" I shouted up at the loft.

"I heard it, Tyler. Let's go," Clovis replied. Clovis descended the ladder, walked right out the door past everyone, fell prostrate upon the ground and thanked the Lord in prayer. I didn't hear the words he said, but I was certain God had delivered us and brought us safely to this day. How appropriate, I thought, to remember to give thanks to the one from whom we received so much. For certain, it was a glorious moment, a wonderful moment, and all the fatigue and exhaustion of the events that had preceded that day were replaced with hope and anticipation. Judy was speechless and Wren's eyes couldn't hold back the tears of joy and delight. Her father was coming home.

Dad, Mark, and Will decided to go back to the ranch. Agent Jones agreed to permit one of the helicopters to fly them back up to the Chinese Wall to transport the body of Little Joe back home for burial. I preferred to go with them but knew that my testimony as a witness to the events that we had just endured would be requested in order for this case to be properly closed. As we prepared to board the aircraft and depart, I grabbed my brothers and gave them a long hug.

"I'll be home in a couple of days for the funeral. Please wait for me."

"Oh, we'll wait," Will replied.

"You know, I'm sure that Mama is worried sick, and it's going to break her heart something terrible when she learns the news of Joe. Just be with her and send her my love."

Dad came over and grabbed me and threw both of his arms around me and buried his face into the nap of my neck, weeping again, almost uncontrollably. Father holding son, son holding father, he finally got a hold of himself. Wiping away his tears, he looked me straight in the eye and spoke words I had never heard him say before and will never forget. "Ross, you make me proud to be your father and I know I've never said it, but I say it now, Son, I love you. I love all of you boys. I loved Joe and I will go to my grave regretting the fact that I never told him." (How does a man explain a moment like this? How does he create a visual image of the mood or climate in a particular setting? I have struggled painstakingly to somehow express or verbally paint a picture describing this scene that might captivate or even perhaps, simply reflect the monumental power of emotion felt and displayed that day. Maybe words aren't always adequate to describe every emotion we feel.)

It's strange to think that those three words, words that mama told us often, seemed so new and foreign as they rolled off my father's lips, and yet I knew beyond a shadow of a doubt that the words were sincere.

"Dad," I said, "Joe *knew* that you loved him. That's what matters most."

CHAPTER TWENTY-SIX

A full-scale investigation was conducted over the course of the next month. AFFA was completely brought to its knees and ruined. Eleven more members of the FBI were sentenced for conspiracy to undermine the United States Government and its leadership.

Watson publicly extended a full pardon to Clovis for all accusations of crime brought against him for anything directly or indirectly involved with the assassination case. He also expressed his deep appreciation for saving his life. For Watson, the fact that Peterson would stoop to murder was a pill he readily admitted was "hard to swallow". Nevertheless, that was a matter he would have to deal with personally.

Clovis instantly became a national hero when the American people learned the truth concerning the events involving the assassination of Vice President Peterson three years earlier. Everyone, it seemed, wanted to write his story, but his answer was always the same. The full editorial rights had been left to me.

By springtime, Mark and Will had moved from Tennessee back to Montana. Dad divided the entire ranch into thirds and gave all of us enough room to build a house.

Jill, Joe's wife, and their two boys did not hang around long after Joe's funeral. We offered them a place on the ranch if they wanted to move from Texas, but Jill declined, expressing that doing so would mean exposing herself and her boys to the likes of me, who, after-all, was to blame for the loss of their father and her husband. She held me completely responsible for Joe's death, a weight I have carried for all these years and will carry—I am sure—even to my grave.

Mama was never the same after receiving the news of Little Joe. He had always been her favorite. There was a connection between Mama and Joe that was unequivocally special. She fought round after round with depression and in less than a year she lost the fight. We buried her beside little Joe on his favorite stretch of the Stillwater River. Losing Mama took the spark out of Dad's spirit. For more than a year after her death, he didn't have too much to say, and then one day he saddled up and rode off for the mountains, giving all of us explicit instructions not to follow. I gave him two weeks and I couldn't take it any longer. I was worried. I saddled my horse and a pack mule and went looking for him, but I never did find him, although I did find his horse. In his saddlebag was his journal in which he addressed all three of his sons and his daughter individually, expressing his love and admiration for each of us. The journal was something we all knew that Dad kept, but never knew what he wrote. We sat down and read it the day before his memorial service. He had started it when he went off to boot camp before the war. Detailed events of seemingly impossible and dangerous situations were recorded. Old photographs of war buddies were buried within the pages, including a photo of a large, young, muscular black man from Chicago, who, after being riddled with shrapnel, Dad had personally carried on his shoulder across a rice field, under enemy fire to his chopper where he flew him back to safety. On the back of the photograph was the date April 6, 1968, and the name Roy Kendall.

We would have liked to bury Dad beside Joe and Mama, but he chose to die his own way. I can think of a lot of ways of dying that would be a whole lot worse. We decided to have a headstone made and placed beside their graves.

After returning from the Capitol, Wren and I courted for only three months and were married. For a wedding present, Clovis gave me his bamboo fly rod, his most prized possession. If God gives me another year or two and the strength and fortitude, maybe I'll write the story of the most wonderful eight years of my life.

Cancer took my Wren in less than two months after she was diag-
nosed with the disease. While my life has certainly seen and experienced its share of heartache and tragedy, losing Wren has been by
far the greatest loss I have ever known. Our precious seven-year-
old daughter Heidi was left without a mama, and I never did
remarry. Right now I just cannot muster the strength to endure the
emotional drain telling her story would tax on my heart and mind.

Losing Wren cast a dark cloud over the life and happiness of
Clovis and Judy. I buried Wren beside Mama and Joe. After the
funeral, it was more than a year before I heard from Clovis again.
I suppose the lack of communication was as much my fault as it
was anyone else's. In an effort to run from my own grief and
despair, I detached myself from those who loved me the most and
turned to the bottle. When I was sober, which wasn't very often, I
engulfed myself in the work on the ranch. Will and his wife
Tiffany took care of Heidi for me during that time.

I have come to realize that God has a way of mending the
hurt. One day I set the bottle down and never touched another
drop. In time, Clovis and I began communicating more with one
another, and we became regular hunting and fishing partners. I
learned more about hunting elk with a longbow than I ever believed
possible and even learned a few new tricks with a fly rod. Mark
and Will, after their children had left the nest, started hunting and
fishing with Clovis and me, and for the next ten years or so, the
four of us always made it a point to get together two or three times
each summer for a fishing trip. Come opening day of archery season every year, we would saddle up the horses and ride into one of
the many wilderness areas of Montana and spend a week or more
hunting elk, mule deer and black bear with our long bows. It had
taken a long time, but we were living the life we always knew
Montana had to offer.

One cold mid-winter morning my phone rang. It was Judy. I
could tell by the sound of her voice that something terrible had
happened. Clovis had met a tragic end to his life that morning
while feeding cows. His prize bull turned on him and gored him to
death. Judy overheard the commotion in the corral and went to
check on Clovis only to find him dead.

Mark, Will and I drove to Augusta to attend the funeral three days later. Judy informed us that President Watson, who had long since retired to his South Georgia farm, had called to express his condolences, and again, he extended his gratitude to Judy, on behalf of Clovis who had saved his life so long ago. How Watson had learned of Clovis's death is something I never figured out. While gathered together with family and friends and surviving comrades of war at the cemetery where we laid Clovis to rest, a 21 gun salute was fired into the crisp winter air, and from out of nowhere, four fighter jets buzzed low over the top of us, simultaneously tipping their wings as a sign of honor, respect, and a farewell to Clovis. I later learned that this event transpired as a personal request made by Watson himself. Chills ran up and down my spine, tears welled up in my eyes, my whole body shuttered. As we lowered the pine coffin into the earth, it occurred to me that Clovis had lived a full life. He was a husband, a father, a rancher, a friend and a soldier. A man, a real man, among men, who stood his ground for what he believed, who lived and loved each precious moment of his life as if it were his last, and who fought to defend and preserve the way of life that allowed him to pursue his passions to their fullest, many of which we shared together. I was humbled by the mere thought of all that Clovis had endured and accomplished in his life, and I do not believe that there has ever been another time in my life when I felt as proud as I did that day to be an American.

With no one to assist Judy with the operation and work, the ranch quickly became too much for her to take care of by herself, so I agreed to buy it from her. Judy moved back to Havre to live the remainder of her days with her sister. Mark and Will's sons now live and work on her ranch for me.

Somehow, life happens, and although we may have good intentions, we just don't accomplish everything we intend to. Writing the story of Clovis and the assassination of Vice President Peterson was one of those things that I intended to do, but somehow, some way, the idea got buried in a chest, untold and nearly forgotten, until now.

Reflecting upon my life now I ponder the absurdity of my wisdom, when for a three-year period in my young adult life, I deserted my dreams and my passions for the pursuit of money. The story that brought me worldwide recognition opened the door to the temptation of greed, and I took the bait like a starving winter coyote, failing to see the trap hidden and obscured from my view by my own lusts. Fortunately, that same story eventually led me home, and while it's obviously apparent that my life has intimately known its share of sorrow and tragedy, I do believe with all of my heart that I have been spared from what could have been the greatest tragedy a man could ever know—to have lived to a ripe old age, only to find that he had never lived at all. One thing I know, I have lived life and I've lived it well.

CHAPTER TWENTY-SEVEN

Preparing to make a false cast to the rising trout before me as the shadows of the warm summer evening began to fall across the water, I glanced at the headstones across the river high upon the bank, and I heard a voice behind me. Mark and Will were stepping into the water, clad in waders and fly rods in hands.

"Hey, Brother, Heidi told us you were down here. Do you mind if we join you?" Will asked.

"No, sir, I don't mind at all. I can't think of anyone in the world that I would rather spend my time with this evening than my two brothers."

Spreading out in the river's bend, we cast our flies to the hungry fish. Lines swished back and forth across the air as the evening sky gave way to the darkness of night, just as they had when we were boys. Laughter filled the air as we each hooked up with a trout and enjoyed the battle and fight of man against fish, listening to the chop, chop of the fish as it thrashed toward the waiting net, where it would be unhooked and released to battle again another day. Even in our old age, we felt young again. Somewhere, late into the night, Mark hooked into a good one. It was a large brown.

Will and I pulled in our own lines and moved closer to Mark, enjoying the scene, watching the battle between Mark and the big brown in the light of the late summer moon. As the great fish tired and succumbed to defeat, Mark reached for his net and gently encompassed the fish. Gathering around to look, Will and I marveled at the size of the wary brown. Mark gently retrieved the hook and held the fish, slowly moving him back and forth in the current to allow it to revive and regain its strength, then let it go. I smiled at Will and then looked toward the barely visible outlines of the headstones on the upper bank of the river. I felt the gentle squeeze of Mark's hand on my shoulder, a twinge of sadness in his voice: "That one's for Joe."

THE END